Imaginary
Crimes a novel

Imaginary
Crimes a novel

Toby
Green

MKUKI NA NYOTA
DAR—ES—SALAAM

PUBLISHED BY
Mkuki na Nyota Publishers Ltd
P. O. Box 4246
Dar es Salaam, Tanzania
www.mkukinanyota.com

© Toby Green 2013

Cover Illustration: Emily Fowke
Design & Layout: www.spearheadbranding.com

ISBN 978-9987-082-39-1

Visit www.mkukinanyota.com to read more about and to purchase any of Mkuki na Nyota books. You will also find featured authors, interviews and news about other publisher/author events. Sign up for our e-newsletters for updates on new releases and other announcements.

Distributed worldwide outside Africa by African Books Collective.
www.africanbookscollective.com

contents

"In a riddle whose answer is chess, what is the only prohibited word?"
I thought for a moment and replied, "The word chess."
Jorge Luis Borges, The Garden of Forking Paths

This novel is dedicated to the memory of Adrián Giménez Hutton,
who took me to Tigre

Acknowledgements

First and foremost, to Walter Bgoya and Mary Jay, for believing in this book enough to take the significant risk of publishing it; to Dave Kerr, without whose incomparable creative energy, and his championing of this book, it would never have found the right publisher; to Ian Rakoff, who read through many drafts of the book with me, and helped me to find the book's voice; and to Maggie Pearlstine for never losing faith in it, and for helping me to make it readable in the first place.

Since I started writing this book in December 2003, so many friends have helped me along the way, and without them this wouldn't have been possible. For our discussions about books, and for giving me little clues as to how to finish this off, my thanks to Shola Adenekan, Catherine Boyle, Stewart Brown, Jamie Crawford, Tim Dowling, Richard Drayton, Paulo Farias, Bob Fowke, Emily Fowke, Conrad James, Juliana Mafwil, Tom McCaskie, José Lingna Nafafé, Insa Nolte, and Keith Shear.

Madrid 2004

I

What would it be like to steal a soul? Had there ever been such a thing except in that blinding flash of fire that heralded this universe of ours and all its joy and suffering?

These were questions I asked myself more and more as I worked in the bookstore. I'd been prompted to do the modern equivalent, to get hold of someone's papers. Few people thought that souls existed any more, it was assumed that they'd been disposed of by the three high priests of the Anglo-Saxon canon, Darwin, Dawkins and Dennett. But I'd read my Gogol and still had a romantic nature. I could still dream that such a horrible theft could be possible, that somehow paper souls could be transubstantiated into that mythical and otherworldly essence which used to provide all of us with meaning.

It was a thoughtless idea, I knew that, and dangerous. Gogol went mad in the end and I didn't want to follow him. So if stealing a soul was even remotely possible I certainly wasn't going to accept all the responsibility. I had read so much since arriving in Europe that I felt imprisoned in the fantasy that people longed for crimes like this, thefts that fed the soul its stolen milk. I wondered if secretly they didn't want what was even more forbidden, a sacrifice in a world where sacrifices were taboo, a crime so atrocious that it might forestall all others and yet stand for them as a totem. Perhaps it's irresponsible to cast all the blame on others and yet without their imaginations, piling up daily in towers of bones in the news, I never would have had the courage to act.

I mulled the idea over for a few days as I worked in the store. Very quickly it became obvious what a brainless daydream it was. For days I tried to spot one from the bookstore where I worked on the Puerta del Sol. There passed the people heavy in the city's lustful heat. Ah, so much potential there was, for just one soul, but there was a constant tugging at the groin, sleepily, just like they were all sucking at one another in the dark whilst only half awake. With their half-formed desires the souls were always just escaping me. There weren't any souls left in the Spanish-speaking capital. There weren't any souls anywhere. The bottom had fallen out of their market and there wasn't even any room for them in hell any more so they had fallen out of there.

I would just have to settle for procuring the papers instead. It would be illegal but that did not matter. Wasn't the law developed by those who wanted to legalise their own crimes? What really bothered me was the moral question of whether I could prevent a crime by committing one. I tried to convince myself that I could, and should. The crime we all imagined had to be possible exactly because we loved what might be stolen or destroyed.

I had plenty of time to think about souls just then. I felt as if this was my job, since customers came to the bookstore hoping for some recommendation which might set them onto a better and more humane path. I wasn't much occupied by the rest of my work. Of course I pretended to carry on doing what my employers thought of as my job, stacking the books on the display tables by the window. I did this work, easy as it was, and I was paid for it. It was all so boring. The only spark of interest was with the manager, who really irritated me. I think he sensed the strength of my emotion but mistook it for something else, which is easy to do in this city where the sun is always jumping you with more energy. He would come close by just to criticise me. But all I had to do was smile, say I'd try harder. *You won't last long, Elena*, he'd respond.

Perhaps I didn't keep my eyes peeled as well as I might have done. I was distracted by the manager and by the activity of the Puerta del Sol where the bleached tourists from the North slobbered over their ice creams and ran their hands over their stomachs like an imperial army coming to terms with its newly expanded territory. I knew I needed to try some place else. One day I demanded permission to leave early. The manager did not refuse me. I picked up a couple of volumes as I left and walked up the hill towards Gran Vía past some of the rival bookstores. Most of the people heading this way barely glanced at the shop windows. They seemed more interested in the trinkets which the African hawkers set out on fraying black sacks curled up at the edges of the pedestrianised precinct. I sensed that it might be just here that I would discover something, in a space which no one else seemed to care about.

I'd been eyeing up the Africans for some time. Finally I'd realised that my best chance of getting hold of some papers was among them and the cheap goods which they sold in the middle ground between indifference and pointless possessions. These were the most vulnerable people in the city. They didn't have the money to leave. Perhaps even sharks worry about the bluntness of their teeth sometimes, since not even credit card companies would take a chance with them so that they could raise 500 Euros and flee back home. Instead the cops used to taunt them by strolling along the road so that they had to wrap up their goods in their sacks and stand back against the shop fronts, innocent and law-abiding citizens. Everyone knew that the cops came down here off duty to see how the land lay, to calculate how best they could humiliate these wretches.

Luckily, the day I found my mark there were no cops about. Soon after leaving work I was sizing up the Africans. I went up and down several times. Perhaps I was taunting them although I didn't mean to. I felt as if souls were rising, as if they'd found their way to the surface and recovered their will to breathe again. Here in Madrid one could spend days, weeks, knowing without thinking that one's soul was slowly rotting like an unpicked fruit on a tree. It was a constant struggle to hold on to the soul, something that required the sort of thought which no one bothered much with any more. It was a battle I'd often felt as if I was losing, so that when I looked in the mirror I would see someone I wouldn't like to meet, someone I couldn't think well of.

Eventually I settled on one. I watched him from a distance for twenty minutes. There was a touch of softness and compassion about him even though he was selling even less than the others. Here was someone whose character might be one that I could touch. Weren't we both immigrants from the same kind of boat, washed up by unhappy circumstance in this city which neither of us cared for and yet which somehow we both helped to subsist? He was unusually tall, thin like they all were, with those ritual scars below each eye which told their own story of a different world and of its losses. He had a gold bracelet on his right arm, though at the time I couldn't understand why he hadn't sold it and tried to better his lot. None of the others spoke to him. He seemed so solitary, and I felt a mixture of sadness and desire when I saw him. Surely, he would want to offer me something. What did he care about his papers? What did any of us care? I hoped he might sell them for very little, next to nothing, provided I approached him in the right way.

"What are you selling?" I asked, and he gestured without words at what was on the floor before him. "I'm interested in something larger than that," I replied. I had decided to create a false sense of mystery, to lure him in as if he were a reader. It was what the professor had done with me. I'd use a trick which would make me and my plan seem much more important than we really were. "What I want is to buy a secret," I told him. "But I can't tell you what it is. Let's just say that in fact, it's your soul."

He eyed me there in the Madrileño late afternoon. I think he questioned my sanity. I suggested going to a bar to discuss it but he said that he needed to stay and earn money. We eyed each other, animals and strangers both. "I'll come back," I told him in the end.

For days I went back to the same place during my breaks from the shifts at the bookstore. He took to smiling when he saw me approaching. He told me his name: Gabriel Cissoko. But he was shy of leaving his post on the pedestrianised street. I think he was afraid that if he left another member of his nameless class would take his place and he would never be able to return there. I joked with him. We kept on laughing whenever I mentioned this business about buying his soul. He'd lead me on. I think he thought it as crazy and senseless and yet as true as I did. So I kept on asking him to tell me about his soul: they were very rare commodities these days, I pointed out, and his could fetch more than he imagined.

He'd laugh, then, his eyes alight with humanity. I was right, he'd tell me in mock seriousness, he'd learnt that no one was interested in souls any more. "It's not just the supply of souls that has dried up," he joked one afternoon. "There's no demand for them any more either."

"How do you know?"

"You're the first person who's come to make an inquiry."

"Perhaps you haven't been advertising properly."

He looked at me strangely, then. I think for a moment he'd thought I was serious, that I believed all this myself. And in a way I did, because of course he was right; souls required a moral sensibility which these days in most fields was a hindrance.

There was a certain absurdity about the exchanges I had with Gabriel, I won't deny that. And in the end it was absurdity which swung things in my favour. One afternoon I brought along a newspaper and showed him a headline from the inside pages: "Divorce Boosts Economy, Experts Claim". It turned out that some economists at Harvard had shown how divorce benefited production and economic growth. With the break-up of the family home there was a need for two dishwashers and two washing machines and more sets of crockery had to be bought. There might even be an extra car. The construction industry was a notable beneficiary. This was how the economy kept moving, it was through increasing separation into parallel realms of nocturnal fantasies that the world did not shatter. He didn't think much of the article. I challenged him: perhaps he didn't have divorce in his country? To that he was silent. He did agree, though, to go with me to a bar.

We went up to Gran Vía and then up Fuencarral towards Tribunal. Walking with him I felt more of a foreigner in the city than I ever had done before. In Buenos Aires we always used to sneer at Madrid. Argentina was richer, and better at football. Those ideas must have sustained me on my arrival and I had never really sensed my inferiority. But the Spanish are a racist lot, even worse than us. We Latinos were barely tolerated and those Africans who did manage to reach Madrid were treated as if they did not exist. That struck me as I walked up Fuencarral with Gabriel, where I swear I saw two old *matronas* cross the road so that they didn't have to share a sidewalk with us. They were such antediluvians that they didn't even realise that they were surrounded by homosexuals. But they knew a black guy when they saw one and that was enough for them, even though they must have hated homosexuals just as much.

When we reached Tribunal we turned down Palma and made our way towards the small plaza in Malasaña where there was a good Moroccan restaurant. I wanted to show him the possibilities of his situation, of course, but also I wanted him to eat well. It had clearly been a long time since that had happened.

"Come on," I told him, "we're going in here." He seemed agitated. It had to be the smell of the food, I thought, the excitement that comes with consumption. "What's the matter?" I asked. For a moment I allowed myself to feel a genuine sense of pity even though I had sworn not to feel any emotional connection to the person whose papers I was after. "What's the matter?" I repeated, as we stood outside.

"They won't serve chicken."

11

"Probably not. They may do, I never asked."

"I don't want chicken," he said, allowing himself to follow me in.

"We don't have to have chicken," I said.

We sat down. It turned out that the last time Gabriel had ordered chicken somewhere, they'd brought him just a plate with some bones.

I ordered a tajine and some houmous. Soon we were eating.

"Tell me about your divorce."

"How did you know?"

I told him that he was sad. It was obvious that he was sad and I recognised that because he touched my own sadness. We were both far from home. We were both prey to the sad desires of solitary people. I could see, though, that once it had not been like that for him.

"The divorce," he muttered. "In my country, it is a big problem. Women marry, the dowry's paid, but there are problems and they return to their family compound, taking the children and the property with them."

"So it was with you?"

He did not reply at once, breaking a pitta. "So I came," he said in the end. "But there is no work in Madrid. Nothing. Everyone says that Paris is better, but I have no money to get to Paris."

I gestured at the gold bracelet on his right arm: "Why haven't you sold that?"

"It was a present from my grandfather," he said. "It is from an ancestor of ours, a man who was saved by a miracle of God from being sold into slavery."

I had nothing to say to that, but in any case I told him that it was easy to get to Paris. The trains left Chamartín station daily at seven o'clock, and if he was prepared to sell his papers to me I'd buy him a ticket. "That could be the price," I told him, "your passage to Paris. I can get you a passable European identity card too. It's all thrown in."

It was no problem, I told him, we could have his real name written on his identity papers too if he wished. The professor had assured me about that when we had discussed our plan involving the books which he had to take to Paris for us.

"Books? The professor?" He pushed his plate away and sat there, taking me in. "This is quite an operation," he said.

"Not really," I said. "It's some mad scheme, really. The professor hasn't even explained all of it to me and I still don't know how seriously to take it. But it's intriguing, and that's something."

I didn't tell him anything about the wider plan, not then. He had to be lured in slowly, by stages. This story he had just come upon was for him like a book whose meaning and emotional resonance would not become clear until the final page. I was offering him entrance to a mystery, a mystery rather like the one which the professor had led me into. Like all stories it moved around, in circles, sometimes seeming to advance and at others to go backwards. Like the most appalling crime, it had to be imagined before it could become real.

"What do you want?" he asked.

"I've told you."

"My papers, yes. But what has the professor got to do with it?"

"You'll meet him soon enough."

"How can I help? I can't justify all the books you want me to transport."

He laughed with a bitterness that I tried to pass over. The waiter came by. I got his attention, and ordered some mint tea.

"The Moroccans do make good tea," Gabriel said grudgingly.

I leant over and touched his arm. There was no need for this ever to happen again, I pointed out. He still had his papers, I could see that, but they were doing him no good in Madrid. No one cared. All he had to do was to pass over all the documentation from his home country. He would be freed then of the identity which had plagued him. He could sell that worthless paper soul to me. What did it mean, after all? Just let him forget about the professor, about anything to do with books. If he did as we asked he could go to Paris and become something more than he was.

We left the restaurant after we had drunk the tea from opaque glasses. It was one of those fresh, optimistic Madrid evenings. People sit out till late and the kids kick balls about until after dark. There in the Malasaña plaza the people were out. The bar was doing big business and a wave of energy and laughter fluxed there in the emptying light. The tables were occupied by glasses of beer and baskets of fried potatoes. Life was full of possibility again. As we passed the tables set out beneath the bare plane trees, a football landed in among the drinking people.

"Those kids again!" I'd seen them do this here many times.

"You watch them," Gabriel said. "You will see that they are not children."

One of the football crowd, an Asian kid with shades pushed up above his forehead, came to get the ball. The old man who'd picked it up refused. *It's the third time now*, he said. They argued for a little while. Then the kid pushed the old guy. But he was no coward, he pushed the kid back and squared up to him. One or two of the drinkers stood up. The other footballers rushed over, bounding up the stairs from the sunken area where they were playing. They all surrounded the old man who still had the ball. They looked cold. Surely they couldn't attack him? But none of the other drinkers had come to his rescue, and a hunted look came over him. I stepped forward, ripped the ball out of the man's arms, and hurled it back to the grey concrete where the idiots had been playing. *There's your ball*, I shouted.

I've noticed that with angry men before. Put an angry woman in front of them and all their threatened violence withdraws. It's as if they've come in their pants. Of course the *cabrones* slunk away. Probably they forgot about the humiliation or turned it on its head and remembered only how their group had humiliated the old man.

"Come," Gabriel said, after the incident was over, "I must go back."

"What do you think of my plan?" I asked him, although I hadn't told him much about it. The professor hadn't fully explained it even to me by that point. He'd talked a lot, and about so many different subjects. He took himself seriously, of course, but that didn't mean that I had to. And in the midst of his discussions of Chinese history and of the possibility that the universe would stop expanding, and crunch, and time would start to implode back towards the big bang, he'd suddenly developed this strange tic, this idea that we were all in danger and had to follow his plan if our world was not to combust. It had all sounded strange but strangeness has its own fascination. That was why I had decided to follow the professor in the first place, to see if he was right about the crime and the plan he had that could prevent it. "What do you think?" I asked Gabriel again.

"I'll consider it."

As he said that I felt I'd made the right choice. He was indeed the type to go for the professor's plan. The apparent absurdity of it all would appeal to a lost soul such as he was. Mind you, I couldn't be sure that he wasn't deceiving me, pretending to be someone he wasn't. That would have made him as bad as me, another person up to no good and looking for a mast to tie themselves to and so find a sense of direction.

"It's easy," I said to him then, as we made our way past international call centres back towards Fuencarral.

"You're the first European ever to show an interest," he said, stopping outside a sign offering cheap calls to West Africa.

"I'm from Argentina, from South America. I'm not European."

"Will my papers really help?" he asked.

"We need your soul," I joked. "It's an urgent matter."

He smiled at that, and then turned to go, adding as he went: "We'll discuss it."

He went into the call centre. He was much too precious to lose, I decided, and as I turned away to carry on to my flat I knew I'd be seeing a lot more of him.

II

At that time I was living not far from the Plaza Malasaña with the neurotic Spaniard, Dolores, who shared her surname with this city and was proud of it. Finding the flat at all had been a relief after my life had begun when I'd arrived. At first I'd been happy to fall in with the Latino crowd in Madrid and had lived with a bunch of them in Lavapiés. That had been a snappy neighbourhood, full of North African tea rooms. It was like Chueca, the sort of place where some Latinoamericanos also liked to live, where accommodation was cheap and no one cared how many people shared a flat or how loud and late you liked to boom merengue out of the third floor window which overlooked the inner courtyard of your apartment block.

It was easy to make friends in Lavapiés and that made finding work easier too. I'd tried my hand at waitressing, then at working at the cinema towards the Plaza Mayor, and I'd spent some time in one of the local bakers. No one really cared if you dropped a job after a few weeks. That was life in Lavapiés at that time and it was fun. There was a sort of parity between the bosses and the workers which followed and it gave the neighbourhood its craziness. This was why we all liked it, because there weren't many places like that left any more. I had enjoyed it all at first and couldn't imagine that the city might have anything better to offer me.

After a time I'd gone back to waitressing and that was how I'd met Dolores. She worked at the same place as me on the Plaza Santa Ana and owned a flat in Malasaña which she'd bought with her inheritance. Her father had died a few years before but she didn't talk much about him. She had fled the country farm in the Moraña for Madrid, and who could blame her? My own father had done much the same. He'd never liked the ranch which his grandfather had started up in Santa Fé after arriving from Poland. He didn't want to be one of Argentina's new wave of gauchos, herding animals in the lands of peoples who'd only been exterminated a generation or two before. He preferred the more banal brutality of a career in insurance.

Perhaps then when I heard of Dolores's past and of how she'd escaped a rural prison I felt a sense of kinship with her. It may even have been that story which deluded me into thinking that there was something kind and thoughtful about her. She wasn't an aggressive type, at least not at first. She even kept pet mice in a shoebox with a bed of straw which she changed regularly. That made me think that she had to have some sort of heart, but it didn't stop her from being withdrawn, the sort who might have jumped if you'd touched her unexpectedly.

The idea of living with Dolores seemed like it would be a pleasant change for me. The crowd I'd been living with in Lavapiés had started shooting up and I was getting tired of the mess. Little bits and pieces were going missing. I was getting a good education in thieving but it wasn't a happy place to live, and when I heard that Dolores sometimes took in lodgers it didn't take long for me to ask her if I could be one of them. I installed myself just a few days later and that was when my life in Madrid took shape.

That didn't mean that the new set-up in Malasaña was perfect. Keeping pet mice was no substitute for sanity, it turned out, and underneath everything it was soon clear that Dolores was disturbed. Soon after I moved in she'd insisted that I buy a separate fridge. It had seemed a fair demand and I'd even been quite pleased as bits of food had always been going missing in Lavapiés, usually at about four o'clock in the morning. The idea was that Dolores would keep to her fridge and I would keep to mine. But after a week or so I'd come home to find that someone had rearranged all the food in my fridge. Everything had been given an external, superficial order, so that the vegetables were all neatly arranged on one shelf, dairy and meat products on another, and eggs and spreads on a third. It was a display to please an absolutely precise, absolutely emotionless individual, the sort who spends their lives filing away atrocities and their paper ciphers whilst longing to commit them.

It was obvious that Dolores had rearranged the fridges, but she denied it. *Come on, nena*, I said, *who do you think did it? the invisible man?* But she denied all knowledge and said that I had to be mistaken. Then a week later the same thing happened again. I realised that I was living with someone who had very little connection to reality. That was quite frightening until I recalled that most existence in our time was dependent on retaining as small a connection to reality as possible.

In these circumstances I soon got fed up of working in the bar alongside her. I started to look around for another job. It didn't take me long to find something. One morning, strolling along the Puerta del Sol past one of the bookstores there, I noticed that they were recruiting. I went in and inquired. I'd always had a hankering to work with books. They had always been important in my childhood in Buenos Aires. During the long, humid summers we used to go out for weeks at a time to our villa in Tigre. My parents would take piles of books with them and we'd sit out reading on the veranda in the evenings, listening to the heavy slap of the water from the delta against the platform where we moored our motorboat. *The thing is, Elena*, my father used to say, drawing on his pipe, *every book is an act of hope, a declaration of optimism.*

He was a sweet man, incapable of seeing the worst in people even though it was so apparent. That was why he was so willing to sell them insurance, my mother used to jibe, he couldn't see when they were planning to have a house fire. She was wiser than him, that was for sure, and used to crack jokes at his pomposity. She was the one who turned me towards exciting and less pretentious ideas. But she too had loved reading. I remember once, she pointed to the pile of books they'd brought, sitting stacked up in an old leather suitcase that she'd picked up from a saddler's in Rosario. *In there*, she said, *I don't doubt that there's a book which could save the world, if only we could understand its hidden messages, and bring them to the attention of others.*

Perhaps all these memories pushed me to look in the window of that bookstore in Madrid. It's almost certain, in fact. Everyone likes the idea of saving the world even though we're the ones the world most needs saving from. Once interviewed, I was able to impress the recruiters with my knowledge of literature. That was an increasingly rare commodity – something which no doubt ought to have worried them – but they went ahead and hired me anyway. I was delighted. I still hadn't formulated my plan then, but I knew that this move would assist me. The bookshop was fresh. For the first time since arriving in Madrid I felt excited.

The store fascinated me. Those words of my mother's had often been in my mind in childhood, that in their library there was a book that could save the world. Perhaps, I thought now, I might be able to find it. I began to bring home some books, sometimes using my store allowance and sometimes not troubling to. I usually took books which weren't selling well since they were often the most interesting. No one cared, and the manager probably thought I was helping. I knew for a fact how much slow sellers annoyed him, so I was doing him a favour.

There was one book in particular I used to read, by Elias Canetti, since my maternal grandfather had known him in Vienna before fleeing to Argentina just before the outbreak of war. It was thanks to him that I was allowed to have an EU passport in the first place, so I made sure to have Canetti. I even read his *Auto de Fe* three times, from cover to cover. Always I lingered over the final set-piece, the incineration of the monumental library of the sinologist, Professor Peter Kien, in a fire which he himself had started. I was scared bloodless by its prophecy of fascism and collective incineration and wondered what it was about fires imaginary and real that seemed so frightening in our world just then.

The books I read gave an added pleasure to my work at the bookstore and I was happy there. Most of our clients were respectable and I got to know some of them quite well. They were usually intellectual types or retirees with too much time on their hands. I serviced their needs without much difficulty and did not spend long thinking about them. There was one older man who was different, though. He was very thin and well-dressed and he seemed to have such a refined taste in books that in my mind I called him "the professor". Sometimes he came in with a cane which he would rest against the counter while he waited for his order. He was obviously well-off. If there was a queue at the till he'd stand checking his emails on his Blackberry, which in those days were still exciting gadgets. When it was his turn to be served he'd put the machine away, fastidiously, in the pocket of his jacket.

There was something compelling about the professor, there's no point in denying it. My parents' psychoanalyst friends would have told me that I found his studiousness attractive because I'd been brought up surrounded by books myself. And it's true that I admire elegance and those who live elegant lifestyles even though elegance is always, when all is said and done, founded on the work and misery of others. But that was so easy to forget in the bookstore, when the professor was piling up another collection of volumes on the desk. He'd often talk to me pleasantly and I found our exchanges engaging because he was the sort of person who could talk about anything and sound authoritative – a charlatan by another name. He began by asking me about Argentina, which was a place he'd often thought of visiting. He spoke Spanish with a strong foreign accent. All of this helped me to forget.

Once I knew him a little, he opened up. He was American, he told me one day, and had been a professor at a big university there. He started to tell some funny stories about some of his students. One of them had asked him why China had so many people if it was only a small country. He didn't suffer fools gladly, he told me: he'd answered by telling his student that that was a bit like asking why the university had so many students if some of them had small brains. Shortly afterwards, it turned out, he'd been forced into early retirement.

One day he asked me for something new. He said it had been written by an Argentinian librarian: that was why he had asked me about it. *I'm looking for this book that describes the crime in great detail,* the professor said, *and can help us to prevent it.* That was the first time he'd mentioned his real obsession to me, and at first I didn't take it seriously. He gave me the title, and I laughed. There weren't many people looking for books by Borges any more. He seemed disappointed, though, as if it was important. I kept my eyes down, looking at the stock records on the computer. For a moment I was afraid. But what was I frightened of? It was crazy. It was just a book.

I told the professor that it was out of stock and he looked sad. He picked up his cane, twisting its knob in its fingers, and repeated that this was the book which could save us. At once, of course, I thought of my mother and of those long summer evenings in Tigre. The memory disturbed me.

"If I can track it down," I told him, "I'll tell you next time that you're in."

I hoped that that would be enough to dismiss the incident. Probably, he'd have moved on to some other subject by the next time I saw him. But there he was waiting for me when my shift ended, and he fell in beside me as soon as I left the store.

"I have been waiting years to meet you," he told me. "It's a moment of great serendipity." The African hawkers were out with their wares on the way up to Gran Vía; I think this was the first time I really noticed them. "How many copies of the book do you have?"

I asked him to tell me more but he demurred. There was only so much he could say about this subject. That surprised me, since ordinarily he seemed happy to talk about anything. I made some casual remark but he responded edgily. Didn't I know how important this all was? The threat was imminent, he told me, in fact it might already be too late.

He stepped to the side of the pedestrian precinct. We stood by an ice-cream kiosk, next to an obese tourist ordering a chocolate-flavoured ice cream. I didn't know anything about a threat or a crime, I told him as we stood there, and I asked him to leave me alone. I walked briskly away from him, running up towards the Gran Vía. I heard him call out something as I went. But I couldn't make out what he was shouting.

I should have gone to the police straightaway. But they had a bad record of coming down hard on sudacas who had scraped a European passport because of some migrant grandparent of theirs. I didn't want to alert them. No one wants to imagine the worst. Or, to say it more truthfully, people love to imagine the worst but they prefer not to do it consciously. OK, so this courteous old man had followed me from my workplace, had grabbed hold of me and talked some gibberish about threats and criminals. So, he hadn't seemed so courteous all of a sudden. But there was a lot of this sort of talk about just then and there didn't seem to be anything that unusual or original about it. I'd enjoyed his company until then. I'd learnt a lot about Chinese history and what he called the cosmic crunch, this idea that the energy from the big bang might turn in on itself making time run backwards as the universe imploded back to the original fire which had given it meaning. Perhaps there was a way in which his elegance was made more attractive and compelling by this sudden hint of neurosis. It's always a relief to discover that others are more messed up than you are.

After I had made my way back to the flat in Malasaña that evening I did my best to forget him. Dolores was never there in the evenings so I had the place to myself. That was one of the best things about living there. I let myself in and poured a glass of chilled water from the jug in my fridge. Her mice were scrabbling around in their shoebox and I watched them for a moment. Then I went straight to my room. That was a place which Dolores, with her mania for order, never penetrated. No doubt in rebellion to her neurotic tendencies I had let my room pick its own route through to chaos. By this time, after two or three months of bringing books home from the bookstore, I had amassed quite a little library. But I had purposely left the books unordered. They were stacked neither by category nor alphabetically by author or title. There were no shelves. Instead the books had been allowed to grow in lumpen piles. The piles grew to possess their own aspect of comfort. To me they were like well-loved pieces of furniture and my whole room was a sanctum, a garden of chaos which I would help to prosper even in a place as regimented as Dolores's flat.

That evening, after meeting the professor for the first time, I must have been a little distressed. I remember that I found it hard to settle on anything to read. My eyes flitted around the piles of books. Clearly he had picked up something about my actions at the store. Yet from this thread of truth he had constructed a fantasy and decided that I was implicated in something I actually knew nothing about. It was the sort of thing that kind and intelligent people did all the time whilst believing devoutly in their kindness and intelligence. For a moment I even looked briefly to see if I had taken the book he'd talked about without knowing it. But I couldn't see it.

Unable to find the volume which obsessed me, I began to circulate through the atrophied columns of books. Those piles had been set up by me in such a way that one had the feeling of walking through a verbal labyrinth. One reached a junction in the collection and made a choice purely on instinct. That choice determined absolutely everything that followed and yet even as one continued on one had the sensation that one could still return to the previous crossroads, or to the one before that.

I was quite lost to that space when I heard the front door of the apartment slam shut. It was Dolores, abandoning her shift. I left my sanctum and watched for an instant from the corridor as she stood in the narrowness of the kitchen with her arms resting on the work surface. She did not even look at the fridges once. She stood, breathing heavily for some time in the disjointed silence which echoed as the swifts circled outside and a moped growled down the street.

"What is it *nena*? Why aren't you still at work?"

"He came to the bar tonight," Dolores said, turning to look at me.

"Who did?"

"My father."

"He's dead."

"I saw him, Elena."

"You have the money from his estate. You own this flat."

"You should not believe everything you hear about a story. Stories are strange things. Anyone can invent them, traduce them, invert them so that they run backwards. And once they are inverted they can mean something completely different."

"What are you telling me? That he's not dead after all?"

"I'm not telling you anything."

She didn't want to talk about it. She was blinking rapidly as she looked at me. Her face had closed in about her. She was like a turtle poking its head back into its shell. I shrugged, then. If she was so screwed up that she had visions of her dead father but still didn't want to talk about it then that was her problem. In Argentina, we didn't have those problems. We had different problems. We had psychoanalysts, whole teams of them.

"Fine," I said, "so he came to the bar."

"It wasn't fine."

"Why did you leave?"

"I fainted. Manolo and Sebastiana gave me the rest of the night off."

"Do you want to go out?"

I didn't suggest talking about it, not directly. I wasn't that stupid. But I knew that a screwball like her wouldn't be able to face the idea of a night in her own company. So we left the apartment and walked down towards Chueca looking for a bar. The streets oozed people. A fury of laughter and foreplay rebounded between the windows somewhere up around the sixth floors of the apartment blocks. Guys were checking out guys. Girls were checking out guys. If you strayed down Fuencarral back towards Gran Vía, the African whores were out there, being checked out. Madrid felt like an uncorked bottle. All these energies were swimming around. But you didn't want to stay there too long in case it all began to smell nasty.

We found a bar a block from the plaza in Chueca. I ordered a couple of *pinchos* and talked inconsequentially about the bookstore for a minute or two. I could tell that Dolores was not listening so I decided to play a little joke.

"Of course," I said, "he came there at last today."

That made her look at me again. "Who did?"

"You know." I looked at her for a moment. Perhaps she thought I was talking about her father. I hadn't meant to tease her, to be cruel, but I hadn't been able to stop myself. Sometimes it seems to me that that's what's happened to me since I came here, that I've just become harsher and somewhat less of a human being. "He kept on saying that we had to act to stave off the threat," I went on, "that it was within our power."

"And you believed him?" She looked very sad and incredulous just then, and I felt touched, though I couldn't have said how. I said that I had, and she laughed: "You thought there was still time?"

I didn't know what she meant by that. Had the professor been talking to her already? Again, I defended myself and my position, nodding fiercely. Of course there was time. There had to be. And things were looking up, I told her, for the professor was talking about export.

I shouldn't have made a joke about it. At the time, I wasn't expecting to see the professor ever again. But I'd noticed in my sanctum that there was a way in which a choice could create a whole reality. Once you'd imagined something it had a strange way of entering your life. By playing this joke on Dolores I'd chosen a path in the forking garden which would determine my fate.

III

I saw the professor at once from behind the till in the
foyer. A very slim, very collected elderly retiree – the sort
who looks like they were probably married to a military
officer – was just paying for a copy of some English novel
in translation. I was looking for her change in the till
when I caught sight of him. By the time I located the right
coins it was too late. He was well into the bookstore by
then, advancing on the till where I stood serving. He leant
against the counter and rested his cane there, fiddling with
his Blackberry while he waited for the other customer to
collect her purchase. He was looking for a rare book, he
told me then, once she had gone, as if somehow this might
have surprised me. He seemed to have forgotten the one
he'd mentioned the day before which he said held a clue
to the crime, the one written by the Argentinian librarian.
This one was about "dark matter", a work of physics and
astronomy. He accompanied me to the bookshelves and I
helped him to find what he wanted. We began to walk back
towards the counter.

"I'll meet you here at eight o'clock, after work," he said.

"I told you last night, I'm not interested."

"Why didn't you get someone else to go with me, then?"

He paid for the book. Of course he was right. I could easily have asked another staff member to help him and stayed serving behind the till. I had gone with him because I was intrigued. There was something so elegant about his tone of command that everything that was suspicious and repellent in his behaviour was somehow overcome. It did not matter that everything about him seemed mysterious and that beneath his veneer of sophistication there was a constant unspoken violence. It didn't even matter that this whole idea he had of a collusion and a crime seemed crazy. What excited me was that his eyes shone with intelligence and purpose and he was interested in me and my boring existence.

Of course he was waiting, as promised, when I finished my shift. "Let's go to the Plaza Santa Ana," I said to him. "There's a good bar there."

He didn't care where we went. There was a freshness in the air that evening, as the city reminded us of its altitude. Winter lurked in the fringes. We moved quickly and he talked in a clipped, antique form of Spanish. He assumed that I knew everything, and reeled off ideas, contacts, next steps, all as if I had helped to form his project. Gradually, I pieced the whole story together and the plan which he wanted us to pull off.

The copies of this book he had mentioned, written by the librarian in Buenos Aires, contained a clue to an imminent crime which would reveal where it would take place, and so could help to prevent it. The professor was buying up every copy available – this was why he was so keen to have one from the store - and they were all to be shipped off to a specialist in Buenos Aires to be studied for the secret which they contained. The professor explained that so as not to arouse any suspicion, the books were to be disguised on their transfer to Argentina by jackets from those many volumes which, he knew, I had stockpiled in my flat. They needed to be smuggled to Paris and then sent on the night flight from London to Buenos Aires. For all this, he emphasised, my status as an Argentinian and my job in the bookstore were essential. That's why he had been waiting for me, he announced, as we reached the corner of the Plaza Santa Ana and saw the bar where I once had worked.

We pulled up chairs at an outside table and ordered our drinks. I couldn't see Dolores yet but I knew she would be around. Some gypsies walked past trying to foist their soothsaying onto the tourists. One of the gypsy women had a long thread which fell from her thick hair and spiralled in the gloaming. The professor pulled at it and yanked it free. At once there was a commotion. We were surrounded by the women, grabbing at us, demanding payment. They were obnoxious. They lived in a filthy camp on the outskirts of the city, near the main railway line to the north. They were so uncivil, I heard it said, that they deserved nothing better. But really, why should persecuted people bother with politeness?

The professor understood nothing of this. He bullied them into silence. Then he screwed up the thread and put it into his shirt pocket. The gypsies formed a semicircle a few metres from our table. Curses were thrown out, talismans of the powerless. The professor shouted to a waiter, clapping his hands, urging him to get rid of them. The waiter clapped his hands, too, in hollow resonance of the client's aggression.

"Worthless," the professor commented, as the gypsies left, "contributing nothing."

"What have you contributed, then?" I asked him.

That was an invitation for him to launch into a disquisition on his career, all the books he'd published and universities he'd taught in. He seemed so impressed by his own importance that I wondered why he was bothering with me. It was flattering, but I realised that probably he talked so much that none of his old friends could be bothered to listen any more. After a time I asked him his name. He was Kent Piree: perhaps I'd heard of him, he suggested, as Dolores brought our drinks to the table.

I put him right but he wouldn't believe me. What, did I know nothing of the North American fraternity of sinologists? I didn't see why he was so upset, but perhaps it was important. Perhaps, even, in some unaccountable way I had been expecting him. I had always been fascinated by eerie premonitions of danger, of the Old Continent scorched. It was the fear I had lived with as a child, an awareness being raised along with me unconsciously. And who was there who could live in ignorance of the potentiality of such vast crimes any longer? This was why the whole world lived in flight these days, why Madrid and Paris and London and Buenos Aires were like blenders of all the peoples and tastes on earth.

In fact, this was what I had tried to write about, on first arriving in Europe, when I had begun trying to compose a novel and burnish a vision of the world in which I felt I belonged. But the effort of creation was intense and that idea hadn't lasted long. It wasn't so easy to belong any more when nowhere was solid. It wasn't possible to belong to thin air, when you coursed like a fluid from one city to the next. And where there was no belonging some other badge of identity or creation had to step in. There had to be some other project which could give me belonging or memory, and if it wasn't to be my novel then perhaps Piree and his dreams of the perfect crime and our perfect prevention of it might have the answer, even if all of it was false.

Once we had resolved the issue of his name and his importance to his satisfaction he ordered some fried potatoes. Dolores brought them to the table and this time she registered us. Her eyebrows rose when she saw us. "Are we familiar?" Piree asked her.

"We live together, Dolores and I," I told him.

"Ah," he said to her, "then you will know the importance of her library."

"She hasn't been in to my room," I told him, "it's my own private sanctum."

"Very good. That's very good. These books need to be concealed."

"Nothing is concealed from me," Dolores said, leaving with her tray.

"I'll meet you there, I'm sure," he called after her as she returned inside the premises. I softened as she went, relieved that they hadn't met before after all. But this softening was also a softening up, a preparation for what was to follow.

Soon after that Piree told me that we had to go to the flat at once. I hadn't expected things to move so quickly but I did not object. I don't want anybody imagining me as some naïve little flower from a backwater, a slow fool who didn't know how the world worked. Of course if I'd invited any other man back to my flat at that time I would have expected to sleep with him. But I'd been feeling curiously undersexed since arriving in Madrid. Perhaps in those early months I'd hoped that finding my belonging as a writer might even be better than sex. But although this was the first time a man had come back with me, I had no expectations where Piree was concerned. He presented himself as entirely asexual and all his drives were connected with his books. I didn't doubt that this was why he saw the situation as so dangerous, why he carried around with him this feeling of an incipient crisis. Perhaps it was because I had this understanding of him that I didn't take him too seriously.

"We can walk there," I told him, "it isn't far." And this eccentric, normally so voluble, slid into silence as we went back up towards Malasaña. I took him the long way round, along Gran Vía and almost as far as the Plaza España, near all the call centres where the Latinos congregated to phone home. The city pulsed in neon, brilliant and finite, and there was laughter and heat in the air. Piree walked quickly, his eyes focused on a spot on the pavement three or four paces ahead. His was a constantly changing panorama yet static in monochrome quality.

We turned off Gran Vía just before the Plaza España, near to a shop I knew which sold maté and *dulce de leche* for Madrid's homesick Argentinians. As we entered the quiet streets of the neighbourhood something seemed to leave him. He began to look from side to side. Probably he sensed that the flat and the sanctum were nearer.

"The books," he said then, "are they all prepared?"

"I have prepared nothing. As you know, this is all a mystery to me."

"We'll have to work swiftly. Everything must be ready in a fortnight."

"How are you so sure it's that pressing?"

"Everything must be prepared now, at once."

It all seemed the most grotesque sort of fantasy. But there was nothing so out of the ordinary in that. These people were always talking about preparations, they spent their working lives preparing for retirement and retirement preparing for their funerals and for the division of their property. It turned out that you could postpone life for long enough so that already one had died. Existence became a fantasy. The most dangerous, murderous fantasies, which had always skulked there in our imaginations, could then become real.

Outside the apartment block in Malasaña we stood by the heavy wooden door. He peered over my shoulder while I opened the lock and turned the brass handle. Neither of us spoke as we climbed the stairs around the central stairwell and went into Dolores's flat. No one knew that I had returned to the flat with him. It was only then, as we stood in the hallway, that I felt disturbed. I did not know who this person was. He had identified himself as Kent Piree, but what did that mean to me? He was an American with a suave demeanour. This was how he had seduced me with his cultured conversation about China and astronomy giving way to this fantasy of a plot, of escape, so that then with his habitual, patrician authority he had coerced me. It seemed as if he had somehow become the person who determined the choices I might make in a maze of paths of his own making.

Inside the flat I made for the fridge. Of course Dolores had been interfering. Whilst I rose early to leave for the bookstore, she had all morning to rearrange things. I had even begun to reorder the fridge myself. It was a gesture, no more, an attempt to placate her. But it had had no effect.

"Look at this," I said to Piree. "She's put the fruit in a separate compartment to the vegetables. She's a neurotic."

"Does she do this every day?"

"Yes."

"And she does not realise that you have noticed?"

"I don't think she cares whether I've noticed or not."

"This is very dangerous, then, very dangerous indeed. She has free access throughout the morning to your fridge. And who's to say she doesn't also have the key to your room? She could be doing anything in there. Reordering the books. Doing anything." He was evidently as much of a neurotic as she was. His mania was only partly disguised by his professed quest to understand the world and its meaning, and the threats to its existence. He strode out of the kitchen and into the gloomy corridor, decorated only with a kitsch china vase and some plastic flowers. "Which room is it?" he demanded.

I opened the door into my bedroom and we entered the sanctum. At once Piree began to examine the collection. He ran his finger along the spines of the books. He stooped down to inspect the piles on the floor. He muttered to himself. A muscle in his left cheek twitched with excitement.

"You've noticed nothing unusual?"

"I find it difficult to keep track of them all. Occasionally books seem to disappear."

"Of course they do," he snapped. We looked at each other. He examined the books again, picked one from a pile, scanned it briefly, and then brought it over to me. He did the same thing with another two, three, four books. "Look at them. What do you notice?" He had ordered the books, I saw, by author name. "She's been coming in here in the mornings and moving your books around. Ordering them alphabetically."

"Why would she do that?"

"You've already told me that she's got a mania for order. Why would she stop at your fridge?"

"She's not just a neurotic," I protested. "She can't have such a mania for cleanliness. She looks after her pet mice, after all, she cleans them out."

I walked over to the window and stood there, leaning against the sill. It was wide open and I could hear people talking below. Their voices carried clearly, like they used to at Tigre, from one house to another across the water.

"What are you remembering?" he asked me.

"I'm just asking myself why I never thought she might have come in here."

"What is most obvious, most apparent, is what is hardest to see."

"But why have I missed her reordering everything from A to Z?"

"Because to you it was unimportant. You did not care for her artificially imposed order."

I became impatient with him, then. I could not grasp the mystery in which he was trying to involve me. Was he having a breakdown, or was there something really serious in what he was telling me? It was his obsession; and I was disturbed at the ease with which I had submitted to it simply through his force of character, because I had deluded myself that crimes could be beautiful and sublime. I had told myself that there was no harm in following him. Perhaps he was not a fool at all: there was the possibility that he was right, and he really did understand something! Maybe in preventing what might prove to be the greatest crime of all I could somehow redeem myself and recover what was left of my nobility. I did not know what it was all for and yet simply by talking about it repeatedly he had made it seem greatly important. Something in his belief

was infectious and I knew as I looked at him in the desolate
silence of my flat that I would not be able to escape it.

IV

There was a harpist who used to play daily in an underpass near the Retiro Park. The subway filled with melody and several times I saw people's souls touched by that unexpected grace. Many of them lived on tight budgets and could spare little. But the soul reasserted itself. Hands were put into pockets and coins chimed in to the busker's hat. In fact, in those days when I was just entering into my alliance with Piree I was one of the most regular contributors. I had begun to do some yoga in the Retiro in my lunch breaks and I always prepared myself with a Euro or two as I arrived at the underpass.

The Retiro was as good a place as any to try and find some peace in Madrid. I'd learnt some basic yoga postures in Buenos Aires from the son of a landowner who'd given up the chance of sleeping his way through the wives of his father's farmhands to go and find himself in India. He had been endearing because of the choices he had made in life and the naïve enthusiasm with which he did everything and so I was grateful to fall back on my memory of him in the Retiro.

I needed to recall those yoga postures and some calm just then since in the short time since first coming to my flat Piree had become more intrusive. He seemed to have lost the urbane elegance which I had seen in him when he had been for me just another strange customer talking about their curious taste. He would appear in the bookstore unannounced and buy some paperback at the till, fiddling with his cane as he did so and behaving oddly, at times pretending he did not know me and at others refusing to talk to me at all before retiring across the road to a pavement café and reading the book in open view. I wasn't sure what to make of him except that his eccentricity was a definitive trait of his character. Occasionally we still had normal conversations. One time, he began to talk about how bored he'd got with lecturing and research in the end, how much he'd needed a new outlet. Perhaps that was where his whole idea of a conspiracy had originated, from his need to create a new meaning for himself.

Yet even if all this was some sort of disorder it was obvious that he suffered extreme anxiety about his situation and that this was something he tried to remedy through his obsession with books. I could spot behaviour like this very easily since it was something that I'd got to understand in childhood, from the way my parents had shut themselves off from all the sadness in their lives and their families and buried themselves in the ideas of others. Of course there was no reason why Piree should not have read his books in the café across from the bookstore. This was something that no one else in the whole of Madrid was going to find suspicious and there was no one I could complain to about it. He remained courteous if anyone asked him a question, and he was polite to me whenever I seemed suspicious. Once or twice he offered to buy me lunch but I made it clear that I preferred my yoga sessions in the park and wasn't prepared to be drawn into a false sense of security.

One of Piree's tics was that he insisted on coming back to my flat with me in the evenings. He knew that Dolores would be at work in the Plaza Santa Ana and that we could carry out the task of switching the jackets on the books unobserved. He'd bring along a leather briefcase in which he would put a few of the traduced books each day as he left. How else were we going to smuggle them out in time? he'd ask. I didn't know what to say to that but there was something coercive about his questions and his manner and I did as he expected. The gay couple who lived across the hallway were convinced that we were having an affair. They mocked me openly on my taste if ever I saw them without Piree. And frankly, who could blame them?

In spite of his perverse attractions, however, I worked hard to keep some space between us. I didn't want things to get out of control. My yoga sessions were a lifeline since the one place that I managed to keep him away from was the Retiro. He didn't like parks, he said, they made him feel claustrophobic. On the days when I had decided to do some yoga, he would leave me free to go and do as I wished there whilst he read. Of course I knew that those lunchbreaks in the park and my moments of peacefulness could only give me a simulacrum of calm. How could I have thought otherwise, with the multi-lane boulevards on all sides? Nonetheless the very fact of finding a square of grass beneath one of the tall trees and of reaching into that space and releasing all the tensions which accumulate in these bodies of ours seemed to be a way of keeping the violent noise of the city, and of the incipient future, at bay.

But one afternoon, as I came back through the subway from the park, the harpist had gone. For some seconds

I hovered there, not moving. The spell of peace which I had always found on those breaks appeared to have gone together with that musician. A very old man passed me reading *ABC*. The name of that paper had always amused me, even when as a girl I had seen editions hanging from the news stands on Corrientes. My parents had often told me that it was a paper of the right in Spain, and that even in the democratic era it had had no problem in retaining all its old prejudices. *That's why it's called ABC*, my mother used to say, *because those fascists have to patronise their supporters, they believe that even reading is a bit of a challenge for them.*

Of course I had no reason to think that the man reading the paper was an old fascist. He laughed as he came past me, growled, *Of course, they have no choice but to submit.* I try not to discriminate against people even when they deserve it but all the same I could not help feeling a little disgusted. The harpist and his music had gone and in his place was someone who for all I knew made Perón and Franco look like liberals.

I decided to return to the bookstore, avoiding the subway I usually took. People were walking down the streets near the Prado and some of the older and more obese tourists were fanning themselves with newspapers. I carried on across the Avenida del Prado and up towards the bookstore. I needed to get back to work before my manager became really irate. But arriving there would also be a way of putting myself back within the purview of Piree.

At that moment, just as I passed outside the Thyssen-Bornemyza Muesum, I realised what it was that had alarmed me so when I had seen that the harpist had gone. Everything about those rests in the Retiro had been a fantasy that I had created, a delusion. The harpist and his melodies had helped me to maintain it, and the delusion of calm in the face of an impending atrocity had seemed so close to being real. Yet the truth was that it was something that I had made and something which the professor and I were now destroying. Gradually, what had seemed like a rant from a delusional older man had become something much more dangerous. I had joked to myself that I was just going along with it for amusement's sake, but perhaps something nasty was really afoot. Here was the fantasy and the dream that the whole world of culture and the books which contained it was on the edge of a calamitous precipice whose fiery breath was already fanning our faces.

Just before cresting the rise near the official buildings, I stopped at a news stand and asked for a packet of cigarettes. As the vendor turned to get them I picked up a copy of *Cosas* from the side of the stand and slipped it into the knapsack where I kept my blue yoga mat. I paid for the cigarettes and carried on, lighting up and inhaling fiercely. Just that process of distraction was a comfort of sorts. I knew precisely how dangerous my situation was, and yet I did nothing about it. Perhaps I did not care. Or perhaps there was something in me that was attracted to the dominance of a figure of imputed authority, a figure like Piree.

Reaching the bookstore, I took off my knapsack in the cloakroom and went back to work. I served clients at the till, accepting their money without comment and putting their books in the bags which they had requested. After an hour the manager asked me to go and stack some shelves. I spent some time heaving dictionaries about in the reference section. When I had finished, I wheeled the trolley towards the service lift at the back of the store. I had to pass through the general non-fiction section, the collections of history, philosophy and politics. There were few clients. But in one of the aisles I noticed a young-ish man, distinguished by his smooth, round face and thick curls. He was standing next to the philosophy section, holding a book by Schopenhauer, *The World as Will and Representation*. There seemed something meaningful about that encounter just then, imagining the world like Schopenhauer as if we had created it. I stopped to talk to him.

"Can I help?"

"No," he replied.

"Do you wish to buy that book?"

"No," he said again.

"Do you mean to steal it?"

"Of course."

"Well, listen," I told him, "you're going about it the wrong way. I like books too, that's why I decided to get a job here. The books come with the job."

"That's good advice," he said, putting the slim volume into the bag he was carrying. "I'll remember it."

"We sudacas have to stick together. Where are you from?"

"I live in Mexico now. My name's Bontera. Raul O. Bontera."

I said nothing to this, though I was thrilled. Bontera was quite a well-known poet, inasmuch as a poet or a living poet can ever be well-known. Probably I was excited because one of Bontera's famous social tics was a fondness for pilfering books. It was Bontera who had blamed the layout of certain bookstores in Mexico City for important gaps in his literary education by making it impossible for him to steal works which would have expanded his sensibility considerably. Others, however, said that Bontera's real name was Carlos Pérez, or that he was really an English aspirant masquerading as a Latin American writer, and that in any case he was a charlatan who modelled himself too blatantly on the life of the late Chilean poet and novelist Roberto Bolaño. Back then Bolaño had only died recently, at a young age, and naturally he was all the rage.

"Bontera," I said at last. "Well you would find getting hold of books much easier if you followed my advice."

"I need the book for a poem I'm working on."

"That's no excuse. Poetry is never an excuse."

"On the contrary," Bontera answered, looking idly at the books on a nearby shelf, apparently to see if there was anything else he fancied, "true poetry is an excuse for anything."

"Even murder?"

He laughed. "Every fascist demagogue is a poet manqué. Stalin, Mao, Qaddafy. You can't argue with history. It's lucky Borges found success as a writer, God knows what would have happened to the world if he hadn't."

Did Bontera also pretend to be an acolyte of Borges then, like the professor? The thought sent me cold for a minute, and I did not reply, pretending I had dropped something. Then I straightened.

"Are you telling me that Borges could have been a fascist?"

"I'm not telling you anything," Bontera said. "Just be careful who you choose to emulate, that's all. Borges the poet could so easily have been Borges the murderer…"

"And poetry?" I continued. "If it's an excuse for murder can it also be a way of preventing it, of finding peace?"

He shrugged. "That's a mystery we all have to try to understand," he said. Then he smiled and continued to look through the books. At length he picked up a heavy tome by Bolaño.

"That novel's all the rage," I said. "We're holding a special event next week to celebrate the author's life, seeing as he spent so much of it in penury here in Spain."

"I'll come," Bontera said, placing the book back on the shelf. "Perhaps I'll make off with a copy then instead."

He made his way down the stairs to the ground floor, holding his bag with a gentle ease. I walked with him to the door. I was excited by the insight into Bontera's obsession with Bolaño, and I must say that his kleptomania didn't bother me, in fact I found it rather reassuring. When I had been a teenager my mother had advised me to look at older people in any career which I was contemplating and then to judge if I wished to end up like them. There was something in institutions and in the ways of life which they prompted which shaped a person's outlook and remoulded their essence. One could not escape this moulding once one had submitted to it just as one could not escape the cultural and physical inheritance which one was born with. And when I looked at the sort of character which stealing books had given Bontera I felt that my own procurement of books was taking me in a valuable direction, even if I didn't think of it as theft.

That afternoon, I was distracted. The manager kept on reminding me to concentrate, lacing his orders with the usual withheld threat of violence. I gave clients the wrong change, omitted additional purchases which they requested at the till, and stacked an entire trolley-load of new novels in among the popular science section.

"What's the matter?" the manager kept asking me, and eventually I told him that we'd had the famous poet Bontera in the store. "Bontera!" the manager spat out in anger. "Why didn't you tell me? The man's a well-known book thief, a thief on a matter of principle." He insisted on taking me to the stock room for a dressing down. I did not resist. I was interested to see how far he would go. He ordered me to sit, and then paced the small room. "It's really very bad to have had Bontera here. He's bound to have taken something. Did you see what it was?"

"No."

"I hope he didn't infect you." He grabbed my knapsack and opened it; there he found the copy of *Cosas* which I had picked up from the kiosk on the way back from the Retiro. "What's this?"

"It's a magazine."

"You've taken it from here. You've stolen it."

I denied it but he shivered with fury and picked up the telephone.

"What's that for?"

"I'm calling the police," he said.

"But I've done nothing."

He took the magazine out of the knapsack and put it on the desk beside the handset. "This is your last warning."

I left the bookstore early. Piree jumped up in surprise from his seat across the road, but I had a head start on him. He didn't manage to catch me up until I had reached Gran Vía. Even then, I turned away from him. I was tired. For months I had been getting hold of books from the store and creating the sanctum in my flat with the disordered piles of volumes on the floor. Why had I done this? It had all stemmed from some mania for collection, the pointless accumulation of property. The pathetic thing was that it had only been when Piree had turned up with this scheme to prevent an appalling crime that my life had taken on any sort of meaning. Until then I had been deadened with boredom.

"Tonight, we'll finish switching the jackets," Piree said, as we waited for the lights to change on Gran Vía. "When that's done, we'll be able to confront your flatmate. We'll be ruthless, utterly ruthless. There'll be no chance of failure."

He continued to talk as we made our way to the flat. He talked incessantly about himself, as most people do. I knew that there was no point in making any comment. My silence was taken for agreement with his madness and my approval of his plan to export the books and prevent the crime. It provoked him. I could not escape him, because our destination was my sanctum, my one small sanctuary in the town. I asked him, did we have to talk about the plot all the time? I'd liked it so much better when we'd talked about other things. I'd learnt something then, something to remind me of the universe's beauty and of the possibility of kindness. I told him how before our meeting I'd known nothing about dark matter and how the amount there was of it in the universe would determine whether or not the universe would implode so that its story ran backwards. I was pleased that he'd educated me, I said. He looked at me kindly, then, smoothing the sleeves on his linen jacket. He was sorry, he said, but the plan took precedence. He wasn't interested in education any more.

We reached the apartment building and in the darkness of the stairwell which we ascended was silence. I rose first and his shadow came rapidly behind. We entered the flat, ignoring the fridge and its soulless mechanical humming. A stillness clung to those spaces which we relinquished as we moved to my door. We entered and Piree set to work, replacing the jackets of the books on the floor with new ones. He proceeded with all the methodical rigour of someone who has spent their life rifling through catalogues, ordering shelves. I remembered the shock with which I'd looked at my first photos of the camps. For some days I had been completely unable to sleep, replaying in my mind the photographs of the uniformed officers assigning new arrivals into various categories: those with a skill, those who could work brutishly, those to be driven to death, those for instant liquidation. Once I had talked about it with my mother. *Those men*, she said, *they too had to organise, to assess, to categorise, that was the essence of their task.*

The sky was shedding itself of colour as Piree worked, putting the books with their false jackets into his leather briefcase. I left him to it, happy to appreciate the evening outside: the couples fondling playfully, the almost sensual roar of the mopeds in the street, the brilliance of the lights flashing on all sides but in the room behind me: all of it was pleasing, an almost lyrical distraction from what really mattered, the madness of Piree in the sanctum and the destiny of that madness.

He finished switching the jackets at nightfall and we sat waiting until the early morning, when Dolores would return from her shift. I felt unbearably tired. My breath came in rasps. I sat surrounded by my books risen up like great waves from a worthless sea. We sat there for many hours in the half-light which glowed in from the city, picking up a volume occasionally and then letting it go. It all rested on Dolores, and when she came in Piree asked her to come in to the sanctum. Once she had come in and seen us there he accused her of acting as if these books were hers.

"But they are mine," she said; then she noticed that the careful alphabetical order had been subverted, the order which she had tried to bring to my stolen books.

"It's too bad," Piree said. "We've switched all the jackets around. There's no other alternative if we're to succeed."

He explained a little of his plan, but Dolores dismissed it as worthless. How dare we interfere! This was her flat, and these were her books. Piree kicked deliberately at a pile of them, knocking them to the floor.

"The export of these books must start now," he told her. "The campaigns for the general election here in Spain are building up steam and my contact is ready."

"The books will no more leave this house than I will change my name," she said, "from Dolores de la Madrid."

Piree was so excited that he was panting.

"Everything's coming together," he said. "The export will begin soon, after we've given the sign."

V

I returned to the bookstore the next morning in a very unsettled state and worked as ineffectually as I had done the previous afternoon. The manager could sense my distraction, and soon enough he sent me upstairs to do a stock check. I found myself in the philosophy section, just where Bontera had stood. There was the copy of the novel which he had examined there, intruding where it had no right to be. My father had always hated it when books were in the wrong place in his library at the villa in Tigre. He would spend hours re-ordering the many volumes he owned about the second world war in Europe.

I don't know what your father expects to learn with these books about war, I remembered my mother saying one year. It annoyed her. It was spoiling her summer! *Che*, he'd had so many books to read that he hadn't wanted to go down and join their friends, Gordo Telechanski and his wife – who everyone called Gaviota, she was such a scavenger - in Punta del Este. That was typical of my mother, of people in general as I was learning, criticising traits in others which she loathed in herself.

"What are you doing with that book?" the manager asked me, interrupting my dream as I stood with the novel by Bolaño.

"I'm just checking something for next week's launch. But so what? Have you come to spy on me?" It was obvious that he had, that he'd come upstairs hoping to uncover my transgressions.

"I'm doing my job, unlike you," he said. "You can't criticise me for keeping an eye on you. You've been doing nothing all day."

I put the book back on the shelf. "I'll go down to the till."

"You never do anything," he told me. I ignored him. "Yesterday," he went on, "you were worthy of suspicion. I told you."

"Suspicion? And what was the crime?"

"Who knows?" the manager asked. "Perhaps you haven't even committed it yet, perhaps you're just plotting."

"What is this? I've done nothing wrong." I began to walk off. I was not going to let him insinuate anything for a moment longer.

"You had your final warning yesterday," he said as I passed him. "Soon, favours may be asked."

Now I had worked all over the city by then, not to mention the many shitty jobs I'd taken in Buenos Aires before coming to Madrid. But this was the first time a *jefe* had come on to me. I was shocked. But I was also pleased. I knew that this guy would never dare sack me while he thought he might be able to cash in on some satisfaction. My job was safe and I'd be able to be as lazy and insolent as I cared. I was in the perfect position to get paid for doing nothing while I did what had been asked of me by Piree. For a moment the manager had even pretended that he knew something about this too. Why else accuse me of a crime in the making? But then I realised that Piree, the manager, Bontera, all of them, they were just drawing in the air of the atmosphere and replicating it in the certainty of the almighty aesthetics of atrocity which lay all around us. Of course he knew nothing about Piree's fears and how I'd got caught up in them. I didn't know all that much about them myself. I knew that I hadn't asked the professor many questions, but why should I have doubted all his talk? He was an expert.

As I've mentioned, Piree had ordered me to steal someone's papers as part of the plan. Finding someone who was prepared to go along with us to that degree was a difficult thing to do in the city but eventually I happened on the Africans and their wares, on the pedestrianised road up towards Gran Vía, and that of course led me to Gabriel. You can see now how all this talk of crimes and thieving got me on to that absurd question, of whether it might actually be possible to steal a soul.

Now I'll be honest. As a child I never met an African. And what I tended to think of when I thought of them were the animals which you see on nature documentaries and which on some deep level, from a young age, I had always associated with them. Perhaps this made me a racist: I won't deny it. But when I first came across them I felt a door open to a different type of sympathy. I wanted to steal Gabriel's papers, his official identity. This was an essential part of Piree's plan, the way that Gabriel and others like him had always been erased from the history books. But I did care about that soul and I wanted to understand it. At least that was what I said to him as I inveigled him into our scheme.

Still if you'd told me when I first met him near the Gran Vía that I would actually come to love that ebony soul, I'd have laughed at you. I wasn't thinking of love just then. I didn't even believe that that sort of heroism was possible. In the end it was my heart that opened in spite of itself, but that blooming was not itself imaginable even after our first meeting at the Plaza Malasaña when I'd seen off the teenagers over their football.

In the days that followed that evening of our first discussion in the Moroccan restaurant I came under pressure from all sides. Piree reminded me of calendar's rabid and accelerating logic. He wanted me to force Gabriel into committing, yet we both knew that he could not be rushed. Piree followed us from a distance as we walked through the city vanishing when we stopped for some reason. Sometimes I'd look back and spot him turning into the nearest kiosk or window shopping wherever chance discovered him. Often his bourgeois airs would get the better of him then and he'd examine the expensive shirts or some luxury gifts. He wasn't on some expenses-paid trip to an international conference any more, but you would never have known it.

Though I'd been living in Madrid for two years by then, with Gabriel the city bore a different pulse. It wasn't just those tight-lipped *matronas* who crossed to the other side of the road on Fuencarral. There were entire neighbourhoods which were closed to us. I felt my own foreignness deepening as we explored, felt that people were looking at me as a *Latina* whereas until then at least I'd had to open my mouth before I was judged. Yet aside from the sense of exclusion there was also a shedding of remorse and of shamelessness. Once, on Gran Vía, Gabriel stood outside one of the sex shops and began pointing out various objects to me. He had never seen anything like this in his own country, he said. He felt no sense of guilt. For him there was a sense of curiosity, of wonder, even. Was everything he had been told about the morals of white women true, then? He looked at me, searching. I wondered if he was hoping for an invitation of some kind, and for a moment I felt my body's desire, both our desires, drifting there. But then I sensed Piree watching from a distance, and I adjusted myself. I walked on abruptly and Gabriel came with me. All the same, I'm not sure that Piree ever spoke to me in the same way again.

Perhaps my reluctance to have anything physical to do with Gabriel seems strange. But it's difficult for me to describe how far Piree had co-opted me into his worldview, how quickly what had begun as a joke and a pastime had become something else. I had become almost as anxious as he was about the imminence of the crime. I itched with the need for action, for everything to become tangible, even for the crime to become almost proximate and real if only so that we could prevent it. And yet I had to be patient. I had to lead Gabriel out bit by bit, so I framed the subject of his relocation to Paris subtly. I did not mention it every night but touched instead on his papers, or dropped in the story of an Argentinian friend and their success in a new job in Paris. I listened to his stories of disdain and failure. Once I even displayed my stupidity as an enticement, and asked him why people like him had come to Europe if they lived in destitution once they arrived.

In all these exchanges the unerring companion was a sort of desperate isolation. Why otherwise would two perfect strangers have happily given up their time in this way? This feeling was one that neither of us had been used to. Yet you could not escape it in this city: it gulped you down from your hollow. There were so many of us in Madrid, transients all, separately spinning our webs across the dayglo darkness. What terrified me most was the sense that the whole rotten place was only supported by these stacks of isolation. Naturally immigrants did band together. We Latinos and the Africans hunkered down in our groups and supported one another as best we could. But it was always in the knowledge that our Madrileño life would eventually disappear.

Perhaps that was why I suggested bringing Gabriel to my sanctum one evening, as a gesture of mutual solidarity. It's true that there were more prosaic pressures. There was not long to go before the deadline for the smuggling operation. By bringing him into this world of jackets traduced and books stolen there was always the chance of him accepting at last the idea that Piree and I would steal his identity. But I think that I also sensed that there was more to unite us than keep us apart, that in our foreignness to one another was also a shared truth and experience of what it was like to be here in this moment.

This was the first time that Gabriel had actually been inside one of these apartment blocks in central Madrid. Nor had he been into one of Madrid's bookstores before, and when he saw my bedroom he chuckled. He said that it reminded him of his home country, where booksellers piled their wares on tables anyhow, waiting for someone with money. Had he read much in Africa, I asked him? He shrugged. He hadn't had much money, of course, but he'd always been interested. He'd always wanted an education and read what he could get his hands on even if it hadn't been much.

I began to show him around. At one point we stopped amid a clutch of books on religion. Novels were one thing, he could understand the need for those. But he could not understand why people had written on the subject instead of reading the sacred texts. It was all too much for him to assimilate. Repeatedly he said "I had not known their heads were so big." By and by we came upon a copy of *Ulysses*, and I told him that he was right: "Joyce, at least, he was certainly someone with a big head."

"There is so much to read here," he said at last. "Too much."

"It's true."

"And from me," – he was still holding the copy of *Ulysses* –"what do you want from me?"

"I've told you."

"I give to you my papers, and in exchange I take your books on the train to Paris."

"It's as I've told you."

"It's all part of your professor's plan?"

"That's it."

"And this professor…" Gabriel came towards me, holding the copy of *Ulysses* in his hands, "how much do you know about him?" I did not answer at once. "Do you trust him?"

"He is very learned," I replied. "He knows what he's doing."

"He has made you feel that there can be no delay."

"No."

"I do not want to delay either. I have been living here like this for long enough."

He walked between the piles of books, stopping every so often to touch one. He seemed to see them as curiosities, the artefacts of a museum that had never been described as such. They were objects that needed caressing. Everything in this strange world was an object, even those pliant women whose doctored faces we had gawped at when we had stood at the window of the sex shop in Gran Vía just a few nights before. That's how it seemed to him, and perhaps how it seemed to me.

"You need our help," I said then, trying to press the advantage.

"I need something," he murmured. And that was when I sensed his own awful solitude most deeply, eating him away with the impossibility of contact, or belonging, or even sex, in this world in which he found himself where there was no one that he would be able to buy. He was ready.

"We need a decision soon," I said.

"I will do it," he said. "Of course, I will do it. Why shouldn't I?"

Piree had been right: everything was coming together. Perhaps too the whole mystery of the plan might be solved before long. The professor was so clear in his vision that human destructiveness and its will for fire needed to be forestalled. It still was meaningless to me, but I felt now that just by following it through with him it would become clearer, together with my own sense of the meaning of my life.

After he had made his decision, Gabriel began to look at the copy of *Ulysses*, sitting in a battered old armchair there in my sanctum and perhaps beginning to wonder whether that strange and distant figure constructed by Joyce was really a sort of modern hero or whether a new model of heroism did not need to be constructed. I did not talk him out of it. I said nothing to him about Piree or the true nature of our plot because I did not want to distract him or make him reconsider his position. He had agreed to give himself over to our plan and it was my job to ensure that he did not change his mind.

It was late in the night when we heard the door slam shut. Dolores had returned from her shift and we could hear her slow movement in the kitchen. I had mentioned something about Dolores in passing and he demanded to be introduced. We left the sanctum and saw Dolores seated by the small table in the kitchen eating bread and cheese drizzled with oil and holding a glass of Coca-Cola in her hand. She rose then and went to look at her mice. We heard them squeak, and she smiled. She looked peaceful. One could have forgotten just then the demons that she lived with. She did not deserve to be disturbed but already it was too late. She heard us, and turned.

"This is Gabriel," I said to her, "a friend I've met in the city. Like you, he's very much a believer." She did not extend her hand. I left them together for a moment and pretended to busy myself in the kitchen. "I'll get you a drink, Gabriel," I said, depositing them in a silence which extended into the background noise of my opening the cupboard, filling the glass from the tap, and turning back to him with it. There was some brief exchange over a passage in the Book of Revelation. It reminded me of how these conversations had seemed to me as a child trapped in a religious studies class in Palermo Viejo.

I couldn't bear to hear them talking over the same old things. I gave Gabriel his drink and went to stand by the window where I separated two of the strands of the Venetian blind to peer outside at the city. It was late but still there were many people below. Fragments of noise assembled so that the atmosphere was threaded together time and again in worn patches as if Madrid had been a barrier of sound in constant breaking. And into those fragments came moments of Dolores and Gabriel talking, a friction overlaying everything. I knew that she hated Africans and that if she had been thirty years older she would have been one of those *matronas* crossing to the other side of the road to avoid him. And yet she seemed to be listening to him. I suddenly had a terrible fear that perhaps she might even change his mind over the whole scheme of the books.

"Gabriel." I walked back over to them. "Don't forget, we have much to do."

"I have given you my decision. What more is there?"

"You are going to help her?" Dolores asked him. "You are going to help with her crazy plan to export the books?"

"Yes."

"But those books are not hers at all. She has stolen them. Everything in this flat is mine. If you take them you'll be stealing from me." She pushed her chair back and stood. "And if you stop at that, who's to say what you might not have done? How do I know that bracelet on your arm is not also stolen? No, in that case, I will have no alternative but to report you to the authorities."

I remembered, then, the conversation which Dolores and I had had in Chueca after she had fainted at the bar at the Plaza Santa Ana. The time she had had a vision of her father! I had told her that I had got hold of books from the bookstore. I think I had been trying to distract her or even to make her feel better about herself. That was when I had begun to wonder if her many neuroses did not have something to do with her childhood. Perhaps her father had molested her. That might have explained a lot. So I had told her about it out of pity, and because I had not understood then how someone like her would twist the most pathetic scrap of information for their own advantage, manipulating it and reconstituting a lie as fact.

It was clear that night that she was out to obstruct us, as soon as she threatened to inform on Gabriel. Piree had implied to me that she would need to be neutralised if we were to succeed. At last I understood his meaning. She was a follower but she did not understand the gravity of the threat and how swiftly it had to be liquidated. At some deep level she wanted to prevent us from carrying through our plans. Yes, there was no question that she'd have to be dealt with if the crime was to be prevented. Here was another soul we might have to do something to for the wider good.

"Is it true?" Gabriel asked me. "Have you stolen the books?"

"I have not stolen them," I said. "She is sick."

"If you take them," Dolores repeated to Gabriel, "I shall report you."

I laughed: "It will be no use if you do. His identity is already ours."

Gabriel decided to leave. I accompanied him down the communal staircase out into the night. It was still warm and even though it was past two in the morning people were gathering at the bars which never seemed to close on Fuencarral. They were drinking but neither of us felt like stopping.

Dolores's mention of the authorities had made Gabriel anxious. "They can just come," he said to me, as we made for Gran Vía. "It has happened to people I know. They are driven off to the military airport, with no chance to appeal. Then they are flown to Dakar, where they use the French military base."

"She will not report you to the authorities."

"You cannot be sure," he said.

"There are many like her, people who like the power of a threat."

"They are dangerous."

We had reached Gran Vía; I wanted to turn back and get some sleep.

"Really, Gabriel," I told him, "they are not dangerous. They are weak."

I was confident because I had seen people like Dolores in action, the snitches of the neighbourhoods. They'd tell policemen where they could make an easy arrest, where there were some Africans staying or which Latinos didn't have the right papers. They were the type who had always admired uniform. Among the Sudacas it was the Ecuadorians who suffered most since they often didn't have the residency rights accrued from some benighted grandparent. There were some of them who used to go around beating up on the snitches, and once when I saw one of them whisper some words to a policeman I don't mind saying I went straight to Enrique *el hueso*, the kingpin of the Ecuadorians, to give him the details. *El Hueso* was all bone, but he was the toughest fighter around and everyone deferred to him. He gave the snitch a lesson, so I knew how easy it was to stuff them and that was why I told Gabriel he had nothing to fear.

We parted at Gran Vía and I walked back towards Malasaña. Yet as I went my confidence began to ebb. There was something of the snitch in Piree, too, I had to admit. He interrogated me at every turn, trotting out his anxiety as to the African's unreliability. How could we be sure that he would do as he had said? These were people who did not think to the same capacity, people who were different. He did not want the success of his scheme to ride on the shoulders of someone like this. How were we going to save things if we had to rely on someone like Gabriel? When I thought of the questions he had begun to ask me from beneath his respectable veneer, I felt quite anxious. After returning to the flat I climbed into bed, thinking about Piree, about the possibility that he too was not what he seemed, that none of us were, and that he'd give me or Gabriel or all of us away. I thought about him so much that I could not sleep. I was worried: I'd arranged to meet him early the next morning.

Sure enough, at our rendezvous over milky coffee in a café near Tribunal, Piree was in a very disturbed state. In the bookstore we were holding the event to celebrate Bolaño and this meant that I would not be leaving work on time. Moreover Gabriel had promised to bring his identity papers so that we could plant them in the appropriate place when the police came along to search for clues. I had told him to bring them to the bookstore. His ticket to Paris had been arranged for the following evening, the Wednesday just a few days before the scheduled presidential elections.

When I told Piree, though, he lost all of his faked courtesy.

"You've already told me," he shouted, "that the manager is worried about the event because of the book thief Bontera."

"So what?"

"He may have invited the authorities. If they are there, they'll immediately want to search the papers of someone like your African friend."

"It won't affect your plans. No one's going to report him to the authorities."

"How can you be so sure? You've already told me about Dolores's threat."

"No one's going to report anything."

Piree grabbed hold of the *churro* which was in my hand, just as I was about to dip it into my milky coffee; he crushed it between his fingers and folded up the remains in his soiled paper napkin. "We can't afford to get this wrong," he said, "just remember that. We can't afford any more mistakes."

That was when the American began to frighten me. He was possessed by this fear of an imminent threat and yet wasn't able fully to articulate it. He sat in the café across from the bookstore, day after day, reading books and mouthing the words in them as if somehow that could help. He would say to me, in great agitation, that I didn't understand how close the danger was. I'd noticed how his usual smart appearance had begun to show signs of wear, how his hair would seem unbrushed and he no longer stopped to get his shoes shined. He'd lost his interest in human culture, in its negligible meaning to the wider universe. For Piree, it seemed, the only explanation that would do was his own sort of staggered sullen explosion, as if his fear of the future had got the better of him and plastered him to every wall of the room where we sat. But this fear has possessed him so fully that he had easily swept me up in it. His sense of purpose had been attractive and I had been too bored and isolated to resist.

Whatever I thought about it at the time, this exchange over breakfast was enough to put me on edge. When I arrived at the bookstore the manager was as difficult as ever. Some notable writers were scheduled to appear at the event and everything had to be in order for them. He sent me up and down the various floors of the store, moving tables of books to create space, shunting aside the works of the lesser writers, or by those who were not well-known, which in his mind came to the same thing. He demanded that I ring the suppliers of the wine which had been ordered to make sure that they were ready. He did not allow a moment to fill with inactivity.

This was one of those rare days when the manager did not flirt with me. Actually, the absence of his leering provoked in me an almost carnal sense of incompletion.

I developed an itch on my left arm. I needed something as a replacement for a scratching which wasn't to be had. I was far too agitated to go to the Retiro for some yoga in my lunch hour. Instead, after a cursory acknowledgement to Piree, seated in the pavement café across from the bookstore, I went to look for Gabriel. Don't get me wrong, there still wasn't anything physical in our relationship. It wasn't as if he was a replacement for the ogling of my boss. It was rather that he was all to the contrary, as we say in Spanish. Probably I looked at him with criminal romanticism. Maybe even this attitude came from those wildlife documentaries. But wherever it came from, I was fond of my African.

Yet when I reached Gabriel's pitch, I saw that another woman was talking to him there: Dolores. I stood at a loss, watching. I could not have said that there was any attraction between them, any sense that Dolores had somehow replaced me. Gabriel was looking uncomfortable. Perhaps he sensed my presence, though he never looked towards where I was standing. Two clowns with flaming wigs walked past, looking for someone to pick on and humiliate. Anything to entice a crowd! Each of the clowns looked pleased with themselves, or at least that's what I took from their show of bonhomie. In their own way they were as bad as the policemen I used to see there, passing slowly and shaming the African hawkers. They knew that most people were frightened by them and by the possibility of being singled out for humiliation by them and yet also that some found that in that fear lay an attraction.

I took advantage of the clowns to leave before either Gabriel or Dolores had the chance to see me. I walked fast. I didn't want Piree to see me either. I knew he'd accuse me of ruining everything by introducing our mule to my flatmate. The thought of Piree's anger frightened me, his suspicion that Dolores would shop Gabriel. I picked up a copy of the first paper I saw at a kiosk and paid for it. It was *ABC*; covering my face with the paper, I walked through the side entrance of the bookstore.

Inside everything seemed calmer. The manager looked pleased with himself. The main tables were piled high with copies of books. There were photographs of the dead author together with excerpts from some critical appraisals of his work. Now that he lay beyond the factionalism of politics everyone was calling him a great writer. The manager chuckled when he saw me, certain of his success. "We'll sell a lot of books tonight," he said. Then his arm was taken by one of the publisher's representatives and he asked me to go up to the stock room where spare wine glasses were kept alongside pallets of books which had just arrived and others which were about to be returned.

I went up there and sat for a moment in the manager's chair. There was a sense of rebellion, even in this insipid act, for it was from here that he had threatened to call the police to accuse me of an act of thievery. I felt no great rush to do as I had been bidden and descend with the spare glasses. I opened the paper which I'd bought outside, *ABC*. It was filled with the usual conservative reports. I couldn't read it for long and flung the paper aside, fired by an unexpected fear. There was no peace. I moved to the back of the stock room, sensing that something of my anxiety was hiding here, that I could still find it if only I looked hard enough. Then I heard a noise. I swung round and saw Bontera.

"How did you get in here?"

"I followed you up. No one saw me."

"What are you doing?"

"I told you I wanted to come to this event."

"You mustn't," I said, moving closer to him, "the manager's very suspicious. He knows that you steal books."

"That's not enough to condemn me," Bontera said, laughing at the idea. "Everyone's a thief of one sort or another, and in fact thieving often seems to me to be something that's just in our blood. You should know all about that." I didn't answer, so he continued, remorselessly. "You're proud of your thieving, aren't you?"

"I'm not a thief," I said. "I have a compulsion to have those books, and they come with the job."

"All of them?" I said nothing. "People like you, you're always compelled. It's never your own fault. You just follow along."

I hadn't expected such aggressive criticism from him. I turned away, unable to deal with it. I picked up the copy of *ABC* and pretended to read it.

"The plan," Bontera said, "is it ready?"

"Almost," I replied hesitantly. I tried to look calm but I began to convulse inside. How could Bontera have known about it? He was no friend of Piree. He had always been a mystery, famous for knowing things that he was not supposed to know. But now he seemed to have transformed this skill into an art more dangerous even than he could have dreamt.

"It will be violent," he said. "You've thought of that."

"It doesn't have to be."

"Most things have something to do with violence," he said. "Even art."

"But you are an artist."

"I recognise my own limitations. Even at its maximal worth, when a work of art is entirely disinterested, aims at nothing beyond itself, it still relates to violence."

"I don't agree."

"Then you need to study some history, to understand our present state."

"I have."

He laughed: "Let's not argue. There isn't much time."

"That's what Piree's always telling me."

"And you're still looking for those lost books to export? Back to my continent, to America?"

"That's it. To Piree's friend in Argentina, who'll help us to decipher the clue."

Bontera laughed. "It's too late for that, I think." I asked him what he meant but he looked at me as if I knew exactly what he meant and then turned and took a book from the piles on the floor.

"What are you doing?"

"I always take one."

He walked out of the stockroom without another word. I had not even seen what it was he'd taken with him. Irrationally, I began to worry that it had been one of the books that we were supposed to be exporting. There had to be some reason that he'd known about our plan. Perhaps he, like Dolores, was out to stop us. Perhaps they would all have to be dealt with if we were to succeed.

I sat back in the manager's chair, breathless, unable to understand my life. I was committed to peace and hated the violence of the past. I longed for calm and to contemplate the beauty of this orb, that infinity that Piree had touched on when we'd first met and he'd spoken of the mysteries of the big bang. But at the same time Bontera was so obviously right, for in spite of Piree's obtuse intellectualism violence underwrote everything he did and yet this had not repelled me. As I sat in the manager's chair, scratching at my arm,

I wondered if it has not been precisely his withheld threat of violence that had attracted me to him in the first place.

VI

When you reach a certain level of architecture it all seems of the same style. What is revealed? A distorted reflection of the self, perhaps, or at least that's certainly what my parents' analyst friends might have said. Their old pal Gordo Telechanski, whose grandparents had run a haberdasher's in Vilna before coming to Montevideo, was always looking for a mirror which didn't work properly. *Make it really twisted*, he'd say, looking round the junk shops of Montevideo and Buenos Aires, *that way I won't look quite so fat, it'll be good for business.* It always surprised me that Gordo's clients returned to him. His obesity didn't originate in some hormonal or metabolic abnormality but from the fact that he was always eating. His inability to control his appetite was hardly an appropriate qualification for someone analysing the psychic problems of others, but still they came back to old Gordo.

There was something about the stock room which made me think of Gordo Telechanski after Bontera had gone. It was his incessant search for a bad mirror. That room, distinguished by its distended web of books, reminded me more and more of my room in Dolores's flat. But the familiarity was troubling also. I began to rummage about the manager's desk. I lifted up a pile of papers, bills, post-it notes and unanswered letters. Underneath was a single sheet of A4 that I'd written.

I'd had some training in the reading of orthography from Marta Olivares, a family friend from Mexico City who claimed to be able to read people's fortunes by studying their handwriting. She'd taught me what was distinctive about my own script, and here it was staring back at me. Here was something I'd produced when I'd first arrived in Madrid and, like so many of my continent's exiles, begun trying to write a novel about Latin Americans living in Europe. "MANIFESTO," it declared: "A novel must be beautiful, cruel, mysterious, unexpected, repetitious, constantly new, fearful, hopeful and sad – to be like life." There followed lines of scrawls and crossings out as I had tried to make sense of a hopeless plan to create something which I called a novel with a palindromic structure, one whose parts could be read either forwards or in reverse order – from one to four or from four to one – each direction offering a different meaning, comprehensible only as a whole that revealed some wider pattern in the world and the universe at large.

I looked at the manifesto for some moments, finding it difficult to believe that it was here in my hands. Although I'd abandoned the idea of writing this book after some months in Madrid, the idea had come back to me since I had met Piree. All his talk of a cosmic crunch had made me wonder whether, if time might go forwards as well as backwards, the same might not also be true for all stories. People's lives could rightly be understood only in forward momentum, perhaps, but it was also true that you could take them from the end and then work backwards to try to grasp how they had reached their final state. In the right mood, this backwards progress was the more revealing. It could then be that the truest meaning in a book might emerge when its parts were read forwards and then backwards, in mirror image to the explosion and implosion of the universe if accompanied by the right quantities of dark matter.

With the manifesto in my hands, I sat in the manager's chair and tried to work out how it had got there. It felt sinister. Definitely it could not be a coincidence. I had written it when I had been living in Lavapiés. I might have slipped it in between the pages of some book and taken it with me when I'd switched to Dolores's flat in Malasaña, but that didn't explain how the manager had found it. The implications were bleak. Perhaps Piree was right and people were out to stop our plans. Certainly, and as I knew from the many rejection letters that my proposed book had already received, there were many publishers who did not want the insidious ideas of my manifesto at large in the wider world.

I sat in the office chair and looked around the room at the piles of books and the cheap furniture shadowed by the smudged off-white paint on the walls. It looked more and more like the room in Dolores's flat. Trying to banish the thought, I rose and moved towards the back of the room, checking the pallets of books to convince myself that they had nothing to do with the ones that I'd stolen from the store and taken home with me. But as I moved I could not escape the sense of being followed, pursued. How else had my manifesto got here?

"This is where she is."

The door had opened. The voices were loud. Gabriel and Dolores had no right to be there but I did not stop them. When you let your life adopt a pattern of concerted deceit, as mine had done with Piree, you stop challenging the crimes of others. Crime was the breaking of rules that had been made precisely so as to be broken and weren't we all criminals at heart? There was no reason for Gabriel and Dolores to obey the meaningless regulations of this store. There was a reason why they were there, why they thought their crime was justified, just as there was a reason why I empathized with Piree's search and had chosen to follow him. All three of us, in our own ways, could easily point to our own justifications.

"Come with me," I said.

We went towards the back of the stock room. I could tell that Dolores had been working on Gabriel, persuading him to abandon the export of the books. Perhaps I hoped that by bringing them further into my sanctum I would divert them.

"He's decided not to follow you any more," Dolores told me.

"You are misleading me," Gabriel said. "I will have nothing to do with your plan any more."

I ignored them. I crouched down among the pallets of books and began removing them one by one. Piree had come to the store in search of this book by Borges to add to his collection of all those that he was going to export to Buenos Aires. Suddenly as Gabriel and Dolores stood like thugs before me I had this dream as to where some more copies of that book were located. Here they were at the bottom, hidden in amongst the last pallet of all.

I pointed the pallet of books out to Gabriel, but he shrugged. "It means nothing," he said.

"This is what you wanted," I said. "That's the book we're all concerned with."

"It's irrelevant," he said. "We've come to tell you that we want nothing to do with you anyway."

They left quickly. Chatter from the event below drifted in. I was needed at once with the wine glasses which the manager had asked me to fetch but I did not move. I knew that Piree would be furious when he heard of Gabriel's change of heart. I picked up the book from the pallet, moved over to the desk and sat in the high-backed office chair. A great swell of emptiness flooded me, so that the jackets, the pages, Piree's plan to export them back to my home country – every thing seemed void of meaning. The noise swam in from the event outside, almost sensuous. Again I felt that familiar itch, when the body rubs against the atmosphere just beyond it and throbs for release. I had seen it all around me in the city but had felt sexless. It was Bontera who had provoked me. Now I unbuttoned myself slowly and massaged my breasts, my sex. What turned me on more than anything else was that I was in the manager's chair. I could feel my body rising up. I touched deeper and harder than I had done in years.

After I'd come I sat there for a minute and then dressed. I opened the door and scanned the store below. Gabriel and Dolores were talking to an expatriate English critic who was droning on about some holiday she had taken in Andalucía. I couldn't see the manager anywhere. Turning round, I picked up my manifesto from the manager's desk and a copy of Borges's *Labyrinths* and left through the staff entrance at the back. Piree was waiting in his café on the far side of the Puerta del Sol.

"Well," he said, "have you got his papers?"

"I've got something better. Here's the book you wanted."

"Where was it?"

"In the store."

He nodded once, twice. "Where are the African's papers?"

"I'm going with him to his room right now, after the event," I lied. "You'll have to look after the books and prepare them for him. Make sure you've swapped all the jackets by tomorrow evening."

In this business, I'd realised, everything was in the implication. Piree didn't even pursue the issue of the identity papers any further. He paid his bill, took his copy of the book with him and hailed a taxi. We'd meet the next day at Chamartín station before the train left for Paris.

The event in the bookstore was scheduled to last for several hours but I could not wait that long for Gabriel. I needed a diversion to extract him from the crowd. I paced up and down the pavement just outside the store. I could see the manager by the till, his winebibbing face brilliant with Cabernet and the success of the event. He'd obviously forgotten all about me. I saw a waiter cross the road bringing a tray of glasses. They had had to send out for some – it was more of an event like that. I followed the glasses in, pretending that I'd had something to do with it. The manager beckoned me over, expansive with triumph.

"There she is," he said to the people in his circle, "our biggest fabulist in the store. Do you know she came to me the other day and pretended that we'd had Raul O. Bontera in the shop?" His voice rose with the laughter of his listeners. "Bontera the book thief, the poet! As if she'd stolen the idea from our late friend's work, another ideas thief like Bontera himself. And I pretended to take her seriously, of course, pretended to be taken in by the whole thing. I was quite severe with her. I told her she shouldn't have let him leave, that it could have led to anything."

"Señorita," a man said, turning to me, "I am Juan Navarrete." He showed me his card: he was the Mexican publisher of their late friend, this dead author whose life everyone had come to celebrate. We moved away to extricate ourselves from the group around the store manager. "Where did you get this...this fantastic idea that Raul O. Bontera, the famous poet, had come into the store?"

The man's astonishment riled me. There was nothing so outlandish about the idea, so I did not let him front up to me like that. "Actually, excuse me, sir," I told him, "but he did come to the store."

The man laughed and led me further away from the press near the display tables. "It was a wonderful idea," he said.

"Perhaps it all happened because of sadness. I thought of Bolaño and then Bontera came to me."

"You are sad?"

"Aren't you when you think of your author's life?"

The obese man shrugged. "No one asked him to be a writer."

"What choice did he have? He left Mexico and went to Chile during the Allende years but then came up against Pinochet and the other South American dictators. He had no money. He fled to Spain and lived off his wits. Becoming a writer was the only choice he had."

"And that gave you the idea?"

"I think Bontera came here out of sympathy," I said, taking my arm gently away from Navarrete's. "Out of the hope that he could steal things, like your late author, and yet perhaps give them a new meaning."

"Here." He gave me his card. "You can ring me tonight."

"Thanks," I answered, smiling, "but I haven't slept with anyone for two years, and when I do it'll be with someone more appealing than you."

Masturbating in the manager's office must have given me a different scent, something that all animals could sense. I straightened myself, aware that Navarrete was still eating me with his eyes. I needed to get away at once before he persisted. I looked around for Gabriel and Dolores. They were in quite a heated exchange, I saw, and people were looking at them as if they were the ones at fault.

"Excuse me," I said to Navarrete.

"Go ahead," he said, looking about the room for someone else. I brushed past him as I left. I remembered a time that the manager had asked me to call a travelling salesman from a North American publisher who had just arrived in the city. I was supposed to arrange a meeting but when my call was connected to his hotel room he was panting so heavily down the phone that it was quite clear that he'd just been making out with some hooker. It was one of the ugliest conversations I'd ever had and yet at the end, when I'd put the phone down, I had felt aroused.

Gabriel and Dolores were leaving the store quickly. I ran after them.

"Where are you going?"

"Leave us alone," Dolores said.

"It's your shift. You'll be late if you don't go now."

"Just shut up," she told me. But she did have to go. She walked with Gabriel to his pitch on the pedestrianised precinct and then left. He watched her go and then laid out his goods on the frayed sacking once more.

"I'd like to buy one of those," I said, walking up to him and pointing to a cheap plastic comb.

"Please, Elena, leave me alone."

"How much is it?"

"I cannot sell it to you."

"What's the price? Two Euros? Three Euros?"

"For you, one hundred Euros."

"That's fine. I'll pay it."

He stood up, very agitated, looking in both directions to make sure that no one had heard. "Go away," he hissed, "I am not for sale."

This was my best chance, I knew, to override Dolores and get Gabriel to go along with our plan. I just had to impose myself. I reached into my pocket and found my wallet. I held out the 100-Euro note. "For the comb," I said.

Gabriel said nothing for a moment. "If she finds out, I will be deported."

"Perhaps she's gone to get the police right now. She must have known that I would try to persuade you again. We'll have to act quickly or else you'll be lost."

"Why? Why is everyone so suspicious?"

"They're all jumpy. Everyone's more aggressive, these days. The police are on the look out. No one feels safe any more, not even in Europe or North America."

He gathered up his things and we walked off quickly.

"Where are we going?" he asked me.

"I'm staying with you till you've agreed to catch the train to Paris tomorrow."

"It's impossible."

"Why? The books are prepared. We have your papers. For the last time, all we've asked of you is that you give us your identity in exchange."

"I will be blamed for something," he said suddenly, stopping by a branch of the *Museo del Jamón*. "I will be like a goat for Abraham's sacrifice of his son. Or like one of those dead pigs in there, a laughing stock."

"You won't be dead. You'll be transformed. You can't ask for more from life."

He said nothing to that. We were walking fast along the Paseo de la Castellana towards the north of the city. Strings of cars passed us beaded with light. We stretched along the sidewalks and beneath the underpasses and on into the neon spaces. For perhaps half an hour, an hour, we did not speak. We passed the desolate buildings erected by Franco in *Nuevos Ministerios*. The streets were full. People had poured out of work and were streaming into bars and talking to each other on their cellphones. The city was a being in the constant stress of possibility, pulled in many different ways at once by desires which could not all be requited. But while there was a feeling of frenzy and excitement Gabriel and I were silent.

In that darkness overhung by tower blocks sprung as if by magic from beneath our feet, I was taken back to Tigre and to the moment when I had chosen to leave Buenos Aires for Madrid. Late one summer's night I had reached the large hangar where my parents' motorboat was kept, the one which we used to go out to the villa in the delta. Carlos Delgado, the manager of the hangar, had greeted me with the news that my parents' boat had broken down. *Don't worry*, he said, *I'm going back to my own house in the delta in half an hour, I'll drop you off on the way*. I waited as he closed up the hangar, locked up the forklift trucks which manoeuvred the boats down from the upper tiers of storage, set the alarm and turned off the lights. We climbed into his boat and soon were off through the waterways. For ten minutes neither of us spoke. We just listened to the motor churning the waters and watched the trees meet almost by their tips above us. Beyond that ribbed nave were vaults salted with stars. The noise of the motor oscillated to fill our silence.

By and by, Carlos had said, "It's many years you've been coming here, Señorita Elena, how many?"

"My parents bought the house in '84, when prices were low."

"After the dictatorship."

"They were optimists, then."

"I remember. I have been doing this job for 30 years, but I can remember you even as a girl. That mole of yours always made you stand out."

That mole beneath my right cheek had been a bane of my life; it irritated me when people drew attention to it, and I tried to respond with an implied criticism.

"Surely you remember most of the clients?"

"No, not all," Carlos said. "Many are much alike. Of course there are some exceptions, people like the sinologist Halbtsen and your family, but most are predictable."

"Does he still live out here?"

"Yes."

The sinologist, Peter Halbtsen, had a villa just a few hundred metres along from my parents. He knew my father, and they often talked about books together. "It's like a labyrinth, Señor Barajo," I once heard Halbtsen telling my father, "literature is like an interminable labyrinth of the human soul, where every turning can be good or bad, and yet you can never tell which until years later." My father would listen even though in truth he had little interest in Chinese culture.

"We were not typical, were we, Carlos?"

"Your parents and Halbtsen? No."

"And me?"

"You didn't look like one of those kids who'd do what was expected of them later in life, who'd maintain the family tradition like everyone else, without qualms."

"Why should they have qualms?"

Carlos turned to me; the waters were phosphorescent with algae, reflecting the sky, and I caught his eyes shining. "If my parents came here at weekends," he said, "I would have qualms about following them into their lives."

He had said nothing more until we had reached the jetty for my parents' villa. I slipped out with a thank you. I'm not sure that I saw him again before leaving for Madrid, since it was that moment which decided me. That dark night, with the trees overhanging in their luxuriance and yet concealing a world desperate to maintain the illusion of civility, the gentle message which Carlos had imparted – that somehow he had expected more, that one could communicate in many ways, that one had to listen to the flux of life to understand its message – all that had been enough for me. But it had begun with silence, in the darkness, listening: as moments of decision often do.

It was the Madrileño darkness which had made me think of Tigre. But soon Gabriel and I had reached the ring road on the north side of the city, the cut through to the airport which people from the north took to save time. Light was everywhere. I turned to Gabriel directly: "You are coming, then?"

"I am still thinking."

"Thinking time is over. I have the tickets."

"It is true." We had stopped beneath a high rise. "Perhaps you are right, and there is nothing for me here."

We stood looking at each other. "You must go," I said. "Take me to your apartment and we will arrange it all."

It sounded like a pass but I didn't mean it like that. I knew so little about Gabriel and his life and yet at that moment in Madrid there was also no one I knew more about. There was so little heroism in my life but I did long to be brave. Perhaps that was why I had followed Piree and his plan. And now when I thought of Gabriel's life and of the pressures which had moulded it my sense of worthlessness ebbed away for existence itself seemed heroic.

I remembered then Joyce's paean for modern heroes, *Ulysses*, which Gabriel had picked up in my room. All of us were dreaming of new ways to begin. Gabriel and I looked at each other, and in some core part of myself I felt that itch which I had felt before, on my arm.

"I'm afraid of just one thing," he murmured then, "that there is nothing for me here." We were almost touching. And that may have been enough to make the difference and bring him over to the plan, the fact that just for a moment we had all but been together.

I didn't spend long in the box-hole which he called a flat. There wasn't even a kitchen in it; he and the two Nigerians he shared with used a communal one which served their whole floor of the apartment building. *But we don't cook much*, he told me, when I saw these arrangements, *we're rarely here to share a meal together*. I asked him more about them. Didn't they get on, then? Weren't they all in this together? He didn't look at me in reply. He was coy, standing in his home there, his gestures quiet and empty. *These people*, he said in the end, *they are angry people*. They blamed others for their problems, it seemed, and found that dislike was an easy path to follow. So, they were human beings just like the rest of us! But he wanted something different, more hopeful.

The flat itself was just a room with a double mattress in which everything was shared, including their loneliness. Really, he had nothing to lose by taking Piree and I up on our proposal. And yet it had been so difficult to persuade him. What was it that had held him back? Fear, probably, for fear was such a strange thing and difficult to pin down: even now, the fear I felt at the impending crime which Piree and I sought to prevent sometimes seemed to be something utterly different, a fantasy instead, and there was a way in which fear could be admiration and even desire in the right circumstances. That's what I thought when I looked at Gabriel and wondered at how long it had taken him to give me his identity.

"Thank you for the papers," I said as I left. We waited for the lift to rise up the shaft from the ground floor.

"Why do you want them? You have not told me."

"They will be very helpful."

"You can do anything with those papers, anything at all."

"And you can do much in Paris."

"Perhaps I will turn on the radio there and hear that I am accused of some appalling crime."

I laughed. "You have been listening too much to Dolores, to her portrait of me as a criminal."

"But you are a thief."

This time I did not deny it. "And you," I said to him as the lift arrived, "you've just sold me identity papers. If you go back to hawk tomorrow, Dolores might be waiting there."

It was a callous remark. I hope I didn't intend it that way. I hadn't meant Gabriel's last night in Madrid to be spent like that, in fear. And yet that fear was very useful: it meant that he would be likely to do as he'd promised, that he'd come to Chamartín station the next evening to transport the books to Paris, since like me his fear was already being transformed into something else, something that could even have been beautiful.

Returning to Dolores's flat, I could not go to bed at once. I made a camomile tea to settle my nerves. Eventually I brought myself to lie down on my bed. I was still fully clothed. For a moment I felt as empty as I had done earlier that evening at the event in the bookstore, fingering myself in the manager's chair. But then I thought of Gabriel, of the moment that we'd almost touched, and that was enough soon afterwards to send me to sleep. Even so throughout the night I was continually waking to see if it was yet light. In the half glow of the Madrileño darkness I would spy the spines of the books which were piled up on the floor. Perhaps I had taken those books from the store on impulse so that I might feel safer, so that I might no longer feel pursued. Yet clearly it had been hopeless. I had never felt more agitated.

At the first hint of greyness in the sky I rose and dressed. In the kitchen I made a strong cup of coffee and then sat at the table, eating some dry bread. There was no sign of Dolores. I knew she'd rise long after I'd gone, that each of us now pretended that the other did not exist. I did not even leave a note for her on the table. I'd arranged to meet Piree at Chamartín at eleven o'clock, so I went down the stairs and out into the morning. I meandered back towards where I'd been with Gabriel the night before. He didn't live too far from the station, and for a moment I considered going to doorstep him, to bring him forcibly with me to Chamartín so that there'd be no chance of anything going wrong. But instead I decided to go straight to the concourse where I sat staring with aimless calm at the departures board as the trains left soundlessly for the north from the platforms below.

In all the time I'd been in Madrid only once had I left the city. That had been from Chamartín – I hadn't been to Atocha at all, not even when I'd been living round the corner in Lavapiés – and I'd gone to visit an old family friend in Ávila, Juan Aristegui, who had been an exile from Franco in Buenos Aires and had returned to Spain in the 90s as an ageing man. It had been something of a relief for me to leave the city behind, to see the Gredos mountains loom as fingers of rock and windswept grass across the *meseta*. We'd passed the Escorial as the track slithered through the hills. I'd spent my time thinking happily about the novel with the palindromic structure which I was then planning to write – the manifesto for which was even then in my pocket in Chamartín, as I waited for Piree and Gabriel – and watching beyond the window.

There were a few small towns up there, places with minor station halts where the official buildings crawled purple with bougainvillaea and the stationmaster didn't appear to have left his seat in twenty years. I'd been delighted at the prospect of visiting Aristegui, who used to play chess with my father in a small plaza in Belgrano, and delighted too at the journey, until I passed one of those stations and realised that the stationmasters here had probably been appointed during the military regime and that Aristegui, too, must have reflected on this every time he returned to Ávila from one of his excursions to the capital, and that this may even have been one of the reasons why he had chosen to live in Ávila and indeed why he had come back to Spain. No one likes to forget the past, especially if it has brought them much suffering and that suffering has become a central part of their identity.

Piree arrived punctually, at eleven. We sat in one of the station bars drinking milky coffee with two boxes of books piled up between us. Once I had shown Piree Gabriel's identity papers and he had put them in his briefcase the atmosphere was relaxed. His contact was waiting for these copies of his book in Buenos Aires, Piree told me. It was unlikely that there would be any difficulty in clearing customs at the airport. Once the African had got on the train, he told me, the plan would be almost complete.

"And what will happen then?"

"Then?" he asked, "what will happen then? Well, the presidential elections are imminent." He was always doing this, referring to the presidential campaign as if it had something to do with the crime.

"These books have got nothing to do with that."

He knocked over my coffee with a violent gesture. "How many times have I told you that we have to act at once, that time is against us? And yet you ignore me."

"I apologise."

"Time is against us," he repeated, shaking his head.

Piree seemed so sure of himself. He knew so much about this crime that for a moment I wondered if he himself was not the perpetrator. But he was so suave, I couldn't believe it. I thought about Gabriel, and tried to relax. We waited until he arrived at four with just a holdall, clutching a book in his hand. For a moment I thought it was that copy of *Ulysses* which he had taken from my sanctum, but then I saw that it was not that new bible but rather the old one, which spoke of God and salvation.

We prepared him with our books as well as his own. I joked to Gabriel: he had forsaken my offer of a new bible for the old one. He smiled, and for a moment I wondered if this could have been my heroic love right here, something to replace the fabricated sense of purpose which Piree's plan seemed to promise. Again we almost touched, but did not. I wanted more time with him. This could have been a promise and an opportunity to make a home instead of this constant wandering without roots burnt up by feelings of lost and vacant time and space that seemed to consume every city of the earth. Perhaps, I dreamed for a moment, it was still within our power to preserve this strange friendship we had developed if those who saw it could just have had enough faith and chosen love over fear.

Gabriel did not seem to notice my agitated thoughts. He looked remarkably self-possessed. I told him he would enjoy the journey; we hadn't booked him in a couchette but in one of the reclining seats, where he wouldn't have to worry about sleeping in beds surrounded by strangers. He smiled. He knew that he would be all right in Paris, he told us, after depositing the books as we had asked him to. Paris was a city with a huge colony. He would find his way. Piree made one last invocation to him not to forget his instructions and then the lift vanished into the earth and he and the books were gone.

As we turned away we heard screams in the departure lounge. Dolores was writhing on the ground, held down by some security officers as she fought the illness that possessed her. Perhaps she had followed, hoping to stop us, only to find that her disease had overcome her. *I wish I had a gun*, Piree said, *to cleanse her of this agony*. It was such a fearful thought that I tried to banish it.

As we left Dolores, trying to ignore her, absorbed in the plan and yet not speaking, an explosion shook the railway station and space accelerated past time for just an instant. I had the feeling that objects were flying before anyone had had a chance to reckon their meaning and that, flying, they would lure themselves and others into a destruction that no one had predicted and yet which everyone had imagined and secretly desired. I imagined that destruction before it happened, orange with flame. I couldn't see those flying objects but they surely were there: they had to be. I wasn't the only one. The tearing noise caught up with the movement of things and I looked around, panicked but also strangely thrilled. Wasn't this the sort of beautiful atrocity I'd been dreaming of, something to stand for everything which this society was unable to recognise or accept? The thrill burnt in me, a personal shrapnel which I had created.

Of course, I wasn't the only one to panic. There were screams in all directions and people fled outside to the road where the buses pulled in. I didn't feel able to move. This was it, I thought, in spite of the beauty of the moment, we were too late. The crime had occurred and we had done nothing to prevent it. What a useless pursuit! Slowly, however, reality got the better of my fantasies and I looked about me. There had been no flying objects, it seemed. No glass was broken. What had it all been about, then? What was that fear all for? I looked at Piree, who was standing next to me and seemed utterly serene.

"It's nothing," he said, "just the demolition of a tower block that has been scheduled for some time, for the building was affected by subsidence."

"Why are they all so fearful, then?"

"There's something in the air, perhaps. We're all waiting for something awful to happen and we don't know when it will be."

How did he know all this? Perhaps that explosion had resulted from a crime and he simply did not want to believe it. Or it may have been that Piree was right, and if that were so his knowledge of the potentialities of our future was one of the most terrifying things of all. As we walked on out of the station I tried to forget what he had just said, tried to forget everything about the lost chance of love with Gabriel and my fears for the direction which I had gone in ever since boredom and intrigue had led me to take up Piree and his cause. I looked instead back at my flatmate. The frenzy after the explosion had subsided. Still Dolores struggled on the floor as the security people sedated her, her arms wild as if disconnected from her being, violent predators by some monster let loose; and on she struggled as we left her and the station behind us and fell back into the city and the feeling which had plagued me ever since I had arrived there, the unending condition in which it seemed that we all lived, in loneliness, in terror.

* * * * *

Paris 2004

I

This dream was the beginning of a journey whose end was still unclear. He had yearned to leave but in leaving he had started to travel in a direction that he did not want to go. Now his dream was confused in his mind. It had almost become a nightmare.

As Gabriel woke with the train clattering through the violent lights of a station he sensed the professor moving closer to him with each breath. He had just fired off a string of hostile words which Gabriel had not understood. Was he dismissed? It was impossible to tell. The professor's face bleached and blended into the inside of a coconut shell with the brown husks of his hair burnt by the sun. As he stirred in his seat he tried to remember what those words had been. In his memory they coalesced into two clipped phrases, military talk directed at him by someone who might deny him admittance: *Fall out*! the man had said, the words clattering over the points, *you have failed the entry test*: Fall out into the darkness, Gabriel told himself, only to find that his mind had been colonised by the professor and that the world and its mysteries already were dark.

Finally his eyes sparked open once the lights of the station had passed and he emerged from that state between sleep and wakefulness when everything seemed dreamlike and yet real. He stretched his hand and felt for his bible. A glow filtered into the carriage from the night and from the umbrellas of light thrown up by the towns they passed. If he sat at the proper angle the light illuminated the page enough for him to read.

He opened the bible at random. It revealed the tale of Jonah, the messenger of God, thwarted in his flight to Tarshish. Cast into the belly of the beast, Jonah was swallowed whole by a monster and yet still touched by the divine. How foolish were the weak men of God not to trust in their allotted paths! That was the message of Jonah, the message for the pilgrim. The sailors had been right to throw the man into the sea; his doubt had been their suffering, and his suffering would be their relief.

Gabriel smiled. Perhaps these were the words of the village preacher, Ezekiel. He could not be sure. Yet though he could not remember Ezekiel's exact words about Jonah, one did not forget him. In a fit of anger he had preached, his fat finger pointing at the congregation, that the devil would inherit the earth, not the poor, or even the rich – but that at least the devil was easy to find, and was here at large, in the village. In the dry season the young boys used to throw the windfall grapefruits which no one wanted at Ezekiel as he strolled through the village in search of his few converts from the Islamic faith. And yet he had carried on, preaching that emigration, flight, might well be the only way for them to find work when they were older but that it would bring them no future happiness or reconciliation with the earth.

Gabriel reclined and clasped the bible to his chest. All he needed to know was that he possessed this book that would protect him from enemies. It was a relief to be protected so far from home. They were heading straight through to Paris. The man sitting beside him was fast asleep, accustomed to the sounds which the train made. Gabriel looked at him and felt surprised at his envy: he himself was too restless and excited for sleep.

He placed the bible in the pocket of the seat in front of him and stood up. He fidgeted with the gold bracelet on his right arm, and walked between the sleepers and into the passage towards the next carriage. A rail pressed against the windows, and he leant against it, watching the forest, passing shadows. Paris would be another new city for him. He was relieved to have the chance to come here and look for a place in the world at last. Many people of his nation went to Paris, speaking a little French because of all the *francophones* that came to their country, and he had been told that he would find a strong colony there.

There was as yet no sign of day. Gabriel looked up and down the train, on guard. He looked out of the window again at the darkness. He listened to the hum of the engine, absorbing the glow from the lights inside the train. There was a stranger coming towards him from the other carriage. Gabriel looked at him in the semi-darkness and started: wasn't this the strange professor, pursuing him?

He looked again and the fear subsided. He did not recognise the other. They had both been jettisoned into the international train. The man was carrying a book in his bony hands, trying to read in the darkness. Turning towards Gabriel, he called out sharply, in surprise, or fear. Gabriel moved towards him. This man was thin, but he was very smartly dressed. He was no patient of hunger. He wore a grey jacket and a suede waistcoat that might have been expected in a first-class compartment. Clearly he was an individual of status and yet he seemed pursued by anxiety. He was pacing from one side to the other, his knuckles flexed, his fingers touching the book at different places.

"It is dark," Gabriel said. There was no response. "What book is it you are reading?" The man stepped back, barked at him as if in command: "Are you following me?" Then the man stared at him and screamed. "Don't come near me!" He held the book between himself and Gabriel and crept back down the corridor; Gabriel followed. "Go away! Leave me with my book. It's nothing to do with you." Yet Gabriel had only wanted an exchange. Did he think that he was a criminal? What was he going to steal? The thin stranger screamed "Thérèse!", looking beyond Gabriel's shoulder.

Gabriel turned round. There was no one there. He turned back. The stranger had vanished. Gabriel knew then that he was in a place of mysteries. The train was a place between places. Here was a cosmic phantasm who looked like the professor and yet surely could not be the professor. Had the stranger been a spirit from childhood? Was he living in his own nightmare? Nothing was certain any more.

Gabriel did not dawdle. The fear had touched him, almost corporeal. Back in the carriage, he returned to the bible. He flicked forward from Jonah towards the Gospels. Here was clemency from the Gods, a touchstone against which to measure the world. He need not fear Paris. All he needed to do was dispense with the books according to his instructions. He knew there were thousands like him there. It would be easy to find them, to find work as he had planned – which was all that he had ever wanted to do.

Violent red light streamed into the carriage with the belated dawn. The man sitting beside him stretched and made noises. Gabriel looked as the other rose and stared out of the window. Rivers of concrete surrounded them, dammed and diverted into bridges and apartments rising in serried ridges. Life, constantly transferred, throbbed like a bee against the window. It was a bright day. The imagined sounds of Paris's morning rush hour spilled through his mind.

"Paris," his companion said, rubbing his stubble. He turned to Gabriel: "Your first time here?" Gabriel nodded. "Some people like it." The other took his mobile phone from the seat pocket in front of him and switched it on.

"Do you live here?" Gabriel asked him, but there was no answer. The man raised his hand, perhaps in admonition, listening to his mobile. Gabriel could hear a chain of tinny, disembodied voices. The bible was still beside him. He reached for his holdall and put it in. The train was slowing, the brakes grinding. Commuter trains passed, filled with workers crammed onto two levels. Some looked at their watches. Papers were scanned. People spoke into their mobile phones, loudly; he could almost hear them. Still the unchained voices dominated the carriage. He felt subdued, forced to listen. The other man had frozen, with his hand still raised, occasionally moving the phone to delete the messages yet otherwise statuesque, so that when the train came to a halt his bags remained unpacked.

Gabriel moved the heavy boxes and his holdall down and joined the passengers queuing to wrestle their bags down onto the platform. He put his hand in his pocket, and felt what money he had been given; he knew he could last for three, even four days while he looked for people who could show him how to survive in this new city. He had been hungry, but the girl from the bookstore and the professor had thrown him a lifeline. Now he had been offered a legal identity, and he would be able to make his way. He was too excited by the life he might be able to make for himself in Paris to worry any more about the uses they might make of his papers. They had talked of a terrible crime but was that his responsibility? What mattered to him was to find work.

There was a long queue of people waiting to step down from the train. Through the open door came glimpses of platforms busy with passengers. The wintry sun glided over the concrete. A loudspeaker commanded travellers to far-off cities. People ran, in the distance, into line. This was an ordered society, Gabriel saw, as he stepped from the train, where workers obeyed. Who was going to scorch it from existence as the girl from the bookstore had threatened? The whole thing had seemed such an absurd joke that he had not taken it seriously. The greatest danger to such a place could only come from within the place itself. If they wanted to give him some legal papers in exchange for this madness he was not going to stop them. He stood for some moments on the platform, the cumbersome boxes inert beside him. As he bent to put them on a trolley the man from his carriage brushed past him, still listening to his mobile phone, not seeing his recent companion: under control at last, moving in desolation.

II

There were storage lockers at the station beside the taxi rank. People just like him manned the entrance in grey overalls that clung to them like some prison costume. They nodded at the flickering security screen with bloodshot eyes. *Just books?* one of the North Africans asked as the boxes passed. Gabriel nodded. That was what he had been told by the professor. He had not checked the boxes, no. They were marked in big letters "DO NOT OPEN".

He collected them and wheeled them towards the grey oversize storage compartments. There was a cold light outside reflecting the city at dawn and the avenues of grey apartment buildings which he had seen from the train and imagined rising every morning as today in death and colourlessness. Gabriel shivered. He looked at the boxes as he moved them off the trolley and into the compartment. He locked the books in the compartment and rang the girl from the bookstore as he had promised. He could hear that other city, now distant, stretching into the morning as they spoke. They were there, he told her, he had done what he had been asked to do. His obligations were at an end. He thought he heard her laugh, but there was nothing more to say and he ended their conversation. Perhaps there had been a possibility there, a chance for something more, but it had gone.

Outside there was still very little heat to the day. He stooped down beside the taxi rank and picked out a jumper from his holdall. As he zipped the bag up again he felt for a moment that someone had been watching him. Perhaps it could have been that strange man who had fled from him down the train? He started and looked around but there was no one in evidence so he shouldered his holdall and made for his final destination: the underbelly of the Gâre du Nord, by the platforms of the RER suburban rail network which he would find there.

Everyone had told Gabriel that there were fixers here and that this was where he would be able to make the right contacts to begin his life in Paris. When he arrived he saw some tall Senegalese men waiting by a barrier. He spoke to them in Wolof and asked where he might find work and a place to stay and a home in this new city in which so many like him felt bereft. They led him over to a kiosk where some friends of theirs worked. There was a loud conversation which reminded him of home. The words floated over him. He was wondering how it would be to feel like these people and have a secure job, to be sending money back to relatives in the knowledge that at last he had a place in the world. *Hey! Wake up!* One of the Senegalese was clicking his fingers under Gabriel's face. *We have found something for you.*

By the evening he had located a mattress in a room near the Place du Commerce in the Quinzième. He shared the flat with two Nigerians who had work as contract cleaners at Charles de Gaulle airport. These flatmates, Ismail and

Ousmane, knew a boss who hired men with no questions asked. That would suit Gabriel better, they said, even if his papers were in order as he claimed. In this environment, it was always better to avoid questions. They took him to the airport the next day and Gabriel was taken on, for women's work.

At last he felt that he could relinquish the thoughts that had consumed him like his hunger in the other city. He was no longer pursued by nameless fears. His was not a life of luxury, no, but it was one where he could begin to feel at ease. The room he lived in was long and narrow, slapped under the eaves of the building. The plaster was peeling and there was mould on the window frame. Outside in the corridor were the communal bathroom and kitchen, though Ismail and Ousmane tended to cook within the room itself on a small stove. There was space for two single mattresses, some suitcases and a chair. They slept in shifts, worked in shifts, and often there were only two sleepers at one time. When they were all there two of them shared one of the mattresses, limbs curled up against one another, as if still back at home.

The airport where they worked was far, an hour or more on the RER. Actually, there was more skill to this cleaning than Gabriel had realised. If you took the mop and just trailed it over the floor without care the floor was not clean. On his second day the airport manager complained to the contractors. The foreman picked Gabriel, Ismail and Ousmane for special criticism, pointing, like a boxer, jabbing the finger: they had to clean the dirt up faster, they were not here on holiday, and he had only taken them on as a favour. So Gabriel learnt to mop with greater strength. Soon he could spot the dirt before it had spread too far across the polished floor, keeping his head down and removing it.

During their 12-hour shifts the cleaners were allowed a break of half an hour. The walk to the back room was the best part of the break. Most of the other cleaners were North African, and they did not talk to him. Generally the small TV was on and Gabriel would catch up on the latest game of football, resting his legs. If Ismail or Ousmane were on the same shift as him they would watch the match together. By the time he walked back out Gabriel was already thinking about the dirt; taking the metal dustpan extended from his arms, arcing through the concourse, dancing unseen among these people who allowed him work.

Only once in those first days did he feel that he was being observed. *Fall out! Fall out!* For a moment the professor had revisited him. He stopped the act of cleaning. *You have failed the entry test!* He looked more closely. Of course, the professor was not there with this fantasy of a crime and Gabriel's imagined involvement in it. Instead, a family was staring at him. They looked concerned. Gabriel had stopped cleaning. He knew that he should stop drawing attention to himself but he did not pick up his mop again. The little boy was saying something to his father: they had a foreign mentality, Gabriel heard him say, it was true even of Elena at home.

The phrase kept in Gabriel's mind as he worked. Here was that name again which he had first encountered with the girl from the bookstore. Now it had pursued him here to Paris. How many people did he know in this city? Ten, twenty? Yet somewhere there was another person like him.

He asked his flatmate Ousmane if he had ever heard the name Elena, that night on the RER as they returned from their shift. She was like him, he told Ousmane, that was what they had said in the airport.

Ousmane mocked him, though: "They could mean anything," he said. "They could be talking about an animal! Elena the cat, Elena the dog."

"No, the boy was meaning a *person*. A *person* like me."

"There isn't anybody like you, Gabriel."

It was late and they almost had the carriage to themselves. There were only four more stops left before home. Gabriel looked at Ousmane. The flecks of white on his hair made him look aged, rather than distinguished. He was a stocky man, shorter and tougher than Gabriel, and wore western clothes which looked as though they had once been a lot more expensive. He had been rich, in Nigeria, something in the legal world, a judge if he and Ismail were to be believed. It seemed to Gabriel that Ousmane saw everything in life as a disappointment.

"Elena." Gabriel shook his head.

"There isn't a mystery about her." Ousmane shrugged. "That boy means, they all cleaners, the same one as another."

In silence the tunnels traversed, the train like a bullet penetrating the flesh of the city. Gabriel remembered Ezekiel at home warning him before he left, warning him to keep to his allotted path. That preacher would lecture those dreaming of escape, weekly, on the futility of their ideals. *I have seen our brothers on the streets, in need. There is no gold there*, Ezekiel would shout, working himself into a sweat, *the only gold is inside us.* And yet he had escaped, and now with the help of the professor he had gone even further. He had done what had been asked of him. Yet he felt that he was still pursued by him, that in some strange way he had not yet left that part of his life behind. Why else had he sensed a vision of him on the train, a vision that had vanished into fearfulness?

It was past midnight when they reached the flat. Ismail was at home, watching a game of football from the Argentine league. He was leaning forward in his chair, hugging his knees with anxiety.

"What's up?" Ousmane cuffed him on the head. "Marseille lost again, right?"

Ismail leapt up in mock fury. Ousmane supported Monaco, almost out of defiance, Gabriel thought, because his compatriot supported their deadly rival. The two were distant relatives, but Ousmane always treated Ismail with disdain. It was the typical snobbery of the educated for the hustler, something that Gabriel had seen often enough around the transport park at Bundung when he had come across travellers with connections to a European income. They had always let him know that he was worth less than them, that his urgent desire for an education would never allow him to overcome his inferiority. They had laughed at him, playing the big man, just as Ousmane laughed at everyone but himself.

A fight broke out in the match, and they stopped the banter to watch. Then River scored, and Ismail did a dance of celebration on the mattress.

"Hey!" Ousmane complained. "That's my bed you dancing on."

Ismail ignored him and when River won the game he danced again. The TV was switched off and they lay on the mattresses. Gabriel moved restlessly, his arms brushing up against Ismail's ribs. He would have to rise in six hours for work but he needed a clear mind. He got up after half an hour and moved over to the stretch of light by the window with his bible.

It was Ousmane who had challenged him to turn to the Gospels again, this time to read them methodically. "We all believe in God," Gabriel had protested one morning on the RER. "Why you want to make me doubt?" Ousmane spoke loudly, as if in a courtroom, his curls bristling: "I want to know who *is* your God. I want to know how strongly you will keep him. How soon will you deviate?" He was of course a Muslim. Back home, too, Gabriel was in a minority, as a Christian surrounded by Muslims. Yet largely he had lived there in peace, and colonists came together in a new place like Paris, regardless of creed or nation. New loyalties were formed, and new alliances. There should have been no reason for them to be hostile to one another unless somehow that hostility was created by the forces around them, the forces shaping their new world.

This was why Gabriel so often turned back to the bible after the television had been turned off. That night the light was dim and Gabriel had to squint as he read. He turned to the Book of Revelation: a new heaven and a new earth, the words of Ezekiel still clear. Gabriel read the verses where the prophecy culminated again and again. Occupied with the Book and with his favourite passages in it the night sped into stillness. It was late. All the other apartments in the block were silent until by and by a vicious yell broke, prolonged, the cry of bondage and deliverance from it reverberating even once it had gone. Was it real? He could not be sure. Since arriving in Paris he had found that there were screams which could pursue him even as he slept, visions of something awful which never quite materialised if he opened his eyes. It was something that felt like an explosion, firing through his being, and smelt acrid. In his dream it felt like he was burning, as if someone had branded him. He did not know where these thoughts came from and they vanished as soon as he was conscious.

It was light almost before he had been aware of sleeping. There was a hurried washing in the red plastic tub and then Gabriel went down the stairwell. The day was a grey wash beneath a film of clouds. He stood in the square by the metro with the city still cold and the flagstones scummy with wet paper: his ticket swallowed by the machine, rolling open the doors with the curved metal handle, standing beside the others, silent again: so much silence. Really, a human being could get used to anything at all. The grey skies were becoming normal, the rush hour was becoming normal, even cleaning, the cries of prostitutes were becoming normal. The village, Ezekiel parading through Fogny and intoning in Mandinka, the professor, those curious boxes of books in which that strange man and his sidekick from the bookstore invested so much meaning - that was unreality, imagination.

At his break that afternoon Gabriel watched the football alone, a match from the Chinese league. He could perhaps have gone to a bookstore instead, read something, but he did not want to waste money like that. At home, at the village school, yes, he had ached for knowledge and even when the money had run short and he had had to stop classes he had not desisted, returning to the classroom six months and even a year later. There he had read the great African writers of the colonizing language, Achebe, Soyinka, even the rebel Thiong'o who had reverted to writing in Kikuyu. His teacher there had told them of their history, of the importance of articulating the struggle in a universal language. He had felt the significance of this message in his heart as if it had been a poem whose beauty transcended the anger which they all felt at times. And yet now that he was in Europe he had lost this drive. There was no point in going to the bookstore, since he could not actually afford to do anything except watch football.

Anyway, Gabriel felt that he had been turned into too much of an obsessive for books already. There had been the girl Elena from the bookstore, pressing this book *Ulysses* on him. And of course, the professor, Kent Piree, with the books he had been asked to deliver as the price of his freedom. Who knew what had been in them? He'd been replaying in his mind the way that he'd been given the books and left the station, the sudden commotion and a loud, distant noise. Had that been significant? For a day or two after arriving in Paris he had followed the news headlines but there had been nothing to suggest that anything terrible had happened and no news about those books at all. It was as he'd thought, the whole thing was a joke, a performance.

He returned from watching the Chinese football match and continued with his work. He was here to cleanse the society of its dirt. Wasn't that like something that Elena and the professor had both said? It felt like it: it all felt the same. He needed to scrub harder and squeeze out the polluted water so that the impurities were liquidated. There was a rhythmic splendour to work's pattern, simultaneously to despise and thank those large men – mostly it was men who made this women's work of cleaning – who excreted dirt, empty cartons, an air to be cleaned, and all without conscience of it: simultaneously to hate and accept the dirt which he personally accumulated, as if it were his own: simultaneously to clean and become dirty. It all felt like a model of the contradictory and simultaneous rhythms that he had learnt first from the drums, reminding him of home, reminding him to be grateful.

Lost as he was he did not notice the disturbance at first. There was a long queue at the freight collection point, most of them truck drivers. They began shouting and whistling at the girl who worked at the desk. She had turned her back and was ignoring them, and they wanted her attention. The noise made Gabriel put his mop down. He saw Ousmane standing near the front of the queue. The old judge was not even pretending to work, as if labour was demeaning for a man who had once worn the robes of justice. He annoyed Gabriel. Who was there dignified and just enough in the world to stand judgement over others?

The noise began to subside. The girl returned to the freight desk. She was talking pointedly to an elegant-looking man at the front of the queue who was supporting himself with a cane. As Gabriel watched the conversation degenerated into what was almost an outright argument. He could not hear what was being said but yet felt that there was something terribly familiar about it. Had not the professor used a cane when he had seen him before? He had seethed with a violence waiting to explode. Where was it if not here? Was that the explosion he had felt, in his dreams, triggered in some way by the professor?

He turned and moved his bucket further away. He pretended to work. He could not work. All the time he suffered from the thought that others were chasing him, just as they had done in his dreams. They were spirits from his village. They could fly in their own magical vessels. They were his own inventions. Was the professor really who he said he was? And was it not him, standing and arguing with the girl by the freight desk? Perhaps he had invented them all, the danger and the attractiveness of the danger, its stubborn beauty: perhaps this headlong flight into the future imagined world of atrocity was what he desired.

He looked up. The girl from the freight desk had appeared with a trolley piled high with boxes. She was talking to the two men who had asked for them. The boxes were marked in big letters, "DO NOT OPEN". Gabriel felt as if he had lost the ability to discriminate for as he looked at them he could not tell if this really was the professor and his Argentinian friend haunting him by day and by night with their talk of a plot and a crime and of the secrets interred in their boxes. He could not tell, for they all looked the same to him. He felt as if he had been through this all before somewhere, as if this western world subsisted in a timeless void. Yes he had shepherded those boxes without knowing them and would do again unless somehow he managed to crawl out from this circle of pursuit and flight in which he was trapped.

They were moving the trolley across the concourse and as they came Gabriel remembered that talk, that a crime was in the offing, that it was stalking them in invisible circles like a spider on its web until they were trapped and consumed by it. He looked at them and felt the crime coming closer, humanity pregnant with its terrible power and unable to hear its screams until it had given birth to it. He could not bear it. He had to escape. He just managed to move his things behind some stairs before they saw him. But he sensed that this had not been a joke at all, that the professor had been in all seriousness: the threat had not gone as they passed him, and in fact it was only just beginning.

III

In those earliest days of spring a thin white coverlet fell upon the city and smothered it. The fog appeared to have descended as Gabriel had arrived, in the winter. There were so many white faces, pallid, as if ill. They passed him, indistinguishable one from another. Soon each day blurred into a likeness of its predecessor. He could not tell the difference between one advertisement hoarding and the next, though he sensed that they changed. They sold and others bought and soon it seemed that for so long everything had been the same, that Paris was static and stretching outside history. As he looked at the selling signs and the fog time for him developed a curious quality. He wondered if it was not running backwards, or in circles. Why did it have to progress? Everything seemed so much the same that the intensity of those dreams of the professor and the girl from the bookstore surely had to refer to what had already happened, a crime which had occurred and which they now needed to solve. Who was there who could prevent the violence of what must be done by those who could not but do it?

A sense of fatalism almost overwhelmed him. In the airport, he read passages of the bible. But he could not concentrate. He took to walking the concourse, trying to maintain the sense of release which he carried into his rest periods. He looked at the queues of travellers and distinguished the religious from the commercial, the students from the tourists, the happy from the damned. He tried to picture their destinations and imagine whole worlds and lives for them. But one day, scrubbing beside the automatic doors that led outside, he realised that this was all a dream. He was not equal to these people whose lives he imagined, even if he was on a paid break just as many of them were. Equality had not been one of the gifts given to them by their maker.

He turned and carried his things back into the concourse with the impression that everyone was watching him. What was there that was so unusual about him? Always he felt these poisoned arrows of energy firing from the eyes of others and yet he did not have the mark of Cain. Simply by associating with the professor and worrying about his pursuit of him he had begun to feel as though he was in some way guilty of an offence that he had never committed.

Gabriel felt wary. He left his mop bucket propped against a shop window and went into the bookstore, grateful for its familiarity. He felt agitated. There had to be somewhere in the airport where he could find a space to breathe. The girl who worked there gave him a fresh smile and he felt a surge of relief. There was something that distinguished her: the rich complexion, relieved by a dark mole on her right cheek and the brown curls set above her high, freckled forehead. Gabriel smiled back, and she said something in a strong foreign accent.

He began to roam the bookstacks. Novels, histories, science, current affairs all struck him as being the same. At home there was only one bookstore in the whole country, in Bakau, and most of those with books to sell crammed their wares onto ageing trestle tables in Serekunda market, the books in lumpen piles, middens of ideas exported and forgotten. He had spent many days among them. There, you could say, the booksellers were representatives of an exotic world, supported by the vanity and charity of those with connections. Yet the aisles of this airport bookstore possessed unending streams of books, piled up, stacked on shelves, on tables, by the counter, propped in the window, categorised by subject and by language. Here was a world of unique creations packaged to look identical. It was just like the store which he had gone to in the other city. Until now he had not realised that these people loved their minds so much that they felt compelled to share them.

"Can I help you?" It was the shop assistant now, standing beside him in withdrawn courtesy. "Are you looking for a book on religion?"

"Is this the religion section?" Gabriel asked her.

"Yes. What subject are you interested in?"

"I have a book on religion. The only one I want to read," he said. She smiled; she had a rich smile, this assistant, one which for a moment made him forget. "These people have also written on religion?"

"All of them," she said.

"Why is that, actually? Why do they write their books?"

She shrugged: smiling again, that woman, taking a step towards him. There was something familiar about her. He was sure of it, he had seen her before: this whole exchange, seemed to have happened before. e was sure of it, he had

111

seen her before.H "You have only arrived recently," she said.

Gabriel nodded and looked at her. "You also are not from here. I have seen you somewhere else."

She shrugged. "I also work at freight collection sometimes." That was not it, of course: there was a falseness about that excuse, as if she knew it had been invented and that her whole existence was a performance for others. Strands of brown hair fell across her forehead, offering and withholding. "I'm an Argentinian," she laughed. "But my parents came from the East, and so they called me Elena."

Gabriel did not listen as she continued talking. Her talk was all a pretence, as was everything else, that they did not know each other: how could they? What was he supposed to think? That this was a strange coincidence, such as he might have found in one of the books in this shop, in a book that was not to be trusted! He knew that God did not deal in coincidences, only in fate, which could be seen by one or two of the old marabouts in the villages even though they used the Qu'ran. Elena was pursuing him and pretending not to. Their lives were connected in some way, and he was supposed to find out how. Perhaps she was telling him how now, if only he would listen. If he could follow her through the books perhaps he might see the hidden meaning which underpinned life, and all the crimes which underpinned the world might somehow count for nothing.

"Why do you work here?" He interrupted without ceremony or invitation.

"For the money," she said.

"But why the bookstore?"

They looked at each other, joined by a mutual curiosity and suspicion. Elena held his eyes for a moment. She was attractive to Gabriel, as when they had met before. She had paid for him. In another time she might have felt that this offered her rights of ownership but time was not static here however much it seemed so. Relationships changed and in the space of these few exchanges she had already come to seem beautiful and important. Yet he knew to beware: a quick movement, a clumsy phrase, these were all it might take to make her frightened of him and ready to reassert her feeling that she was better than him.

Gabriel told her he would return the next day and ran to continue his shift, picking up the mop and bucket just as the foreman was wandering over. It was enough for now to continue cleaning the dirt, to think about the mystery of his own life - of this person Elena who appeared to have been sent to him, if that was possible.

It began to rain outside. The wintry light vanished, taking with it the work he had done on the concourse as people came in with their shoes, muddying the floor and then departing. Time took on a sudden, immediate quality. He worked so hard that he could feel himself age by the mop-stroke. He was absorbed. A man kicked his mop, moving too rapidly towards passport control to notice it, and began to shout obscenities to someone behind Gabriel, pointing his finger, his face twisted and seized with anger: "You are all the same," he shouted, "all the same: you try to make our lives a misery, to dominate us." His face was wet, Gabriel saw, his jacket spotted with sweat, or rainwater. People tutted as they passed the scene, looking at the person behind Gabriel with disdain. He shook his head at Ousmane, who was on the same shift as him, and turned to catch a glimpse of the offending party only to find that there were so many people that it was difficult to see who it might have been.

Gabriel glimpsed Elena coming along behind the upset man, chaperoning him. There was no doubt: this was certainly the girl he had met before, in what seemed like another life, before he had taken the train to Paris. They seemed to be coming from freight collection, just as they had done that other time when he thought he had seen them. This time, however, he could not escape them. She smiled as they stopped near to him. She was pushing a trolley with several large boxes which were marked in big letters, "DO NOT OPEN". Apparently, they contained books. The man was still shouting: "You make it impossible to prevent the crime," he shouted, "you hate us, because you will never be like us!" Then he thrust a piece of paper in front of Gabriel. "Here, at the very least you must sign this!"

Gabriel understood none of it. He looked more closely at Elena and her patron. The lines of his face began to take shape, curved and hard. There was a sharp frown mark between his eyebrows. He seemed different to Piree and yet he had to be Piree. These big people all looked the same. They were like brothers of the same mother, very difficult to tell apart. But beneath his anxiety and compulsion there were certain signs, signs that Gabriel was learning to recognise. The man was well-dressed. He was charged with books. He had to be the professor.

Gabriel grabbed Elena's sleeve and pulled her aside as if for romance. What was this? Why were they pursuing him and pretending not to? Why had they tracked down the books from the locker if only to parade them in front of him again? Did they think that he would suspect nothing? Were they trying to implicate him? What had he done? What was the crime? Was he guilty of anything more than the desire to work?

She could not tell him much. She did not even acknowledge their previous meetings. All she could tell him was that this man, Kent Piree, was an important professor from an American university and it would help everyone if they extracted him from the airport as quickly as possible. So Gabriel signed, in his bewilderment. Piree continued then, as if satisfied. Some gendarmes played with their guns and looked over in their direction and Elena, in the process of gathering the boxes, managed to whisper to Gabriel: "Don't worry, I've got him under control. He won't disturb you again."

Gabriel's shift finished. He returned home on the RER. Elena had said, in a whisper on the concourse, that they could meet again tomorrow. It was a strange task she had set herself, to push the professor's books for him through the concourse. It was as if she had known that Gabriel would be working there at that moment and had again designed their second meeting to seem like coincidence.

With that thought, he became anxious. He could not rest when he reached the flat and sat up watching out of the window into the darkness. Only when it was late was he able to fall asleep and he was woken early the next morning by Ousmane banging the door as he came in from the night shift. Ousmane saw the film of alertness in Gabriel's face and began something in Yoruba, as if in friendship, before reverting to their common language. He asked if Gabriel had seen the powdered milk but Gabriel lay too tired to answer.

Ousmane began to rummage through a holdall. He and Ismail were going to a festival in La Villete that night: did Gabriel want to go with them? But he was busy with Elena, and when the old judge found out about the girl he began to mock him with the loudness of authority, even using

Gabriel's surname, Cissoko, as if he was some low-life brought before him in a case of petty theft. Gabriel looked at the whitening curls on his flatmate's head and realised how small the defendants must have felt in that courtroom in the central plateau of Nigeria when Ousmane Agbyeni had donned his wig and performed against them.

Gabriel felt angry. He was not a criminal. He had stolen nothing. He was not like Ousmane and Ismail, wasting money at festivals that their families needed. He was not escaping, but following his path, as the preacher Ezekiel had told him to. He did not respond to Ousmane with the deference which was expected and muttered something about all of it being down to fate.

Ousmane exploded. He jabbed his finger in Gabriel's direction like the foreman in the airport, imposing himself, trying to dominate. All those years running the courthouses of Jos had woven into his every movement. He was tired of fate, tired of it! Gabriel ran about, a decapitated chicken in the city compound, trying like the French to be free, but it was impossible. He was working here, that was his purpose. Did he think that any of them could forget where they were from? Didn't Gabriel know what people like that girl thought of people like them? "We are all of us slaves here," he said to Gabriel angrily, "but slaves of a different God. We all accept it. We do nothing! It is not right, no it is not right. We should do something. We should be planning."

"No one can be free who is not with God," Gabriel answered, in the end.

"You will lose Him here, Gabriel," Ousmane said. "With your girl."

They spoke no more about it and Gabriel was able to sleep a little more before the light came. Later in the morning he returned to Charles de Gaulle. He did not know why God had thrown Elena and him together, but he knew that it was so. During his break he turned to the passages from the Gospels which dealt with reprieves which almost saved Jesus from the Cross, but again he could not concentrate on the words: this time the North Africans were joking about something, and the noise of the television was loud.

Even so, when Gabriel met Elena later that day he knew at once that this remained his path. She was annoyed because he was late, but she was welcoming. She was still open. She told him not to apologise, yet of course that was his first reaction. He had encroached upon her free time without thinking about it, but she insisted that it was not a problem. He apologised again, the words almost a whisper, a recollection of how he had learnt the colonising language. She was still looking at him, still open. She had not sent a message: she was a message. She suggested they went to look at the bookstore. Why, he asked, what did he want with the heads of others? Each book was a head, after all: the bigger the book, the larger the head. The bible, too, was a long book, she pointed out, but then, as Gabriel reminded her, God had a right to a large head.

She laughed, and turned away. The night flights to South America were beginning to board and the concourse had filled. Elena beckoned, and he followed, out of a sense of mystery, thinking that perhaps even here he was touched by the breath of God, and stillness. It was so easy to walk where the path beckoned, imagine fields of maize and sweet potatoes, forget the present and the choices he made in it: it was dangerously easy to follow. Elena seemed in control of her movement through the concourse, the white sea parting, for the first time in his life, following *their* path, it seemed: except that the moon, barely visible in the

Paris night, began to exert its power: the waters began to press them.

A woman in one of the queues moved out and slapped Elena in the face, without ceremony or invitation: "You bitch!" she screamed, "you thief, you fucking bitch!" She grabbed Elena's hair, scratched her face, tried to bite her. Elena fought back and the two women grappled, twisting around the concourse like hysterical dancers, screaming insults, scratching, screaming, crying: "You bitch," the other woman kept screaming, "you've stolen him and he's mine."

It was time to intervene. If Gabriel left it too much longer then people would label him a coward. "Stop that," he called out, grabbing their arms, separating them violently: "that is enough of that." A streak of blood ran down his arm, drawn from Elena's cheek. Her eye caught his, but only briefly. "Of course you take her side – you're her slave!" The mad woman was talking to him: he looked at her for the first time, caught the wildness in her eye, shadows, clutching her black hair, all in shadows: a mystery. "You're her fucking slave! Devils, the both of you." She hit him in the face too, but then the security forces intervened and she was marched off the concourse.

None of the onlookers spoke. Again Elena looked at him, only to look away. They were both injured. They had both been attacked without cause. Yet as the crowd dispersed and the airport recovered its dignity he sensed that many of the onlookers felt the attack to have been in some sense merited. Had the mad woman gone any further, some might even have joined her.

"Come on." Elena spoke as if nothing had happened. "We are going to the shop."

Gabriel followed her. The words of their attacker had struck him. They were both devils, she had said. It was difficult to know if a path was always as true as it seemed. "Elena, did you know that woman?" She was fumbling in her pocket for the swipecard to the store, and ignored him for a moment. "Did you know her?"

"She insulted you," Elena said. She would not answer him directly. "She should not be allowed to get away with it. She should pay."

Hopelessness settled on him. He just wanted to move on from this strange violence, this incomprehensible new world where crimes and their criminals were pursued without pity and without end. He followed her into the shop. "Let us look at the books instead," he said, feeling that this showed already how much he had learnt – that the key to the crime which Elena was tracking lay here.

Elena closed the door behind them. He felt a touch of the freedom which Elena had mentioned before. The freedom settled in the pages, the millions of pages around them, seething, constantly reforming, breaking apart. He spied a copy of Sembène's *God's Bits of Wood*, and picked it up, comforted with the familiarity. Slowly he returned to that classroom and the memory of reading that book, the anger which the students had felt about colonialism. But as well as the anger there had simultaneously been an optimism at the thought that those days were past.

"This is a good place." Gabriel looked around. He knew he would not be attacked here. No one would run from him, along the night train. No one would shout at him, mistaking him for someone else. He would not be pursued. This was, in fact, some kind of *inner sanctum* – the words of his teacher at Fogny school – a place free of the violence of the concourse: a place free.

"Look at the books then," Elena said to him.

"This was your idea. To come and look. I am looking." He looked at her, his eyes drawn again to the mole on her right cheek, to the freshness of a face that loved life.

"You're not interested."

"You interest me." He could not withdraw the words.

"Look again." She walked to a section of shelving near the tills and picked up a book, caringly, flicking the pages and helping them ebb from one end to the other. "I look at the books because they interest me." She held the book out to him. "Perhaps you're right, and these books are like heads. I'm a stranger here, like you, and each time I read one, I understand this place and the way it thinks a little better."

He took the book. It was in English, he saw, and it was very long. "The man who wrote this book – he had a very large head."

"Gabriel, you're funny. But you are right too. Joyce had a big head."

"Have you read this one?"

"He finished it here in Paris. People call it a great book, a bible of modern literature."

"Is that so?" He knew it: it was *Ulysses*, as she herself had told him before, written about a single day that had passed exactly a hundred years before but whose tragic, complex relevance had yet entirely to wane. Once again she was plying him with the same ideas that she had done ever since they first had met. But he tried to dissemble, to show that he was unaffected by her crushing, tedious pursuits. "Is that so? A bible?"

"Of course you have your own bible. I understand that. But when I came here from Buenos Aires, I wanted to read it."

"I will buy it." He spoke without thinking.

"There's no need. You can have it."

"That is stealing."

"No. I'll take it from my allowance." Still those soft, measuring eyes: she turned and walked away among the shelves of books, and he followed. This was a world so utterly strange. Time was like a labyrinth and things repeated themselves as if it had ceased to exist. And yet he felt that there was a pattern and a code to it all and in that too a meaning. First though one had to break through the labyrinth and here among the books it was all the harder, with the heads of all these people preserved as if in ice for their fellows to know them. He could understand now how people like Elena and Piree saw these objects as mysteries which had to be broken. The books, the heads, hemmed him in; hewn from the trees, filled with a version of life in their lifeless pages, talking like the trees beyond the dreams in his head. This chatter began to press down on him. The voices were inside him, talking. All this noise! He clutched his head for a moment. "Gabriel, are you all right?"

"Where are you taking me?"

"Just to a different way out."

"There are too many books in this place. Too many!"

"That is what I thought when I first came here. But now I like it."

"It is like a puzzle," he said. "You feel you can never escape it."

"That is the thing about the crime," she said, turning to him and acknowledging for the first time what had gone before, the violence and the pursuit, the coercion and the madness. "But it is a puzzle we are obliged to unravel before long. Something that is urgent."

"Where is it going to take place, this crime?"

Elena shrugged. "We still don't know. That's why we're pursuing it so hard."

She moved up a winding stairway. He could see another exit above, leading out to a different concourse where there were more shops. She understood them, she said. Yet he had read the bible many times, and now in Paris had tried again. Still he did not understand his place in this city. Perhaps that was why her talk of a new and different bible had excited him, why he was willing to return to *Ulysses*. Perhaps he would do as she said, and enter some of these heads a little, in the hope that the path in would also lead him and all of them to a way out.

IV

It was easy to become lost. The lesson had repeatedly been given to him in life. First by his father, who as a young boy had been sent into the bush clothed in white rags for circumcision, ignorant of the missionaries' truth – deep into the forest, his father had told him, until none of the boys had known where they were, or how to return, and they had clasped some small talismans and bracelets of love and protection that their parents and grandparents had given them as if in them to seek their salvation. And then in later years the lesson had been given to him by Ezekiel, who had talked weekly of the evil one's facility for luring people until their souls were quite lost, and they had almost forgotten that they ever had had one. And then, in this Europe, it was quite easy to become lost.

It was because he felt lost that he had accepted Elena's invitation into the bookstore. She had given him the book, the new bible. He read it. Ousmane mocked him when he first appeared with it in the flat. Wasn't he reading the word of God any more? And then the old judge laughed, in some way superior. Yet their lives in Paris were almost the same.

Superiority was a myth, however tenacious the judge's grip on it might have been. He was the one who was really lost, Gabriel felt, imagining a sophistication which he had never had. But he didn't condemn his elder, not openly. He couldn't do that. He was silent.

Instead Gabriel accepted the gathering distance between himself and his flatmates. It had always been there and it had been ridiculous to pretend that it had not, that somehow they could all be African brothers together. It was never so simple as that: time and stories were never so simple. Ismail and Ousmane were angry: angry at their place in the world and angry at the causes of their place. They were disgusted by history, and frightened of it. They did not have the strength to confront it. They talked wildly instead of some impossible revenge. Gabriel could see that they were letting in bitterness to cover their joy and so he wanted no part of it. When they went out to drink, once or twice in the week, Gabriel let them go. At home Ismail and Ousmane had been free from all intoxication except that of the divine. But they had forgotten themselves here and were easy prey for new alternatives.

When they were gone, and the flat had retreated back into a pulsing quiet that reminded him of home, he read *Ulysses*. Elena had told him that the book was about heroes, and he read of them by the light of the bare bulb in the flat. Why did he bother with the book? Perhaps it was because it did not present the false promise of an easy story with an easy moral, because it was not the sort of story that he was learning to distrust. He read, too, because he sensed that every story was connected to every other in turn up to the very first story that had given birth to the world and all its painful beauty.

In the end, everything he did was prompted by the mystery of his presence there. Everything was connected. He had begun to wonder if everything was not a clue which had been laid by the professor and the Argentinian. The clue to the crime which they sought to prevent lay in a book and here was a book, *Ulysses*, which lay in his hands and had been placed there by them. Perhaps this was the very book of dreams and nightmares which they were so desperate to smuggle out of Europe. If he read it, he might understand before it was too late.

It was as well for him that the book was written in the language that had colonized him. And even then, it was nothing but pages of words, amassed as if a treasure, at times not seeming even to connect with one another, ideas released just for the sake of being free of them. Pages would lapse with Gabriel certain that he was reading each one, absorbing each word, only then for him to realize that it was in fact some time since he had been aware even of one thought that the writer Joyce had placed in his book. But perhaps that was the point: that the path to peace and understanding did not go forwards but sometimes backwards and in repetition as if never breaking its way to an end and its consolation.

Elena asked him how he was doing with *Ulysses* a few days later when they met during their break at the airport. It wasn't easy, he replied: the man Joyce was like a judge or a lawyer, he was a monster who used words not easy to understand. No, she replied, it was just that Joyce was like God: creators of monsters both. She looked at him but she did not laugh. Why were they both talking of monsters? Were they afraid of each other, or of something else? He could not answer that question, did not even know if there was an answer. So he told her how he felt, that the story and its meaning went backwards and then forwards, but never in a straight line. She looked sad, then. She touched his arm. He'd surpass them all in the end, she said then. She'd been thinking about that subject for months herself, for years, and ever since the professor had started to talk to her about the universe and the eternal fires of its expansion and implosion, she had found these ideas almost overpowering. How had he known to touch her like that? He was smart.

After a week or so they started to meet outside the airport when they both had some free time. They did nothing extravagant on these occasions, strolling past the delicatessens and antiquarian booksellers of the Rue de Bretagne in the Marais or relaxing in gardens. At times Gabriel remembered the shrill voice of the madwoman from the airport concourse, screaming about devils, or the command which Elena and the professor had taken of him. He wished he could have pulled himself away, but there was something that fascinated him in this whole game, in her. He could not say what it was, and as the attraction was nameless he was able to ignore its hold on him. She made no attempt yet to seduce him beyond her simple presence, which was enough to remind him of everything that he had had at home and which here was absent.

Sometimes, on the Champ de Mars, he found that his two worlds collided. As he strolled with Elena, he would see men selling crafts from home. Groups of Wolofs, their heads cupped by berets and flaunting colour from their printed shirts, offered miniature djembes made in chains of workshops along the road from Yof airport to Dakar, carved figures from the dusty hinterland, cowry necklaces. They were always pestering and upsetting people. He would nudge Elena when he saw them and disparage them as soon as they were past. Did these Senegalese want to sell their world, here in Paris? Was it worth so little? Why was he so angry about it? Elena wanted to know. And this he usually met with incomprehension, silence. He had too much anger, she said. He needed to read the book she had given him, to understand again, as he had already shown that he did.

She repeated this so often that he did as she asked. He began to read parts of *Ulysses* again. He read with more concentration. He read at home, or during his breaks at the airport. It was so easy to get lost. The main protagonist of the book was certainly lost: his friends, mocking his religion behind his back, even when he himself no longer believed in that God: looking at the women of his city with unceasing surges of desire: his desires always failed: could this man possibly be a hero for this world, a Jesus Christ figure from a modern bible? and could his heroism really be a clue for the location of the crime?

Gabriel could not see it. Heroes prevented crimes, they did not commit them. Who was this character of Joyce's to restrain anyone? Such an ordinary and God-forsaken man as this Leopold Bloom surely was not equipped to seek out atrocities and prevent them. His was a desolate world which sometimes seemed as forlorn as Gabriel's. The idea that the clue that Elena and the professor sought was in *Ulysses* had to be discarded. This was not a book that could prevent anything: it was not the book of fire that they talked about.

The more that Gabriel immersed himself in Joyce's work, the more obsessive he became. He began to interrogate Elena when they met, asking her who had chosen this book for him, and if the hidden meaning was not in it. "Why else thrust it on me?" he asked. "You have something in mind in that forest of words, you must do. Or else, perhaps you are trying to mislead me. Perhaps the real clue isn't in this book at all but something else entirely." He laughed.

Elena denied everything and so he demanded to ask the professor about it, but Elena started at that. He could not. The professor had no time to deal with him. There were much more important things afoot. He was liaising with his contact in Buenos Aires over the transfer of books and he was not to be disturbed at a time like this. What about the boxes of books, then? Gabriel demanded. Where were they being kept? She would not say, but he knew. He sensed everything now. It was not for nothing that she was moonlighting at freight collection at the airport. He remembered how she had wheeled them past him with the professor, and how he had started with fear: all of it had been a parade, a demonstration of power and secrecy.

Gabriel took to carrying *Ulysses* with him wherever he went. It reminded him of this desire he had always had, to read, to learn. Neither of his flatmates could understand this obsession. Ousmane would chide him whenever he saw him for deserting his Bible, mockingly but perhaps also with a certain anxiety. Ismail barely seemed to register Gabriel's presence in the flat any more, since he supported no football team and did not come with them to meet girls and use them. The two of them talked together in Yoruba. They excluded him as in a way he had expected and even hoped that they would. He accepted their exclusion of him but it was not something he wanted to share with others, and certainly not with Elena.

So when Elena asked to see where he lived he refused. Elena insisted that instead he must come to her flat. She lived in the high-rises of St Denis with a Spanish flatmate, Dolores: he'd like her, she told Gabriel, for she was very religious. He looked at her without expressing surprise. Of course: he could not be surprised. Did he not know that her flatmate was Dolores? The Argentinian always lived with her. In the repetition of a pattern of subordination and patronage there should have been no shock. It was an expression of the madness and timelessness that he found here in Europe, which made it seem as though things moved in circles or did not move at all even though they were thrusting on with frightening velocity. So what if the two women hated each other? There was a familiarity about hatred and haters often depended body and soul on each other to such a degree that without the hatred they died swiftly. Dolores had behaved coercively with him before, it was true, but he wondered if she had really meant to. She knew how to be kind, too, to care for creatures that otherwise had no defences. Perhaps that was why he had irked her so, because of his ability to resist.

He began to smile as he agreed to Elena's plan. Did Dolores still insist they keep to separate fridges? he wanted to know. What did he mean? Elena seemed angry. It was obvious wasn't it? Gabriel persisted. Surely she couldn't be surprised that he knew details of their arrangements? But Elena seemed prepared to exhibit shock when everything was normal, even though it was the most atrocious and frightening of plans which for her had adopted the veneer of the ordinary.

All the same, Gabriel went with her as she had asked. They travelled out to the flat on the suburban service one Sunday afternoon and then walked from the station towards the tower blocks. They passed a group of North African youths and one of them barged Gabriel with his shoulder as they walked by. This was not how the Moslems had treated him at home, not at all. Though tempted to react he took a deep breath and went on. Skateboarders cruised past them, checking to see if there was a bag they could steal. They passed halal butchers, grocers with their fruits laid out in trays on the pavement. The tower blocks neared. Elena led him through a short underpass and then up to the entrance of a block of flats. They rose in the lift silently. Always, there was a sense that the entire neighbourhood was bursting with suppressed fear. Only when they got out and began to walk along the featureless corridor did either of them speak.

"Why have you brought me here?"

Elena said nothing. She was continuing to walk, and Gabriel felt a sense of anxiety. She said that she had wanted each to see the other's life, yet perhaps it was not that. This Elena, who had dropped as if a gift into his life, appearing to open paths where previously the bush had been thick and misunderstood – did she not sense that he was a man living alone, with other solitary men, all of them aching for release? did she not imagine his weakness, his ability to follow?

Elena had stopped by the door to her flat and was fumbling for her keys. She had not answered him. She was not looking at him. Her motives were not pure.

"Elena!"

"Dolores is waiting for us now." She had not heard him. "She is expecting us." She opened the door and called out. Gabriel advanced slowly; when he reached the entrance to the flat he saw the two women talking in Spanish. Elena turned to him with a smile. "She's like you, Gabriel," she said, gesturing at her flatmate, admitting nothing of what had gone between them before. He could not hide now. "Always got her head in a book."

The Spaniard held her hand out and introduced herself as Dolores de la Madrid. Gabriel started but it turned out that Madrid was just her family name, something that he had not been told before. He began to relax and ask her about her books: what was she reading? Dolores told him that she was on Fs this week and Gabriel pretended to be interested. People always did this in Europe: they spoke confidently, as if all intelligent people should understand them, even when they were mad. Elena told her flatmate that Gabriel was reading Joyce. Dolores asked him why and he admitted that it was a good question, since he found the book revolting. Dolores seemed pleased at this. She asked him to sit down with a gesture of warmth. Why was he reading it, then? He almost mentioned the crime and the secret but did not. He had to be silent.

Elena had said that they would find friendship between them and it was so. While she prepared some drinks, he talked with Dolores about faith. They spoke in a language foreign to them both, but he could see that she looked at him earnestly as he talked about his father's conversion from Islam forty years before. And yet all the time as he spoke there was this same pretence that he had had with Elena, that they had never met before. Gabriel began to wonder, was he dreaming? Was all this talk of a plot and a crime and a salvation in the making something which had been invented? Perhaps none of it existed.

He carried on speaking as if nothing had happened. All the same it began to unnerve him. Perhaps this woman was not quick-witted. Perhaps she was not. Perhaps she had not even recognized him. There were people like that, he was learning in this strange new world, people for whom all others had but one face.

The women had begun to talk in Spanish. They were all foreigners together, all with their own reasons for leaving, their own ways of serving. Elena had told him that Dolores was a waitress, serving. He asked her where she worked. A bar in Montmartre, Dolores told him and Elena interrupted with delight, saying how fashionable it was. That was where they had first met, when Elena had been waitressing there, long before she had begun to work at the airport. Dolores confirmed the story. They were talking slowly, so that Gabriel could use some of the Spanish he had picked up to understand. It seemed that the bar in Montmartre was important to Elena: it was when working there that she had started writing.

"You, too, are writing out of your head?" Gabriel asked her, remembering something of this ambition. Elena was very pleased with herself. She stretched, as if in invitation. "What are you writing?"

"It's a novel about immigrants," Elena told him. "It's their fantasies and fears mixed with harsh realism. It's about their hopes, their dreams, and truth."

Dolores was dismissive. There was nothing new in it, and other Latin American writers had tried similar things before her. Elena flushed with anger: What did Dolores know about it? She hated Latin American literature! And her book was very different. She had this idea, she continued, a crazy idea. She opened a dictionary, looking for a word, and then slapped it shut.

"What is the idea?" Gabriel asked, breaking in at last.

"For a book which can be read as if like a…palindrome. You could read it either in the order of the parts in the book, such as from one to four – or backwards, from four to one."

"And what would the point of that be, then?" Gabriel asked her.

"Each direction offers a different path, a different meaning. The book would contain two meanings in one text. Depending on which way you read the book, you'd find a totally different meaning. And then again, it's like the professor has said, like the cosmos itself. It expands up to a certain point, everything seems inevitable, and then the greed of its expansion and its overweening weight brings about a swift implosion, a firestorm, so that everything reverses. It's the cosmic crunch that is the deepest heart of our place in the universe, that makes our beings whole, only relocated in literature."

Dolores countered quickly: the idea just showed how worthless the project was. Gabriel knew nothing of this strange argument, these strange ideas they spoke of. Dolores leant forward then, touched his arm. She asked him how long he'd been in Paris. He was still getting used to it, Gabriel admitted. It wasn't long since he'd arrived.

After he said that, the conversation drifted back to Elena's work in the bookstore and its clients. One man had come in two days before. He had told Elena that the store had a book with the secret to a crime. When she'd asked which book he meant, the man had laughed: surely she knew that, it was a book by Jorge Luis Borges called *Labyrinths*.

"And what was the crime?" Gabriel asked.

"He wouldn't tell me." Elena shrugged; always this defiance and insolence, Gabriel thought, as if to say that she would not tell him, that the atrocity they all sought and sought to prevent must always remain a mystery.

Dolores rose and went into the kitchen, where she began scrubbing thoroughly, washing dishes: far away from the curiosities of Elena's clients.

"What did you say?"

"I told him we didn't have it, but he wouldn't listen. He went over to the bookshelves and pulled books off at random. He said the crime would happen at any moment. It would burn us all alive."

Elena's voice wavered. Gabriel could hear Dolores scouring the cooker, scrubbing and scratching like a dusty cat in a village compound. That man sounded like Piree, or any number of the old babblers he had known in childhood, people who learnt how to mistake their own madness for signs of divinity or predestination. Such people were the same wherever you were, in the village or in the bookstore. This was something he had begun to see.

"The man was mad," he told Elena.

"Yes." She called out to Dolores. "He was mad."

Dolores came back into the room. She had on a plastic apron decorated with a map of France, neatly tied behind her back. She had rolled up her sleeves, and put on some gloves.

"He sounds like the writers who come to the bar." She walked up to Gabriel and held his arm. "You'll come now, to be with me there."

She went back to the kitchen. He did not understand. But there were so many foreign ways of behaving. He had worried that Elena might be from the devil, luring him there so that he might lust for her, but actually the devil worked here with much more intelligence than that. You could not tell where he was, stalking the city, threatening to destroy it.

V

There was something hopeful in him in these weeks, he could not say what. This was hardly a feeling that he was used to. Arriving in Europe it was not hope but fear which had consumed him. He had been afraid of both these women, Elena and Dolores. Still neither of them would release him. They wanted him in some way that was certainly more than physical. It felt almost as if he had a secret which to them was lost, something they needed to steal back again. Was he taunting them by playing along? Gabriel could not be sure. He did not stop himself, though. He went often to the bar where Dolores worked and Elena introduced him to the crowd that gathered there, guitarists, poets, singers, people with long hair who played at creation. It often seemed that they believed that such a matter was easy, and to them perhaps it was. They had never had to nurture anything other than themselves.

Elena was evidently on good terms with this crowd. They called her by her surname as a sign of familiarity. *Barajo!* they cried, when she came in and flicked her brown curls away from her smile in greeting. She had been going there for some time and so her friends accepted Gabriel easily. Sometimes they asked him questions: Where was he from? Were there famous writers or musicians from his country? So Gabriel told them about the kora masters. And writers? No, he once replied, there may have been big names with big heads in his country but he'd always thought it a good thing to avoid them. The people had ignored him for the rest of the evening. On their way out Elena told him that his answer had been misjudged.

"Do not let them believe that you are smaller than they are," she told him

"That is not what I said."

"That is what they heard. "

"I did not say that. I said their heads were too big. They did not listen."

"Gabriel, they think it shows superior evolution: their heads are even bigger. Once they think that, they will ignore you."

"These people are not creative: they are *small-minded.*"

That was the word. He had heard it somewhere. Or he had read it, in passing, in one of the newspapers. What Elena had said was true. These people wanted larger heads. And the more that he accompanied her to the bar, the more he felt that Elena was placating them. The more that she sold the books, the more she was tending to their madness. She knew that there was a dangerous touch to those books, that they held a destructive secret. That was why they were all here in Paris. And yet she could not stop selling them and helping those ideas and that danger to spread. Why did she long to prevent the crime so? Perhaps it was because she herself was a criminal.

There were very few people who Gabriel felt would share this response. Ousmane had all but forgotten the Qu'ran.

He and Ismail seemed increasingly strange, and angry, withdrawn from the faith that had brought them to engage with the world, and yet unable to replace it. Ousmane felt that everything was beneath him, while Ismail missed the years he had spent hawking at the transport park at Jos, the great deals he had made, the small triumphs which had lit up his life. Cleaning the airport was no substitute and Gabriel barely spoke to them either there or in the flat.

Curiously, and despite her odd doings at Elena's flat and the threats she had made to him before, it was only Dolores who seemed to have this feeling, of incipient madness, in common with him. At the bar he would watch her serving people and see that a sudden question or unexpected situation would cast her compact face into confusion. Who were all these people to order her? Wasn't she always receiving orders? Hadn't she seen them somewhere before? Of course she would manage, but Gabriel felt that the confusion was directed not only at the matter in hand, but also at this strange world, and her role in it, serving. Perhaps, like him, she did not understand the coincidence of their meeting again, or how one city and time could seem so much like another. Everything seemed so accelerated and yet so frozen in time that life and its potential atrocities sometimes appeared no more real than dreams.

Once Dolores said to him, without warning: "I'm very grateful for your presence."

"Why is that?" He was standing against the counter as she served him a drink.

"Because you are like me."

She was called away to another client and he was left alone with his drink. He had wanted her to say something else: that it was because they were both prisoners of the secret crime and yet somehow would endure it. But he could see that Dolores was too distracted to acknowledge this.

There were times when he did manage to articulate these feelings. He shouted at Elena, one night as they made their way back to St. Denis: Why had she forced their relationship to continue? He had brought the books to Paris, hadn't he? What more could be expected of him? Yet she was pale like a corpse in its burial sheet as he held forth. He had felt attracted to her when they had first met and now in Paris, but this attraction was threatening to give way to something else. And what followed attraction and its charge if not hostility, and fear? He could see, she was scared. The professor had told her, the date of the crime was closing in. They had to act. Could he not see that she lived in fear, that it pursued her even as she pursued him? Perhaps he owed her more pity than he realised.

The argument on the train back to St Denis that night upset her. "You will sleep in the living room tonight," she told him when they reached the apartment building and rose in the lift. Her fear had transformed itself into anger. She was cross. They walked along the corridor to the flat, her words resting almost as a threat, perhaps precipitated by the lateness of the hour and any expectations which he might have had.

"You get angry for no reason."

"You will sleep here." She had opened the door, was gesturing at the sofa. There was a nocturnal stillness in the flat, something that reminded him of home. All it needed was a soft light to simulate the moon and everything would have returned to him. He walked away from her and looked around, wondering why he felt so on edge.

"Dolores will not disturb you," Elena said. "She works until late."

"And what will you do?"

"I have had enough for tonight. I am going to write."

"You must empty your head each night?" She did not answer. "Yes, you must."

It was true, what he was beginning to learn. If you waited long enough people's behaviour was explained, even here, in Paris. That curious emptiness with which Elena moved, the sense that something was always reserved for her: it came from her arrival, late by night in the flat, her need to create even at that late hour.

"You will sleep well, here," she said, with a turn of sympathy.

"And you will write."

"My manifesto," she said. She smiled, as if this explained her oddities.

Once she had gone he thought with his eyes boring into the darkness, sparkling as they reflected the gold of his bracelet and his memories of how he had been given it and of how that time had passed, those sparks and memories welding his sadness to the restless glow of the Parisian night. He thought for minutes at a time until he realized that he could not single out any of the thoughts that had passed. Dolores came in and turned on the light. The birds were singing outside in the wintry dawn, and she must have seen him there, thinking in emptiness, for she came over and kissed his forehead, so gently, and then went into her room to sleep. But afterwards he could not decide if this had been a dream, and he struggled with the thought for a time before lapsing again into dreamlessness.

On waking he did not mention it. He was friendly, though, to Dolores. He asked her about the church she attended, and which passages of the scriptures she preferred. She was most struck by the Book of Revelation.

Sunlight streamed through the windows, and they could see the lines of planes descending towards the airport on the skyline. The Book of Revelation was also one of his favourites but it was a frightening book.

He offered to help her tidy the kitchen. But at that Dolores backed away.

"I'm quite all right."

"I would like to help. Now I am a cleaner, you know."

"I prefer to clean it myself." Almost smiling, she was, as she insulted him. He noticed a tic in her right cheek. Anxiety brought lines in a rush to her forehead, but soon she had them under control. "I will clean it on my own."

Gabriel and Elena soon left for the airport. They made no conversation in the underground. In the airport they rose the moving stairways that catapulted them into the terminal building. Light bored through the windows in cylinders, drizzled the passengers and their passages across the concourse with brilliance. Arrows of silence bound the space between Gabriel and Elena. The bookstore was ever closer. He remembered how swiftly she had switched from anger to intimacy the night before. They were afraid, he saw it at last, lately as the windows of the shop approached. Fear had rarely troubled him in the past; but he felt his chest clench as he saw the books approaching. It seemed that what he and Elena shared was fear. And fear between a man and a woman was natural in the beginning, but who could say where it might end?

They had said nothing since leaving St. Denis. He saw that there was a man waiting at the entrance to the bookstore. It was the professor, Kent Piree.

"I'm waiting, I'm waiting." Piree was pacing; he tapped his watch. "I want the books before the flight is called."

"One moment, professor." Elena turned to Gabriel, her eyes hovering as if in apology. "I'll call you." Her eyes still wavered. "You must see more of me, and Dolores."

"What are we afraid of?" he said, without thought, the words launched from beyond him: her eyes pale and startled now: shrugging to rid herself of discomfort, awareness of her eternal physicality. "Elena, what are we afraid of?"

She turned away and reached for the door. "What books do you require, professor?" Piree followed her into her private domain of control. Elena did not look at Gabriel as he went after them. Piree was talking about the libraries. He mentioned his colleague in Buenos Aires and his expertise. His gestures were expansive, concealing oceans of feeling; Gabriel looked at them, refining the process of acquisition. Piree's eyes drifted towards him, displaced the feeling from his gestures and the goods which they had secured onto Gabriel:

"You!" he said with authority. "You have done your job now. You have been our mule. Now you can go!" Was it true? Perhaps he had signed the paper and carried something. He could not remember. Without being asked, it would have been all too easy for Gabriel to fall into the role of carrying books for the professor again. "You can go!" Piree repeated himself.

"What about the books?" Gabriel asked him. "What have you done with them?"

"It's not your concern any more," Piree told him. "You've done your bit."

"Will you prevent it? Will you manage that?"

"Prevent the crime?" Piree moved towards him through the stacks of books. He smoothed a crease on the lapel of his jacket and looked at Gabriel with complete disdain. "I don't know," he said after a moment, "for the more I read the more the identity of the criminal eludes me. I've come to wonder if it hasn't really been you, all along."

Gabriel started. "But I've done nothing."

"So far," the professor said. "Nothing so far."

Elena grabbed Gabriel's arm and steered him towards the exit. He had to go. But he should not worry. The books were going to be transported to safety, wherever that was. He'd heard talk of Buenos Aires again, and even of Madrid, and of their fear of what might happen whenever, wherever. It was impossible to know what their plans really were, of the true destination of the boxes. Piree was now saying that they'd have to be moved to London first, but how was he supposed to believe that? It was so difficult for him to challenge Piree after everything that had happened. Sometimes he wondered if it wasn't Piree's hope that he might incite such a fated challenge to his authority which had brought him to enter into this pursuit in the first place.

He left the shop swiftly. Perhaps this had been the exchange intimated by his dream of the teacher shouting at him, *fall out*! And now the fore-dreamt assault had come in his place of work. It was not so bad for Piree to assault him now: he had been living in Paris for long enough to be able to fight back. He was not too distracted by the confrontation and actually the cleaning was as easy that day as he had known it. Corners behind the stairways and beside the telephone booths were less troublesome. The task of purification took on a new drama; sweeping without thinking and so without suffering, he was controlled by each threat of dirt and yet readily able to liquidate it.

That evening he returned home to take himself back to his reading. He carried the copy of the book by Joyce with him to one of the bars on the Rue du Commerce and immersed himself until the river of words had swum by. One spent years at home, dreaming so hard of Europe that it was almost present: then in this Europe new dreams unfolded, already realized, filling all the bookstores: he could pull one down and enter it without trembling, dream a way into the future.

He cupped his drink carefully, reading. Joyce's dream was clear and dark, filled with longings, boiling there, a vat on fire in the centre of the compound to which all residents were expected to contribute. It was a world everyone would struggle with: you would enter it and hate it at first, reject it, fail really to see it: then you would return to it again, embracing perhaps its ugliness, its invention begging beside its grey monotony, its lack of discrimination: you would see that its subject was everything that could be conceived of in that time and place: that its subject was immediacy weighed down by everything that was finished and not immediate: drinking, you read it, from one bar to the next: forced into drunkenness, with the book your guide to the future: until, finishing, you returned to your cramped flat drunk and solitary with your own longings, knowing that this too was part of the book's experience, that life should not be easily understood, or wholly enjoyable: and thus in biblical meditation he raced up the bare concrete steps to his flat, entering without thought.

"How long you going to be reading your bible, Gabriel?" Ousmane broke into the sports commentary.

"I come and go with it." Gabriel put the book under his pillow at the end of the mattress, and sat down.

"Hey Gabriel, the girl from the bookstore." Ismail stretched and tapped him on the knee. "Is she reading tonight?"

Ousmane laughed. "That must be a good book, Gabriel! Keeping you from her."

Gabriel tried to shrug the mockery away. He didn't know where Elena was. And she was not his woman. They were friends. He turned his eyes to the television, but they would not let it go.

"You seen her Ismail?" Ousmane asked. "You seen the girl at the airport?"

"Once," Ismail said. "Elena. She also works at freight collection."

"I told you that," Gabriel broke in. "I told you that already Ousmane."

Ousmane walked to the end of the mattress, getting in the way of the television. "You reading this book because of her?" He rustled under the pillow. "You think this all a sign, Gabriel?"

"Leave the book alone," Gabriel said.

"Do you care about it that much?" Ousmane asked him. "What happen to your God?" Gabriel shrugged. "And your family? That money you sending back – what happen to it?"

"Sending more than you."

"Listen, Gabriel." Ousmane flicked through the book, every gesture an imitation, mockery. "You think this reading makes you good. You think this Elena is a sign from your God." He paused. "You just believe that." He let the book fall, and Gabriel snatched it up. "You carry on."

Ousmane walked past them both to the corridor. He left the door open, and they could hear him banging pans in the communal kitchen. Ismail called out a remark to his compatriot in Yoruba. The flat increased its foreignness for Gabriel, and he clutched the book to his chest even harder, hearing the television without listening.

Gabriel turned it off at last. Ismail had gone to argue with Ousmane. He watched lights flickering between the rungs of the blind. Somewhere from within the building a prostitute's cries savaged the night, and he thought of Elena. In her hands Paris was reassembled into the deadliest of weapons, lying concealed beneath the streets and behind the counters of the *boucheries* and *patissiers* and *fromageries*: the constant danger that control would appeal more than love, that all of this could be destroyed by an atrocity that everyone imagined but about which everyone was silent.

Ousmane stood by the door, a bowl in his hands. He offered the food to share. It was baobab and peanut butter. He'd got the baobab from a Senegalese store. Ousmane put the bowl on the mattress and the three squatted around it, picking up the wooden scoops. They blessed the food in Mandinga and Yoruba, and ate the thick paste. Ismail asked him if Elena had any friends, and he told them both about her flatmate, Dolores. Eating again, the scoops cutting into the paste, levelling it, axes into the thickness of the forest. Silence again: this connection to rituals once practiced almost daily, yet now known only from memory, repetition, stubbornness: the meaning of life as it had been voided and a vacuum festering, waiting to be filled by a new and frightening pursuit.

VI

It was Elena who suggested that Gabriel's two worlds should meet. She still hadn't been introduced to his Nigerian flatmates. Why not? she complained. He wouldn't let her come to his flat, that was one thing, but surely they went out together at times. Couldn't she meet them then? All this talk of a secret seemed to have affected him since he treated that co-habitation as if it was the greatest secret of all. He had spoken of their fear in the airport but really it seemed as if it was all his. What was he so afraid of?

She looked at him. He did not want to tell her about their resentment, that he could not predict how they would behave. But then why should he care about her feelings? Her expression was supercilious. She was the one who knew the secret, she intimated, and all it entailed. Did he want to know the answer? Did he? Yes, she was teasing him, like a streetwalker, but things were not going to be as she expected. Why should his African and European lives not meet? In fact, as he had guessed, Ismail and Ousmane were pleased to be invited along to the bar where Dolores worked for they were as intrigued to meet the girl from the bookstore as she was to meet them.

They all went to Montmartre on a Wednesday evening. There was still light as they walked up the streets away from the Boulevard de Clichy. They walked past the shutters of the shops selling cheap clothes picked through by exiles from their continent and drawn faces wreathed by scrapings of stubble, awkwardness of gait, the ill-fitting. Everything about the streets seemed grey to Gabriel. Even the gardens below Sacré Coeur were dark as the light drained.

The bar where Dolores worked was at the junction of two quiet streets on the hill. It was a place for regulars. The doors and windows were opaque. They encouraged those who did not know the place, and its methods, to move on.

Gabriel led the way in. There were few people there as yet, and Gabriel looked about for familiarity. Elena had not arrived even though it had all been her idea. Dolores was in the far corner of the bar, cleaning glasses. He pointed out Elena's flatmate and the three men approached her. He introduced her to his friends.

Dolores turned; her eyes widened with her smile for a moment, then lapsed into a thin line, a harshness they saw a thousand times daily. "Ah, there are three of you." She took a step back. "I had not realized."

Gabriel laughed. "I told you many times, Dolores. I live with two friends."

He introduced Ismail and Ousmane. Dolores nodded. She smiled, and touched Gabriel, said something more friendly to them all. Then she gestured towards a different part of the bar in pretence that some pressing matter called her, and walked off quickly to some tables by the window where she picked up an overflowing ashtray and tipped its cigarette ends into a bin. She cleaned one of the tables, excusing herself to the clients there. Gabriel and his friends had to stand without drinks for some time while gradually the bar filled and Dolores did become busy. She carried trays of drinks through twists of smoke, her limbs poised, unflinching. She laughed only occasionally, her thin lips spreading without intention, closing with definition. It was among the throng, Gabriel saw, that Dolores lost herself and seemed almost happy.

Elena arrived at last with the bar crowded. Gabriel knew of it before he could see her when he heard the familiar cry, *Barajo!* She made her way over towards them and Gabriel introduced her to Ousmane and to Ismail. They shouted to be heard. Ousmane tried to impress her with the career he had had in Nigeria, desire getting the better of resentment just for once. Words were lost, misunderstood. Ousmane laughed: Elena was the girl corrupting Gabriel with that book. But Elena rejected the charge, for had he not followed her and read it of his own free will?

Ismail drifted away and talked to a girl. Gabriel felt flushed. His head overheated and an invisible force pushed him back against the wall. He could not hear what Elena and Ousmane were saying to each other. He did not need to know what Ismail was saying. He felt himself trailing through the wall of noise, the sound filling him. His head was bouncing, being pummelled, held fast as if by one of the wrestlers whom now the tourists went to see at home; it was being towed over the dust like a toy in a village.

But who was attacking him like this? Where had all this anxiety come from? It was a crowded bar but there was no one nearby to touch him. Now someone was pulling at his sleeve, vexing him. He remembered the professor, Piree. He felt his presence in the bar but could not see him, felt the threat and the crime interred in that book of his but could not touch them. A spear of anger shot through him, thrown apparently from nowhere, and he raised his arm.

"Gabriel." Of course, it was Elena. Piree was a force marked precisely by how invisible he was, how elusive and unworldly were his appearances. "Have you introduced them to the writers?"

She gestured through the crowd but he could see no one.

"I cannot."

"Why not?"

"They are not friends for me. You know them. You write together."

"They like you also." She leant forward, then. Her chest was touching him. He had longed to be touched by someone ever since he had begun his work in the airport.

"You two are close," Ousmane said, watching them both, "it is true, you are close."

"Come on," Elena said to Gabriel. "There are two writers through here. Show them."

"Who are they?" Gabriel asked her.

"You know one of them, of course. Professor Piree has come with a friend."

She freed herself and walked through the crowd and Gabriel pushed through the crowd after her. Suddenly he felt this ache and longing for her. Could she really be a new beginning for him? He was beginning to believe that it might be so. Between him and Elena's wake a man interposed himself. He had his mobile phone before him and was exercising his thumb. Gabriel could see Elena beyond, approaching Piree. The man in front had lowered the phone and was looking down at it. Gabriel knocked it out of his hand without thinking, and the man dived after it so that at last he could get by him.

Elena was introducing herself to the writers. "Gabriel, here is Professor Piree." She put her hand on the shoulder of the other man who was there, on the point of introducing him also, but the two men ignored them both. Piree leant forward and grabbed the other by the elbow. Their heads locked. Gabriel could not catch their remarks. He looked round to see if Ousmane was nearby, but his flatmate had not followed him. He turned back to look at the two writers. Piree definitely considered that he had the edge over the other, while they both thought themselves superior to him and ignored him with contempt. Gabriel decided he would not be treated like this, as if he did not exist. He stepped forward and demanded, was this other fellow involved in this plot in some way? Was he not the Argentinian contact that Piree had spoken of? The man deferred to Piree, who stood and put his hand on Gabriel's shoulder.

"What is it?" Gabriel asked Piree.

"Do not interfere with what you do not understand."

"What about the books? Where are the books?" Gabriel asked.

Piree laughed. "Oh, they've been dealt with. They've very much been dealt with."

"We've already begun the process of decoding," his friend added.

"But where are they going?" Gabriel insisted.

"Madrid knows."

Piree nodded towards Dolores, and Gabriel started. He had forgotten that that was her family name. It was another piece in the labyrinth which Piree was constructing. Did he mean for Dolores to return to her city, again, with the books? But he had told him: everything was supposed to be arranged, that they were going to go on to London for transfer to Buenos Aires and he had to come too. Why did the professor have to swathe everything in such mystery when it should all have been so easy? Gabriel sensed that this, too, was part of the plot. It was all connected through the professor's disdain for him.

"Madrid knows." Gabriel repeated Piree's words, but they turned away, and ignored him again. "Elena!" Gabriel had to shout though the hot, sticky air of the bar to be heard. But Elena did not answer. She withdrew. He had to move after her. "Tell me, Elena. Who is this Piree? How is he so important? What is his subject of expertise?"

This she was prepared to answer. "He is a professor of Chinese history," she told him. "He has one of the West's great libraries for the study of the Chinese world. He is also very interested in astronomy. I see him here and there."

"And his friend is also a writer?"

Elena laughed. "He also is expert in Chinese culture and history. A sinologist." Yet they did not look at all intelligent. Their bodies were weak, and were not exercised properly: the mind had taken over, like a spoilt youngest child, demanding to be fed.

"Elena, I am going to be honest with you." Gabriel could not be silent any longer, or accept the unacceptable. "I am going to tell you what is true. Your work in the bookstore is not good for you." He had to shout in her ear above the noise. "You should leave that job." She said nothing: it was so loud, perhaps she did not hear. "You are not understanding this place any more. You are accepting it. You are doing nothing to stop the crime from happening."

There, he had said it. Life required people to resist evil. This constant chatter obscured life here. It made nightmares appear at every turn, even though they were supposed to be buried more deeply. Life was further away than he had ever known it, easier to ignore. These people could not foresee the dangers as he saw them, they could not see crimes even when the criminals were poised to commit them.

Elena did not respond with anger, or disdain, when he told her to leave her job. She reached out for his hand, squeezed it. She then turned, reached up, and kissed him. After those seconds of touching, she moved away, struggling to the bar, where she spoke to Dolores. The Spanish waitress then came over to speak to Piree. The intellectual ignored her, and began to make a point forcefully, jabbing his finger at his colleague's jacket. The other seemed somehow compliant in the aggression. Piree jabbed his finger again, sensing superiority. His body was angled in, poised, predatory. Gabriel moved towards them to try to intervene. He could hear Piree talking about a crime, and blaming his colleague. Gabriel listened to their talk, half hearing only. Here it was again, this talk of danger.

The two intellectuals had reached a height of discussion, their words scything, reaping, levelling: forcing. Piree rose abruptly, and the other followed him. He was moving to prevent the crime, Piree shouted. A crime which was not yet a crime: and what kind of a crime could that be, Gabriel wondered? Piree's colleague looked numb. Perhaps he felt nothing any more. Piree was not even looking at his companion as he forced him outside so that they soon had gone.

The bar forgot the two sinologists. People talked loudly, and drank their drinks. Dolores moved to collect empty glasses. Her tray filled. Gabriel wanted to talk to her about Piree, but then the American professor returned unannounced, alone, and sat upright, brooding. He was twitching, patting his pocket. Gabriel moved towards Dolores's corner, just as she turned, fully absorbed in her activity, with the tray. She raised her head, upright, as if marching, and began her advance towards the bar with the empties. Her eyes focused on something, apparently behind Gabriel, and she stopped. She quivered, holding the tray, as if about to snap: and then the scream.

"Don't come near me!" She stepped backwards; her tray dropped to the floor. "I'm sorry. I'm sorry." She was cowering: had bent down, almost to the floor. "I'm so sorry." Gabriel was nearby, and he moved to touch her, but Dolores screamed even more loudly. "Don't touch me!"

She had begun to shake, seeming like people he had seen in his village when they had opened to the Ancestors, as they had said. Dolores did not believe in Ancestors, and yet she was pursued by her own nightmares. Gabriel saw that now. The nightmares of them both had touched there, in the bar in which she worked, when Piree attacked and Dolores had seen her fear lurk somewhere beyond Gabriel.

"Your friend is mad. Look at her!" The old judge Ousmane was there next to him, mocking as ever.

"She is screaming, Gabriel," Ismail joined in, as Dolores shrieked again.

"She has no shame," Ousmane said.

"Be quiet, Ousmane!" Gabriel shouted. "You are the one without shame."

Gabriel turned his back on his friends. A broad-shouldered man with a crew-cut barged through the crowd and ministered to Dolores. He was someone from the management. His back to the clientele, he made it plain that he would deal with the matter. He leant down to her ear and whispered something, hands firmly on her arms. In spite of the restraint there was a kindness in what he did, something which Dolores needed, Gabriel felt, which was necessary. Some of the onlookers took up their conversations again. They drank. Dolores's fit was easily absorbed. Soon it would be gone. And at that thought Gabriel felt an unheralded sense of peace, and freedom.

Dolores was still struggling on the floor, even some minutes later. She was calling out, asking for her flatmate. Elena was over by the bar, struggling to get through the throng. Dolores called out again. He remembered how on the train which had brought him to Paris a man had screamed at a figure hovering behind him, and in the airport the same thing had happened. Was his life shadowed? He had never seen this agony that tracked him before, never sensed it until now. Would it follow him to the next city too if they all went there in the pursuit of these books and the hidden truth they were said to contain?

Dolores was carried past him. Elena had reached them at last and touched her flatmate on the hand briefly as she went. Then Elena stood next to Gabriel, and he felt the charge that was growing there, between them, in spite of everything that had made them who they were. The warmth was gathering itself and making him think that perhaps he could live in hope. Perhaps he would finish Joyce's book and find that there could be new heroes in the world after all, and a new sort of love to shield them from the future.

He followed Dolores's going by with his eyes and then walked after her with Elena. As they went he saw that Piree was still in the bar, twitching. The professor rose. He was laughing at Dolores as she passed him prone. He pulled something from his pocket and toyed with it. He aimed it at her. Surely, it was not a gun! He could not see properly. Here was this figure, talking of crime, and yet he himself seemed about to commit an appalling atrocity. Gabriel shouted at Piree. He ran at him, knocked him down. There was a struggle, and then Gabriel felt himself being carried as if in dreaming through to a room at the back of the bar.

His eyes were closed. He was not even sure if anything bad had happened or if it had all been in his imagination. Perhaps no one had died and the crime had just been a fantasy in the world which they all had made together.

* * * * *

London 2004

I

She was not dead – she would not give them that satisfaction. They hadn't killed her yet even though she knew that that was their intention. Every time she moved they tracked her. It was like a game of chess in which the powerful pieces were advancing from both sides. They pursued her from city to city. They were hunters, but she refused to let them hunt her for to be hunted meant that everything would end.

Were things really any different in the English-speaking capital? It seemed a straightforward question but Dolores knew that were no straightforward questions. The eyes of Pepe were just like the eyes of her bosses in other cities. *Look busy*, he told her, and she – was she not in permanent business? – gathering the glasses, clearing the stacks of plates from the dirt-encrusted sink and loading the industrial dishwasher, wiping the bar clean. *Look busy, Madrid*, he told her, his command accentuated by his use of her family name. *Ah that's it*, he said – Pepe was not even looking at Dolores, as if knowing how she would try harder to satisfy – *that's it, clear it all up, clear away all the empties.*

Pepe was Dolores's patrón. His wife, Sebastiana, tried to ignore the violence of his every motion. But even the crisp rustle as he turned the pages of his newspaper betrayed him. He had chosen to employ Dolores just as he would choose when she should be fired. He filled the doss-rooms above his bar with illegals from Cuba, Colombia and Ecuador, and flirted with them nightly. Thus did he construct his world, utterly false, utterly fantastic, just waiting to disintegrate.

Tonight Pepe was in expansive mood. It was after all the winter time. People came in earlier and drank more quickly, so to line their veins against the coldness that was outside. They were the ones in command, the supremacists. Profits soared, and even Dolores was all the busier. *You'll get your reward, bonita*, he would say if ever she mentioned a raise, reminding her of things that she had heard in childhood. But naturally Pepe's intentions were dishonourable. *Hey bonita*, he admitted to her once, with Sebastiana sitting beside him and thereby dignifying his coarseness with the respectability that might have fitted a sociable crook, *this city is the arsehole of the world, that must be why I'm at home here. Hey bonita* – yes he was feeling expansive tonight, things were busy, after all, in the arsehole of the world – *don't worry about clearing up behind the bar tonight, I'll hire some Polish scum tomorrow, throw them a tenner.*

Dolores could feel his eyes sucking her in through a straw. It made her feel like one of those Poles who Pepe mocked. She loathed it, loathed Pepe acting as if he was one of those who had arrived when he was imported scum, just like her. There was no sense of generosity or charity in him. He did not reach into his pockets to give coins to one of the begging poor under the arches of Waterloo Bridge. To him stories of such selflessness as this, of men like St Francis, meant nothing. Already her thoughts were wandering away from the bar as she worked to clear everything. She was thinking of those beggars she saw every night, of her conflicting responses to them. *Hey bonita, are you deaf or something?, I said you can leave it, clear off home* - Pepe eased himself towards her - *You're a vanishing breed,* he said to her then, *working because you want to get the job done, and not resentfully, thinking the world owes you something better.*

Dolores turned to Sebastiana, dressing her face with kindness, and made her excuses. She didn't know why she had bothered as she knew that Sebastiana would hardly acknowledge her. Her mistress no longer tried to pardon the patrón his ugliness. Dolores couldn't even be sure that Sebastiana noticed it any more for she was much too busy smoking Marlboro reds and cross-checking the account pages. Sebastiana smoked too much and had a bad cough which rasped across conversations and cut them dead. Sometimes if custom was slack she would tell Dolores of her family in Galicia, all these years separated. It was because of war, and disagreement. Conflict did that to you. It ate you, like a client in the bar, ominous of a disease which had yet to manifest its deadliness.

Dolores had a book to read, something by Cela, and so she was content to accept Pepe's invitation to leave. She would forget the bar and her pursuers and lose herself in the book. After saying goodnight to Sebastiana, and ignoring Pepe, she retrieved her bag and walked up towards Waterloo to catch the night bus. By the Old Vic some drunks jostled each other. One of them barged her with his shoulder. They did not apologise and their laughter was still with her fifteen minutes later as she boarded the bus. To her it sounded like the sickest part of the throbbing disembodied noise of this city and all others.

It took nearly an hour for Dolores to reach her stop. In Camberwell the streets were crowded come night or day and she peered out into the unfamiliar darkness and the fear which lay there. The bus continued on east into Peckham. She grabbed her rape alarm when her stop neared and waited by the exit doors, tapping her finger against the bell. Then she got out and walked her solitary path to the tower block.

When she opened the door to the flat she found darkness. Her Argentinian flatmate was already sleeping. She would not be able to threaten her tonight, nor pressure her into doing something that she did not want to do. Dolores felt relieved. She went straight into her room and found the Cs on the shelf. This was her escape when she returned from work, to retreat into the pages and find comfort in the authority of a different voice. This was what a great writer needed, the power and ambition to declaim with authority. Her father had told her so: *Authority, flor, authority is what makes for greatness.*

She stood in her room for a while, holding a copy of the book by Cela. Her father had liked Cela and had been quite overcome when he had been awarded the Nobel Prize. The blood rushing to his head, he had run to her with the wind rattling the empty barns, shouting of the long arm of justice and heavenly reward. She could still remember the pinched expression on his face. When he had neared her his voice had lowered. The sun had been setting, lightening the heat from their griddled world in the plain. He had spoken unctuously, in his black T-shirt, like a priest. He had wanted to look like that. He had hoped that the trappings of religious authority would cling to him in the place of the dreams of his mother, who had hated her obligations to him so much that she had longed for him to be a priest before settling for compromise. Hatred ran like a stream, linking the generations, and when the old horror had died suddenly, of a coronary, Dolores's father had still felt such attachment to her that he had abandoned his literature studies at the Complutense University and returned to run the farm as she had commanded in her will. *There will always be hatred*! her father had screamed, listening to the socialist filth, homosexual liberals criticising the award to Cela because of his political stance.

She read until it was late with circles of lamplight revealing the pages before she turned them. When she closed the book she returned it to the shelf next to Calderón de la Barca. She could hear her flatmate rustling about in the kitchen, metal against metal ringing like church bells across the void of the flat. No doubt she'd be scaring the mice in their box, driving them to burrow deep into their straw beds. That was the sort of thing she did, and without thinking twice about it. *Che, nena*, the Argentinian used to say, whenever she came into her room, *you spend all your money on books, don't you?, it's like a library in here, a fucking library, you should work in a bookstore, like me, then at least you could steal the books, or get a discount.* Her flatmate polluted her room just with her presence in repetition of a pattern that could not be escaped. Dolores had thought somehow that by uprooting herself the dynamic might have altered but it had not. Elena had tracked her down, even in London, even after they had brought over those books and deposited them she knew not where. Dolores knew that she should have gone straight to the authorities. But no one would have believed her. They were probably all colluding in the plot. So she had decided to bide her time and gather her evidence, pretending that everything was all right.

Elena spent every day as if nothing had ever passed between them, that everything was fine, that she was not her hunter. She said nothing about the crime and the conspiracy that had brought them here. Instead, she mocked Dolores's reading habits. *All these Spanish authors,* Elena would say, the mole on her right cheek twitching in repressed desire, *all these classics, che, are you trying to live in a museum or something? Why don't you do something useful and burn these old relics? Put all that inquisition stuff to good use! That's what they used to do to your beloved authors! Light some fires!*

Dolores never replied. Once, when the Argentinian had really riled her, she'd almost laced her salmuera pickle with some of her urine. Frustration could do that to you sometimes, overcoming the better instincts, the ones that made you loveable. But her flatmate understood none of that. This idiot didn't understand that the further that Dolores felt away from home the more she wanted to recreate her home around her. She had left on a whim, chasing criminals, she'd gone from one place to another, and now here she was in the English-speaking capital without any sense of completion. Even if hers was a sanitised, idealised vision of home, it felt like an answer to an empty question. And the noises clattering from the kitchen that night renewed the emptiness within her. For a long time now they had been echoing like thunder across the Moraña. She was ready to defend herself. This was a typical lack of consideration from the Argentinian.

She put on her nightshirt and opened the door of her bedroom. The words had already been formulated, the method of attack long considered in her dreams and in the waking fantasies that absorbed her mind on the bus through Camberwell and when she was unable to sleep late at night, listening to the overland trains struggle in the darkness: *You are so aggressive, in constant confrontation with me, pursuing me without rest, it's enough for me to want to destroy you.* The words had been inside her, formulated silently and without consciousness, waiting to be provoked. *Che nena*, she was about to say with an imitation of the irony that was usually directed at her, presaging her aggression with the withdrawn calm which she had absorbed as a child: except, as she looked into the bare light of the kitchen she did not see her flatmate at all: at first she saw no one and then in the living space between her and the unit a burglar, lying on the couch, a negro africano.

Her first thought was to flee. And yet flight might lure the threat into her room. Ever since Dolores had arrived in the city she had felt a creeping advance of fears as she had noticed that London was filled with people like this burglar, like that friend of Elena's who she had been forced to meet before. Sometimes it felt as if she had been transported to the slums of some Latin American city, as if in some nightmare she had returned to her flatmate's own Buenos Aires where things were not properly ordered. They sat next to her in the underground, in the buses, this Peckham was filled with them, and they threatened her. Given everything that had passed in the world, she suspected their hatred: it was certainly what she would have felt had she been like them.

Secretly she had been expecting the confrontation with an intruder for a long time. She had anticipated running away, sitting on her bedroom carpet with her back pushed against the door to prevent it from being forced. She had dreamt of the anger she would feel at being invaded in this way and of her relief at the thought that there was nothing that cleansing could not resolve.

The intruder was sleeping. He looked like Elena's friend, but of course she couldn't be sure. He was a thief, that was for sure, lying there with a golden bracelet on his arm as if it was some sort of family heirloom. Dolores found it impossible to tell these people apart. As long as he lay there curled upon the beige couch, his head resting on a patterned cushion, she had no need to fear, but when he stirred she almost screamed. She stopped herself, but he must have sensed her since he woke. He looked at her then like an animal who knew that there was no love, only beatings.

It was vital to show that she was expecting him. The most powerful form of control was a demonstration of love. So easy to kiss him, lying there, he had probably come in looking for some warmth and humanity. So easy to walk up to him and kiss him, which she did there in the bare light as if in a photographer's flash. He did not respond. Perhaps she could have killed him and he would have done nothing in return. He did not move after she had kissed him, present there as Dolores had imagined him, as captive as she herself felt, and under orders.

II

Elena often asked what she was doing in London. *Look at you, Dolores,* she'd say with a big yawn, *you hate it here, you're always talking about Spain, you can't stop torturing yourself because you're not in Spain, I don't know why you don't just go back there.* There was no purpose in responding to this kind of attack. Didn't she know, she had only come to escape from her and already that escape seemed to have failed? Perhaps she'd find her way back there sooner than any of them imagined. The woman came from Buenos Aires, the global capital of psychoanalysis. It was typical of Argentinians, they had to be the best at something, even if it was only psychoanalysis. Dolores would ignore the Argentinian bookseller, smooth back her hair, leave the high-rise and take the overland train to London Bridge. *You never talk, nena*: the words would still be in Dolores's ears as she waited for the lift by the filthy stairwell: *you're like a clam on the beach waiting to be torn open.* Ay Dios, the woman was more dangerous than an intellectual!

What did Elena expect her to talk about? They were both here to foil conspiracies and so each was the foil to the other. Here was this ball of arrogance from South America pretending that she had some grand scheme and a secret and could prevent what could not be prevented. She made it seem as though she was outside time and could even reverse it. She had smuggled those books over somehow and claimed that any minute she would decipher the essence of the plot and yet all the while she seemed to be laughing and to take nothing with seriousness. No, she challenged Dolores and implied that it was she who threatened the order of things when it was seekers of freedom like Elena who made destruction ever more inevitable.

At the bar where she worked Pepe did not bother her anything like as much as her flatmate. He was a lout, of course, full of coarse lusts which Dolores could not abide, but at least his urges were directed at controlling those who had to be controlled. He was much too interested in his own problems to take heed of hers and often seemed barely aware of her existence. This was one of the reasons that she was content to work for him, since work was a matter of keeping to a routine and serving the customers and thereby reinforcing the hierarchy of authority. She was pleased to do what she could to reverse the situation in this God-less country where children no longer respected parents. This was why everything was in decadence, for was it not obvious that if a parent's authority could be questioned then so could a priest's, and God's, and that nothing would be sacred? It had been Padre Ramón, a priest from Arévalo, who had told her this.

What did interest Pepe was not the reason for her presence but her behaviour in his restaurant. *Hey bonita*, he said to her when she arrived the next morning at eleven, in time to prepare for the lunchtime rush, *what was it with you last night?*, *why didn't you leave like I told you?*

Sebastiana chided him, calling from the kitchen, he should leave Dolores alone, she was the best worker he had, not some second-rate Latin American hooker who never got out of bed. But he persisted, *You can't take orders, is that it? you don't know how to obey in a world that demands it?* Then he laughed, as if to say, it was all harmless fun, wasn't it? and if she went along with it he might have to give her a pay rise.

Dolores sneezed. It was cold in the tapas bar, just as it was everywhere in the infernal city. It was cold almost as if to convulse you. She sneezed again. She couldn't help wondering for a moment what it might be like to touch Pepe, to be touched.

"Are you OK, bonita? What's the matter ?"

She backed away, even though she had not meant to. He smiled, then. She must be unwell, he said: perhaps she needed to see a doctor. He reached out to touch her but she couldn't bear to be touched, no: you never knew where a man's hands had been. Everyone said that he and Sebastiana had come to London way back as refugees from the military government, that they'd built up the bar from nothing on the back of sixteen-hour days. But Dolores knew better. Pepe was not one to be in opposition for the sake of it. He did not appear to have any need to resist those human forces which were irresistible. He would have been one of those to join the generalíssimo in repressing filth which should have been flushed out of the system long before. In her heart she trusted Pepe, even though the main emotion she felt towards him was one of disgust.

"I don't need to see a doctor," she declared, almost moving towards him as she answered the challenge in the end. He remained there, still: he was only trying to help, he said. She ignored him, and proceeded. She had to proceed because it was only the exactness of her routine which allowed her to be ready for the lunchtime rush when it came. She recognized those who were out on business, or had come in a party from work, or who were treating themselves to a more elaborate lunch than usual. You could tell that you were in a country lacking in culture through the greedy solitude with which so many workers took their lunch, devouring sandwiches frilled with rumpled plastic as they passed in the street or gobbling down their chorizo a la Española as if this would be their last meal on earth. It was always the English who did this. You could see it in their eyes.

Pepe allowed her a one-hour break between lunch and the evening shift, and that afternoon she walked up to Waterloo and then across the Thames. The second-hand booksellers were laying out their wares on trestle tables beneath the Hungerford Bridge. The discarded books lay as targets for the pigeons, grey like the London sky, like the city itself. Everything was monochrome, mass-produced. Even people. Even the negros, the chinos, the indios, gathered from every corner of the world by some mysterious act of alchemy, were mass-produced, their desires predictable, individual.

At the corner of Trafalgar Square and the Strand Dolores went into a bookstore. The quantity of volumes made it apparent that ideas could be mass-produced like anything else. She passed the piles of gaudy paperbacks, the self-consciously worthy and exclusive hardbacks, and went up to the second floor. The availability of works in Spanish was unpredictable, but she often managed to make special requests. Elena did have her uses, it turned out, and her job here was one of them. Dolores loathed the Argentinian and yet here she was in her break, seeking her out. What was most repulsive was also, in a frightening way, what attracted her the most.

Dolores hesitated when she reached the upper floor. She saw that her flatmate was dealing with another client.

"I must have it. I must have it at once."

"Could you remind me of the title, sir?" Dolores did not catch the response. The man had leant his cane against the counter and was drumming his finger there. "I'm afraid I have not seen it in stock," Elena said at length, tracing her finger down the computer screen.

"You must have it!" The man was louder, now, more insistent. "It's a famous work. Jorge Luis Borges's book, *Labyrinths*, was a classic of the 20th century."

Elena shrugged. "I don't know if it's escaped your notice," she said, "but we're not in the 20th century. We haven't been for a few years now. Things have moved on."

Elena pretended a certain triumph, as if that should have been enough to end the exchange. But they all knew this eccentric better than that: they knew Piree and the anxiety which filled him with an appetite for pursuit, for deferred destruction. He insisted. He explained how Borges's collection, *Labyrinths*, contained a story called *The Garden of Forking Paths*. That story was about a sinologist trying to locate a hidden meaning in an old book. The clue was found in a Chinese classic that was both a book about the meaning of time and a labyrinth. It was about time because it never mentioned it. And it was a labyrinth because the book had been constructed in such a way that time was never referred to.

Elena looked at him with disdain: of course she must have heard this many times before, but for Dolores there was something new about this whole revelation and she listened with special attention. The Argentinian was smiling: surely what he was looking for was more important than that? Oh it was, Piree said. One of the characters in *The Garden of Forking Paths* had a name which provided a clue to a city which would soon be destroyed. Like something from the Old Testament? Elena laughed, but Piree looked at her with fury, as if it was intolerable that still his sidekick did not take him with the seriousness that he deserved. He was shouting now, attracting attention.

"You know," he said, enunciating each word clearly and with menace, "that we haven't got long."

"An atrocity!" Elena laughed. "Is that what your book's about?"

"One that can be prevented or permitted, as society sees fit."

"We don't have it, sir," she told him, removing her finger from the screen, and pressing a button on the keyboard. "I'm afraid atrocities are in high demand at the moment and we're out of stock."

He began to laugh, taking his humiliation with something like good grace. *That's hilarious*, he shouted as he was escorted out of the building by the security guards, *you're surrounded by rubbish, and yet you have no copy of one of the few books that could help.*

As he left Dolores recalled the church, and the farm, where at times she had been reminded by her father or Padre Ramón that those involved in public displays had often been executed. Perhaps those victims, too, had been actors, just like Elena and Piree here. Dolores felt as though they had acted through this entire charade for her benefit. Couldn't they see that she knew that they were pursuing her? Didn't they realise how obvious it all was? She would just bide her time before finding the right way to be rid of them.

Something about Piree in the bookstore had brought the farm back to Dolores. She struggled for an instant to gather what the connection was. Perhaps it was nothing more than a sense of frustration, as she recalled the studied fury with which her father had always held books, sad beyond keening that he had never realised his ambitions. After his mother had died and he had returned from the Complutense he had read more and more, finding solace and sadness in the whiteness of the pages and the rustle they made as his own pale hands had turned them.

Piree's mad fury had seemed like a memory of all that for a moment. But now Elena had raised her eyes from her computer screen and was looking at her. Dolores moved forward. Nothing was said about that which both had witnessed or about the strangeness that was between them. They'd pretend that nothing peculiar had happened. Even more than that, they'd pretend that nothing peculiar was happening at all. It was better. Instead they discussed books, and Dolores declared that she needed something new now that she had finished Cela's novel. Elena's lips twitched as if in repression of a smile. She turned and picked out some of the experimental Latin Americans. *Something with a bit of violence*, she said, *with a hint of the fire.*

Such subversion was not what Dolores had intended. She left without buying anything. She went through Embankment underground station to the river. By the steps up to the footbridge an old tramp was being prodded by two policemen. Lights beamed from beyond the grey water beckoning her across the river in their collars aureate. She had to return to Pepe's bar. The darkness was falling across the South Bank and the long night shift stretched ahead. As she began to descend the steps near the Festival Hall the whole afternoon seemed unbearable. The return of Elena and Piree to her life seemed all a part of her failure to escape, even though she had fled and had come to a country where she was not at home. Why were they pursuing her like this? Were they mad? How imminent was the crime anyway? It felt as if it was touching her. Dolores shuddered. She could bear the conspiracy no more. Soon something would have to be destroyed, she sensed it and knew it and in a terrible way found it reassuring.

III

For some time Elena had been surrounding herself with foreigners. They eased in and out of the flat as if they felt perfectly at home in their collected foreignness: Brasileños, Mexicanos, Cubanos, forever they seemed to be separating and recombining around the loveless table in the salón. Sometimes they came back from a night out in the tapas bars in Stockwell, full of their exploits. *We had such fun there*, el hueso the Ecuadorian once told Dolores, *drinking rum and laughing loud enough to annoy the English, pretending that just for tonight we were at home.* He didn't make it sound fun to her. One night, when João the Brazilian electrician made a pass at her, she only just managed to hold back from lacing their drinks with urine. But then you couldn't judge them all by João. He was an odd case, really; everyone called him *Gol* because of the way he celebrated scores at football matches.

Dolores felt that Elena had surrounded herself with these incomers as some sort of diversion from her true obsession with the atrocity which she and Piree sought to prevent. She herself tolerated them as best she could and did her best to be welcoming in her own style. Often she exchanged pleasantries or offered coffee, although Elena's crowd preferred alcohol. Feeling a stab of pleasure at the inevitable rejection of her generosity, she was happy to offer her excuses and retire to her room.

Once in her sanctuary Dolores usually felt unblocked. Often she farted, taking a certain satisfaction simply from the fact that the smell was hers. Soon she would start running her finger along the spines of the books stacked in the cheap plywood bookcase, allowing it to rest on the title of a favoured book or author. All she wanted was to be drawn in by these books, to be consumed and in that cannibalism and incorporation to find her meaning. Sometimes she dreamed of finding something written especially for her, a romantic book, one which her father might have hated, in which she was the heroine and a suitable future had been mapped out. Her finger often dwelt the longest over precisely those books which had helped her to develop this dream most strongly.

In London, she felt that with the books and the process of cleaning she kept reality at arm's length. Soon after confronting the burglar in the flat she found herself reading with greater conviction, hoping that she would be able to ignore Elena and Kent Piree and the books they desired to export to Argentina. She did not even tell Elena what had happened. Instead of sharing her fear she divided the next few days equally between books and cleaning therapy. After reading in the middle of the night, she removed the cushion covers on which the intruder had rested his head and washed them in the bathroom sink. She hung them from a pulley-line attached to the discoloured wall of the apartment building beyond her bedroom window, and then dusted the sofa cushions and the handles of the external door. In this methodical process she filled the air with so much disinfectant that Elena complained of irritation to her eyes when she next rose in the dark morningtime.

Even Dolores was agitated by the chemicals of the disinfectant spray. After the ritual cleansing it was a pleasure to return to her room and the books. There the Cela was substituted by *Don Quixote*, not of course because she had not read the epic before but rather because she found the pages of the master delicious. Her body flushing, attendant to the desires of the prose: transcending for a moment the knight's paramour, Dulcinea: lustrous: in order: ready to submit. But five days into the Quixote and Cervantes's refusal ever to engage the reader with the longings of Dulcinea herself began to frustrate.

"You are a great romantic, aren't you?" Elena asked her that fifth day, breaking into her thoughts in another minor act of violation.

"Romantic?"

"Yes, all this dreaming of a golden knight, someone from a chivalrous novel…"

"I have ideals which I dream the world might live up to."

Elena laughed. "I've developed my own sort of romance now," she told her.

"A romance?"

"I've found a man," Elena said. "You'll meet him this evening, I'll bring him home after I've finished work."

"You're always finding men. Your life is full with men."

"It's not one of the Stockwell crowd."

"Why not? Was there anything wrong with them?"

Elena laughed. She left the question hanging in silence. Her head retreated beyond the door, leaving Dolores to her sanctum. Dolores fretted. After ten minutes, unable to concentrate, she left *Don Quixote* spine upwards and returned to Pepe's. Sebastiana had gone to visit her family in Coruña for a few days and there was something ominous in Pepe's attitude that day. He occupied the bulkiest chair of the bar and dispensed orders to her with waves of his butcher's hands. There was no need for her to clean the tables as he saw fit, or to perform the tasks in the manner which suited only him, but he did not seem willing to countenance opposition. That morning she longed to be Dulcinea, saved from her fate by an impossible act of chivalry.

"Hey bonita," Pepe said after a time.

"What is it?"

"Hey bonita, you working like a shepherdess whose sheep have been stolen." He was still sitting on his chair, complacent. "You should try smiling some time, you might like it."

"If you hate me, why don't you just fire me?"

He laughed. "What's all this talk about hatred? I'm not as bad as that."

"You don't like me," she said. "You could just get rid of me. It would be easy."

"Ah no," Pepe replied gravely, "there are laws which have to be observed. I cannot just get rid of people, like that. We have a contract which requires two weeks written notice, on either side."

He buried himself in his newspaper and ignored her. She felt like a mistreated puppy furious at the removal of its innocence. Pepe coughed, buried in a fug of cigarette smoke and yesterday's *ABC*. For a moment he even looked pathetic so that she almost felt pity for him. There was something about him that had changed now that Sebastiana was away. She could not put her finger on it but she knew that she did not like it. She collected herself, smoothed down her skirt, and made for the kitchen. The swing doors creaked as she passed through them, and she heard him cough again. He was always saying that he wasn't as bad as she imagined him but she knew it wasn't true. Perhaps she hated him. She hadn't realised it before, but as she worked she was in a permanent state of desiring revenge, and knew that it was the constant thwarting of this desire which excited him so and gave their respectable relationship of master and servant its charge and definition.

She worked that day in permanent rebellion. When she was preparing to leave, he called out to her – *Bonita, anyone would wonder why I bother with you at all, it's like employing a statue, one of those silent witnesses erect before Buckingham Palace, all stiff-necked* – he turned to one of his drinking friends as she left – *but there's no way of getting inside her and knowing whether she feels things like we do, whether even she's actually alive in any meaningful way.*

She left slowly. She did not want to return to Peckham. Elena would be there with her new boyfriend. No doubt they would be all over each other, in contact in places which for her remained untouched. But the bookstore was closed. She had nowhere else to go. In that instant she regretted her decision to leave that other city and come to London.

She arrived at the flat at about ten o'clock. There was something awesomely familiar about the man who sat with his hands clasped in his lap, the new boyfriend of Elena – *Ah Dolores, at last! Nena we have been waiting for you!* She introduced her partner. They'd met in the bookstore, she said. Elena began, in her usual self-absorbed manner, to discuss the books which he was reading, her voice carrying disembodied through the void of the flat as she moved from room to room, supplying drinks. Her boyfriend was, so the Argentinian informed her, a believer. He talked intelligently about the Book of Revelation. Yet then his obsidian presence engulfed her. He was another foreigner, like them, an immigrant. He spoke with all apparent civility. But was he not exactly like the intruder she had found in the flat those few weeks before? and to the African that Elena had introduced her to elsewhere? It was difficult to be sure: they all looked alike.

She made some excuse and returned to her room. She cast her eye along the spines of the books. She looked at the Cs, the Ds, and the letters still to come. She stared then at the black wash of the London sky and at the lamplight stars crisscrossing the horizon with the sadness of their endlessness. She tried to recall the way she had dealt with that burglar's intrusion and the violent fear which it had prompted in her. She had not confronted the intruder but kissed him on the brow. Imagine, she had never done that with *El Hueso* or *Gol* but she had bent to kiss that criminal! She had trailed her lack of character through the city, her desire for all sorts of domination even when exercised by the lowest individuals in the hierarchy.

She returned to the salón. She was sure of it: this was the same man Elena had introduced her to before. She had even told her his name. Yes, it was the same Gabriel, and he was sitting there as if he were in state, and in some way heroic. There was a desperate need for new heroes, of course, new figures of authority. She was not the only one to feel that the world increasingly craved such satisfaction. Only leaders, great men would do. And here, instead of that, she had been pursued by this immigrant thief for weeks, months.

"There is something about you," Dolores told him then.

"About me?"

"You are so familiar," Dolores went on, ignoring Elena as she spoke.

"Perhaps you are dreaming," Gabriel suggested.

Dolores needed him. She would spite Elena, the Argentinian would see. She grabbed Gabriel's hands and commanded him to come to Pepe's, there to exorcise everything that pursued her. Had she not picked up the books because she could not let her father's thwarted, bookish ambitions go? Perhaps that was why Elena and Piree were pursuing her, because they sensed this. But she and Gabriel might yet be able to reject them. She realised then as she held those alien hands that this might be her last chance to bring her world back so that it was in her control, to thwart the plan which Elena Barajo and Kent Piree had concocted to destroy everything which kept her sane.

IV

Gabriel's cleaning job at Paddington station finished regularly at five. It never took him more than an hour to change out of his navy blue uniform and make his way to Pepe's bar in Waterloo. This was always a quiet time of day and he and Dolores would talk at one end of the bar to Pepe's irritation. *Hey*, he said to Dolores once, *I don't pay you by the word, bonita, you're not some fat-arsed journalist, there's work to be done.* When Real had lost at the weekend he tended to find Gabriel's presence insulting and he would tug at her sleeve and say, *Don't forget to wash his glass twice by hand, bonita.* Before or after, she asked once, as if she didn't know what he would say.

The patrón could not understand Dolores's relationship with Gabriel. He could not see that it was as great a mystery to her as it was to him. He seemed laden down with suspicion at times, staring at them as they were talking, coming close, trying to eavesdrop and making no effort to hide it. It was his bar, he could do as he liked. People would not be allowed to plot anything dangerous here, he told them. He suspected them just as they lived in constant suspicion of the others in their lives who seemed to desire the construction of a dangerously beautiful, even perfect crime, something which could have the power in the future to act as a constant warning from a past that never died.

Pepe seemed to fear that there was more to their relationship than really there was. Dolores longed to ask him, *Do you think I've asked him here as a friend*? Didn't he know that they were mystified by their apparently recurring meetings, that they compelled each other through their familiarity even though they did not understand the pattern of their lives which threw them together? It was as if their lives were already broken by some all-powerful demon always just out of sight. Pepe had a good sense for the demonic, Dolores knew that. Probably that was why he was so vexed by the whole affair. Dolores enjoyed what little power she had over him, confusing him, telling him nothing about what was going on. She wasn't going to share with him the curiosity of their repeated meetings. Sometimes she caught her face freezing in a moment of falseness as she looked at Pepe, with the corners of her mouth flatlining.

At times the emotion made her think of the catechism which Padre Ramón had taught her all those years ago. She had often gone over to Arévalo for these sessions. Señora Valverde used to bring in a tray of drinks and some turrón for the priest from the kitchen of the parroquía. Then they would sit in his living quarters overlooked by the church and Padre Ramón would begin his instructions, interrupting his monologue occasionally to await an answer. In this pause he used to fill his mouth with food. He would excuse himself as he ate: there were fewer priests, his district grew by the year, like an empire, so he had less time to rest and to consume what was necessary for his work. Sometimes she managed to respond by raising her eyes to his, thinking of her father. She'd been too young then to know what it was that she was feeling, but she recalled those times in staggered instants, as she talked to Gabriel and hoodwinked Pepe and felt the corners of her mouth pushing down.

During those evenings what they discussed most of all were books. They never discussed the plot or the crime, at least not directly. Everything, including their fear and foreboding of the direction in which they were being taken, was manufactured through manipulation. Dolores could not even once imply everything that had gone before, the threats, the veiled desire which had always been thwarted. All of it was too much to bear. All of it, everything, was best forgotten. Amnesia was the only cure for pain, perhaps some doctor had told her that.

And so as they talked, Gabriel pretended that his main concern was this book which the Argentinian had told him to read. Daily he would attempt to explain to Dolores its contents, daily emending them in one way or another. This book: this *Ulysses*! It seemed natural to her that Elena had peddled such filth, a book about heroes which really was not about heroes at all, which revealed only her own tendency to everything that was dangerous. And so as Gabriel spoke, Dolores pretended to listen, admiring her own restraint. The author was not even Spanish. And yet she listened, smiling with a sort of intellectual coquetry, amused by his doggish gratitude for her attention.

It could never have lasted. One night Dolores looked at Gabriel, dressed in his cheap garish shirt, and felt flooded by a hatred she had not felt for years. She had not asked for it, and she had tried so long to bury it. She had tried to cultivate kindness, to give to the poor and care for helpless little beasts, and yet it had returned. She hated this person in front of her, hated everything about him. What was she supposed to do? She realised that she had to bring Gabriel under her command, or there would be no hope: no hope at all. This did not suit the ideas she had about what sort of person she ought to be, about the kindness she had tried to cultivate, but it did fit with the talents which her upbringing had given her, the talent for hatred which her father had been careful to nurture.

There was also a way in which this new feeling could be helpful. The evidence had to be gathered, and, somehow, the conspiracy of Elena and Piree had to be stopped. An intense emotion could help with that. It could be a relief. As these feelings rose like waves inside her she herself felt relieved. Pepe's bar was crowded, yet she did not pause in unburdening herself. She turned her backs to the people waiting to make their orders and stared Gabriel down.

"On one thing, at least," she said to him, "we are agreed, and that is the need for great heroes." He did not deny it. "And in the past, heroes came in the form of prophets and saints. They were fighting to ensure that the divine message was not lost." He muttered his assent – he had no choice. "Today, more than ever, the world is in need of heroes, great leaders. People are crying out to obey," – here Dolores turned away for a moment, accentuating the command which she had taken of the situation – "and the problem I have with the heroism of which you talk, this heroism of Joyce's, is that there is nothing divine or remarkable about it." He could not deny it. "And so," she told him, "it cannot be the path to salvation."

It had been so easy, this taking command of a situation. He was new to thought, and argumentation. It was easy to twist thoughts, an argument, to impose oneself in a battle of wills in which you had set the rules and laid out the dispute and the terms of your victory.

"You are right," he said then. "The Argentinian has misled me." There, his hands crossed on the bar, and Sebastiana taking a leaf out of her husband's book, shouting out from behind her wreathed cigarette smoke that he looked so pretty there and would look even prettier if he bought a drink. "Yes actually, I should reject this book, and reject her. What business of mine is this crime she discusses, these books she wants rid of? I am not responsible."

Of course, Dolores agreed. He was not responsible but she could see that he had an important clue. He denied it angrily: he had no clue, he just wanted to escape them and make sure they didn't blame him for something. She persisted: there was no chance of that if he worked with her, she told him: he had to tell her which books he had carried for Elena and Piree. But he said he did not know.

"I heard the name in the bookstore where Elena works," Dolores confided, then, showing her superior knowledge. "The story they are interested in is *The Garden of Forking Paths* by Jorge Luis Borges."

"And what is that story about?"

"An atrocity that must be committed even though the perpetrators know not where."

He laughed, as if he could not quite believe in such a possibility. Was it a perfect atrocity, then? It was something beautiful, she agreed, something that had to be imagined. Atrocities could only occur once they had already been imagined, in art and in countless individual minds, daily and for a great length of time. There was nothing more beautiful than an idea that had found its roots.

They were interrupted. Pepe called over, gesturing at some new clients, his face flattened by a scowl. She went to take their orders. Then she wiped down the bar with a moist cloth and fiddled with the glasses beneath the drinks on the wall. With the sensation of control, she felt at ease. She returned to Gabriel, smiling. She didn't know what the atrocity was, she told him. But perhaps what Elena and Piree were trying to tell them was that Borges had already imagined this atrocity, that somewhere in that obscure story about a sinologist called Stephen Albert whose name conceals the location of the crime is a clue to the horror which they had imagined, which they feared and desired, which they said they wanted to prevent.

He said nothing when she had finished this. His eyes were open, as he considered it. He desired her then, Dolores could see it. But she wouldn't be touched. She would remain in control.

The next evening she pressed home her advantage. She insisted that they must challenge Elena personally. They would meet her the following day at her bookstore during her shift. Dolores told him repeatedly that nothing would be the same afterwards. He would have to transfer his affections to her, as she instructed him. Gabriel made no protest, as she had expected. She could not imagine that he might have his own motivations, his own feelings ripe for transformation. His way of thinking was beyond her.

She told Pepe she would be in late the following evening. Then she met Gabriel the next day outside Waterloo, after he had made his way over from Paddington. Dolores felt fresh and confident. She made a joke, that now it was she who was picking him up. Decidedly, she was not herself. For a moment she forgot him. There, Gabriel was saying something to her, asking what arrangement they might make with Elena, his questions mounting up in her ears like featureless corpses: *Stop interrogating me!*, snapping in kind at his mouth, *I cannot provide an answer for everything* - watching for a moment his face merge with the twilight and the trains as they broke free of Charing Cross and crossed the river in splintered torrents of metal - *No, then, don't say another word, follow me in silence.*

Elena was waiting for them. She kissed Gabriel on the cheek, smoothing back her curls as she did so. She did not seem to appreciate that things had changed. Dolores told her that they had to find a quiet place and so Elena led them past the tables piled high with books towards a back room.

"Gabriel," Elena called out as they passed a table of books in the store, "here's a copy of your book, your new bible."

Gabriel smiled for a moment, but then recovered himself. He managed not to reply, Dolores saw, intimating his new hostility. But the Argentinian had not understood her situation. She gestured with the tome she held, proffering it at Gabriel with that smile born of false conscience. She did not betray awareness that they were not to be distracted by slight gifts such as this book. She held open the door to the stock room, keeping the copy of *Ulysses* in one hand. The room was a jumble of books and papers with several pallets from publishers stacked one on top of another at the back. She moved over to the store manager's chair and sat down, fiddling with a piece of paper on the desk.

"What's that, Elena?" Dolores asked.

"This?" Elena held the sheet of paper up. "Nothing much. Just something I've been writing."

"I should have told you, Gabriel," Dolores said. "She is writing a book. She is inventing our stories for us."

"Is it true?"

"Yes." Elena sat back, looking pleased with herself. "I've just been working out my manifesto for writing. What a book must be if it is to be of value, in itself."

"And what is that?"

"Here, Gabriel." She showed him the piece of paper and he read out: "Manifesto: A novel must be beautiful, cruel, mysterious, unexpected, repetitious, constantly new, fearful, hopeful and sad – to be like life".

"It's all nonsense, Gabriel," Dolores told him. "Worthless talk to delude you. She's probably stolen it from one of the authors she's always trying to get me to read. One of those damned Latin Americans."

Gabriel looked at them both. Then he turned to Elena and found the force in his balls at last. He told her that he would not be reading *Ulysses* any more. It was worthless and he had learnt nothing from it. Was she just trying to distract him? Why couldn't she let him go now that he'd done what they'd asked of him? He didn't work at the airport here, he couldn't help them any more. He didn't want to know what happened when they managed to export the books and didn't care. He had a feeling that he would find out about the crime soon enough. He even wondered if it hadn't happened already, if there hadn't been some explosion and a reckoning with it.

And yet after all this Elena was calm. She did not seem to care and her indifference was crushing. Did Gabriel think himself that important to interfere with the plan? It was too late for that, she laughed, far too late. So it was Dolores who had to complement the words with decision. It was she who led the way back through the books as the African followed her. *Come on*, she hissed at Gabriel, *you're with me now*. They left the stock room and found that the bookstore had filled with men and women. None of them had come to buy books. Rather they flirted stickily in groups that expanded and shrank in sudden spurts. It was a book launch: Elena had told Dolores about these events. They looked at the room. One could sense the despair as shelves were scanned, that the writers gathered there were never going to be free of the competition except through genocide or political extremism.

Gabriel took her arm. There was a tremble in his hands which had been absent in the stock room. Here one was surrounded by leaders, or those who aspired to be leaders. It was not something that those who were born to serve could deal with. She reciprocated the pressure on his arm, and they turned into a cheerful woman struggling to maintain the generosity of youth when her shapeless shoulders and the severe frown mark between her eyes revealed bitterness.

Ah, the woman said to Gabriel, *do you have any more wine?* She offered him her empty glass. Gabriel took it without question, gazed at it. The mistress had not dared to make visual contact with him and she was unaware that her glass remained empty for some time. Of course: she was still talking. They had visited the Alhambra, she said, and even lodged there a night in the Parador – such a secret, her eyes glittered – and moved on to the priceless mosque of Córdoba, and from there to Ronda, the terrific chasms opening up beneath the city. *Do you know,* she said, *that Franco's army threw scores of Republicans to their deaths, down those very chasms where I stood with Michael just last week* – her eyes straying, in animal thirst to her glass – *and it is difficult to stand in a place of such beauty and imagine such barbarism.* And still Gabriel trapped there, holding in his hand the empty esteem of those whom he served.

"Why?" he asked her.

"Why…" The woman looked at him.

"Why is it difficult?"

"Because…" She could not finish. "Have you got my wine?"

"I do not serve here, but at Paddington."

"We didn't go by train. It takes too long, and is too expensive."

He returned her glass. The guest averted her eyes. Dolores throbbed violently, in silence. This London was full of people like this, people who trampled through the cities of her country and believed that a few raciones of patatas alioli and a cursory examination of some mudejar architecture gave them a right to an opinion. They dismissed the violence of the military regime. They declared that they "could not understand" the motivations for such violence. They found the carnage of the guerra civil "incomprehensible". With their deep-seated homosexual inclinations, their fascination with the impossibility of their own violation, they sided with the oppressed and the defeated. They loved their fantasy of Republican Spain. They had no respect for the authority of triumph. And yet they had emerged from the culture which was the most triumphant of all cultures.

"What were you doing in my country?"

"Usted vyaynays de Espanya?"

"Si."

"We have a house there in the Alpujarras."

"And here?"

"It's a great event. A launch to celebrate the centenary this year of Bloomsday, the day on which all the action of Joyce's *Ulysses* was set."

Gabriel's pupils dilated. "*Ulysses*, you say, by the writer Joyce."

"Yes."

"But Bloomsday was in *June*, I think, not in *February*, when we are all still cold."

"Oh, you know…" - the woman laughed – "any excuse to sell a few books."

The woman had turned from Gabriel and was deep in discussion with someone else. Yet he would not let her go. He touched her on the shoulder. He persisted.

"What is this? You do not work here! Release me!"

"Do you know the assistant here, Elena?"

"Of course not!"

"But she is an expert on *Ulysses*."

"Are you pursuing me? Is that it?"

The fear had transmogrified already into violence. People were beginning to look in their direction. There was the sense that the hostility, so swift and manifest, might be channelled into an act of aggression. It was clear that Gabriel understood none of it. Everyone was staring at him. They had realised that he was out of place in their gathering. He was surely the cause of their discomfort. Peace was so easily broken into the pieces of the soul, cast into a depth from which no one could reassemble it. *There will always be hatred*, Dolores's father had shouted, in the daylight.

They had to leave. Dolores dragged Gabriel through the crowd, and they only spoke once they were outside. Gabriel was shaking, she could feel it as they walked along the Strand. He told her that ever since he had arrived he felt that he had been pursued by fear. People looked at him as if the fear was just over his shoulder, as if he was being pursued himself and in his pursuit was pursuing them. She felt a sadness welling up in him, in her, deep down from many generations. Where was this shadow of fear? he asked Dolores. Could it really exist?

She hesitated. She did not want to share her own sadness but there was no purpose in shielding from him the reality of his position. There had been no doubt in his mind, she pointed out as they crossed back over the river towards the London Eye, that his meeting with Elena had been no accident. Everything had counselled against coincidence, for in his world coincidence was the unexpected soldering of fragments from the one spirit. He had then set out on the path that had been determined, but had he ever wondered if it had not been Elena herself who had been the determining factor?

They stopped midway across the thick grey river suspended above the barges and their overspill of tourist waste. Many people passed them with their mobile phones. Of course, she continued, there had always been calculation. The whole thing had smelt like a pretence. From the beginning Elena had implied that theirs could be an equal friendship yet had seen herself as ascendant. Always Elena had despised Gabriel and believed him to be easily defeated. And was that not how one treated animals, the animalized, or those in whom such a condition was always incipient? Humanity was finally an arbitrary value always within the power of the aggressor to bestow and to remove.

That was how she saw it, she went on, why else did he have the sense of being pursued? It was the Argentinian who had pursued him more than anyone ever since his arrival. And Gabriel had to acknowledge that it was so. He unfurled his hands upon the dirty handrail, turned side-on to her so that she could not see his eyes. He had not quite given himself over to her. There was still a shred of something that had to be overcome if they were going to stop Elena and Piree.

Dolores took his hand again, leading, as they crossed over the river and descended onto the concourse by the Royal Festival Hall. For Gabriel the people must have seemed as dead as the stones the place was built of; it was like those old ships, once you went in there you might never come out. She explained how she could see that his mind sometimes wandered back to Africa, perhaps to a beautiful beach, a famine-strewn wasteland, or some horror of a village or a city stalked by Death. Yet all of this was far from the manipulations of an individual like Elena. For Elena was not merely mendacious, she was in fact a devil. Oh yes, Dolores went on, when Gabriel responded that these also existed in Africa, but Elena was certain to outstrip them all in cunning. There was no doubt that she had planned a terrible crime.

A crime? Gabriel stopped there on the promenade beside the river. His eyes had emptied with unease. Everyone was talking about a crime, he said, and he was beginning to wonder if they did not think that it was he who was the criminal. Dolores laughed. Of course not! Could he not see that it was Elena, that she was in league with Piree? Surely, it had been their own crime that Piree had been talking of when Dolores had seen them confronting one another in the bookstore. That scholar had mocked them all with his performance, and yet he had intimated that the criminal was deep in the person he spoke with, in himself, in everyone, rising to the surface and ready at the slightest charge to catapult itself into the atmosphere of this London that haunted them all.

After that they were both silent. As they moved on again along the river Dolores asked herself if there had been any hint of Elena's wickedness. Perhaps she had been stealing those books, pretending that she was entitled to them as an employee. Perhaps hers was the largest fraud of all. It was something that would have to be cleansed and expiated, the most terrible crime of all.

V

To escape fear you had to cherish it: this was what her father had told her day by day and night by night as each of them had brooded on the farm. Human life was nothing without a little fear, he used to say: without a little reality. And so this haunting tracked Dolores in this English-speaking capital which had seemed to offer so many avenues of escape.

The farm would not leave Dolores in London. Did she cherish those memories even here, when she had spent so long trying to escape them? They came to her by day and by night and whenever she woke. She would catch herself as she climbed out from her dreams with a hint of those previous awakenings. She had risen daily on the farm for twenty-three years to take in the air. From a young age her lungs had drained of phlegm which she had spat onto the cracking yard as she had breathed in the air between the house and the barns. Then every morning she had gone to the bathroom to dispel something that had festered by night, shitting there in the darkness. Her father never absent and whistling in the breakfast room as they ate in silence, contemplating through the dust-edged windows the clouds rolling in the oceanic sky. Not a hill nor a forest was there to break the plain, and in the silence a fear and a sadness because even in the very prospect of fear there was an animal excitement.

And statuesque in the sunlit gleam of the breakfast table only once did she recall him having broken the silence. *Here is a story, hija, one that always reminds me of how much I admired my father. As you know he fought hard to defeat communism. He was at Toledo in the alcázar. Because of his blood pressure they despatched him to Coruña, to check on those who were trying to leave the country. Now of course the patria was lucky to be rid of those who fled. Most of them were communists who thought that patria itself was some sort of oath to be sworn at the military. We all wanted the rabble themselves to be gone – Argentina, Cuba, Chile: who cared if the Communist threat went to Latin America! My father, stuck out with the doltish Gallegos, did his best to fulfil his task. The rabble we wanted rid of, but the rabble rousers were wanted. And there was one man against whom he had fought at Toledo, whom he knew personally, and your grandfather recognized him at once there at Coruña and said, with such simplicity: You have no choice but to submit.*

It was far better not to inquire as to the origins of stories. When she had left her childhood farm she had told herself that it was because there was no work in the Moraña and no peace in Madrid. But as she was pressed into the flesh of another on an overland train or a bus and her eyes were absorbed by the repetitious journey, she would feel as if she had stepped back into the threat of that old breakfast table, the drone of the radio, the heavy rattle of the wind in the corrugated iron barn roofs. She never knew what had thrown her back like this: some familiar smell, perhaps, or touch, some unexplained pathway in the sight of blind memory. She had fled from the past but the past had not fled from her. The threat was growing on all sides. She was its consumer and the being who by fearing it so had created and nourished it and given it strength.

She needed order. The flat required new patterns. She gave the mice she looked after to a homeless man in Waterloo whose labrador had been run over and missed the company his pet had given him. Then she devised routines so that she never had to meet Elena, far less share the same crockery or bed linen. It was enough that the Argentinian had coerced her into sharing the flat when they had run into each other in London, pretending that it was chance, that in this city things would be better between them. What a farce! She no longer wanted anything to do with her. She knew that the books were supposed to be loaded any day, in Heathrow. She did not care about this, nor about amassing evidence. Who needed evidence when there could no longer be any doubt as to what was afoot?

No, the most important thing was to ensure that she never had to see Elena. She passed whole passages of time on public transport or when working at Pepe's bar devising further strategies of separation. She bought a new fridge and left a note out on the kitchen table: now all their food could be arranged shelf by shelf with no risk of contamination.

Gabriel did not stop coming to the flat, but she made sure that he never saw the Argentinian. She asked him one evening at Pepe's, when already it was dark before half-past six, why had he followed the Argentinian to the London flat at all? He did not seem to know how to answer. Sometimes, he said in the end, it was just easier to follow than to ask questions. Didn't she know that? At first the idea of it all had seemed intriguing, alluring even. There was this beauty to danger and even to talk of danger because it touched on the permanent fragility of life which gave its every instant meaning. There had been nothing sinister, no, not when he had first got involved. *And now?* Dolores asked him, and he grimaced, because now it was different, and Piree even talked as though he, Gabriel, was the criminal, the one accused. Dolores laughed at that: *And that is when as yet there has been no crime at all*, she told him, *when we just have the dreams which will make the crime possible.* He asked her, were they dreaming? But she did not reply.

Instead she moved away from him, down the bar, pretending that she had to serve someone even though her colleague was already there. They were never busy at that time of night. When she came back towards him she challenged him, why was he still reading that book *Ulysses*, when it was a perversion? when he had agreed that Elena's whole scheme had to be discarded and sunk? Gabriel defended himself: Elena had told him that Joyce himself had been a sort of immigrant, travelling through Europe teaching English to support his impoverished family: a foreigner, like them, a totem for modern life. *That is different!* Dolores shouted, *a hundred years different.*

And he complied. He began to support Dolores's attempts to bring order to other areas of her life. She had always kept the books on her shelves in a strict alphabetical structure, by author. At times she had even dallied with reading books alphabetically. For weeks Gabriel had mocked this practice, but by and by he encouraged her in it. Had she not said to him that a well-ordered narrative memorialized the divine story, while those books without a rigorous order betrayed a challenge to authority? So, she needed to ensure that her own books were always in precise order, that they did not fall out of line.

Dolores began to pursue the alphabetic mode more thoroughly. She did not skip a letter or backtrack. The only exceptions she made were for oddities like the "Y" and "W" which did not rightly belong in Spanish. The probity of her enjoyment with the books warmed her whenever she thought of it, bringing her numinous glimpses at the oddest moments. This delight in ordered reading gave righteouness and purpose; it was the negation of the nothingness which suddenly descended on her in the small hours, that nothingness which in those sleepless moments she feared lay at the heart of her existence.

She had placed her flat in Peckham increasingly off limits and Gabriel stopped coming. He did not mention Elena. Nor was there any talk of her coming to see the flat which he shared with two Nigerians, two individuals not dissimilar to his previous flatmates in other capital cities. Instead they met at Pepe's, or else in a neutral place. They walked in Battersea Park beneath the trees and the power station. They roamed the city in the last days of winter. There was no question of them touching. There was nothing physical to their relationship. Yet Dolores felt a sense of delicious lightness, as if nothing was real or mattered. Even the forthcoming presidential elections back in Spain, where the candidate of order and justice seemed sure to win, were a cause for optimism. Everything was moving in the right direction. The evidence and the confrontation with Elena and Piree would come at the right moment. She felt in control.

She did not imagine that Gabriel could challenge the hierarchy which she had created. She had grown fond of him, as one might of a childhood pet to which one has developed a certain attachment that will not outgrow its inevitable demise. It was a learning curve, that of how to control that which was less than human. It was something upon which her father had expounded his philosophy: *one begins with the animals*, he had said, *one studies the mice, tortures them, observes their response to pain, one gasses them when they are no longer of any use, and then, when the intelligence has been attuned to its task, it is ready to turn to other non-human groups*: at that the blood would rise to his forehead, harbinger of his final stroke.

In these days there was nothing which did not bring her rapture. The fear of those mornings in the farmhouse receded as she felt that although she was not in a physical relationship with Gabriel he might do anything to please her. Dolores suggested an outing and it was done. A criticism had its effect. An opinion produced a conversion. And with this unlikely friendship she learnt not to judge the people of London too harshly. She had never understood the willingness of so many among them to holiday in such filthy places, in Africa or India, where there was dirt and disease and the disgrace of poverty. She loathed the conversations at Pepe's bar as they boasted of their adventures. But at last she could see how attractive it must be to journey in a place where people were always serving you and reminding you of your status.

At Pepe's, Sebastiana noticed her happiness. *You must like him*, she would say to Dolores at quiet moments, and Dolores would withdraw, still smiling. *Perhaps it's the first time*, Sebastiana pursued. Sometimes she would share her cigarettes and with that the two of them found a certain solidarity. Then Dolores would laugh, and pretend that she had some business to attend to.

Sebastiana was pleased for her – she was still generous enough for that - but for Pepe the change was troubling. *Have you seen?*, he called to his wife one night, *she's screwing that immigrant.* But Sebastiana ignored him, her head down in the account books to see when she might be able to afford her next trip back to Coruña. Dolores knew that she couldn't bear to hear her husband when he spoke like that; Sebastiana knew him well enough now to give him no more credit than any other customer.

Dolores understood people like Pepe, impelled by blemishes in the purity of others where they had already polluted themselves. It made her think of books she'd read on the Inquisition, the stain of this and the colour of that. She came to laugh at the conversations that Pepe would have with Gabriel, as he railed against the new immigrants. *It is just like that in Coruña*, her boss would say, *we are invaded by these wretched Ukrainians, Poles, call them what you like, they will still do a day's work for 20 Euros, we never asked for them, we are pursued by them, I would hunt them like mice in a cage.*

Dolores accepted the world she had wrought for herself just then. It was what had happened when she had allowed these old feelings from childhood to return, and she did not imagine that it could change. It could have been the happiest she had ever been in her life. But one day Gabriel came to her with a proposal. A friend at Paddington station had given him some free flights to Paris. He had some contacts with the airlines because of the check-in facilities for the express train to Heathrow. They could go even if it was only for the day. Perhaps they would enjoy it, he said, the opportunity to visit somewhere new. She started: somewhere new? Her eyes quested at his. Still, everything was a pretense.

Dolores found no answer. She felt wary. This unexpected turn suggested that her careful plea to unmask Elena and Piree might be at risk. Gabriel told her that he would reserve some seats in two weeks' time. Yet until now it was she who had proposed and disposed. The collapse of her authority suggested that the whole structure might be creaking. The atrocity might be more imminent than she had allowed herself to realise.

In the days that followed, Dolores withdrew. Gabriel still came to Pepe's yet she took little pleasure in directing their conversations and in her nightly journeys home across the city the dread sharpened. There would be Elena, if not sitting in the living room then perhaps sleeping with some man. She could not forgive the Argentinian her promiscuity. She ought to speak out. And yet she was voiceless. Was this not how the worst evils were perpetrated, flaunted before people whose goodness did not overcome their fear? For three nights in succession Dolores gnawed at these agonies in the neon half-light of the London dark. Yet when the lift reached the fifteenth floor and she stepped out into the antiseptic corridor of the high-rise, opening the door into the flat, she was met only by silence. On the fourth night she consoled herself that the sequence of events would be repeated, she opened the front door, and there awaiting her was Elena.

"Ah Dolores, we have been awaiting you, nena." She was sitting there with that scholar Piree, both of them poring over a book. "This is the American scholar of Chinese culture, Professor Kent Piree," she said, as if Dolores did not know him already.

Dolores stopped. The parroquía in Arévalo swam into her consciousness, where she had always stopped and waited to be permitted entry. She looked at the dapper professor. He was always so well turned out, with his shirts and trousers pressed even though as far as she knew he lived without help and did not seem the sort of person who would do that sort of thing for himself. He was self-possessed, obsessed. He never had acknowledged her more than necessary, and was not going to start that evening. He turned instead to Elena.

"The important thing," he told the Argentinian, "is that the books should be packaged so that the wrong person cannot open them once they reach Buenos Aires."

"They're dangerous, you've told me that often enough."

"Only in the wrong hands. But if they find their way there…" Piree left the words hanging for a moment. "The material could start something that could not be stopped."

"Where?"

"Who knows? That's what's at stake. The constant movement of fire that began with the beginning, the first explosion. The quest to stop it from consuming the end."

Elena smiled at him for a moment, as if humouring him. "Would that really be possible?" she asked him.

"Anything can happen," Piree answered. "There's so little time left."

"So little time." Elena nodded, as if at last she understood.

"We must get them to Buenos Aires," said Piree. "My friend there will take care of them. At the right moment, the books will reveal the location of the crime."

Elena did not reply this time. She turned to Dolores. It was like she had said: they had been waiting for her. Piree also turned to Dolores, for the first time. He sniffed: he had not been waiting for her. Fire glazed the irises of his eyes, the code of obsession. Dolores knew that he was not the first to pass on that drive to the books. Her father had told her: among other things that he had learnt before returning to the farm from the Complutense was that it was not for nothing that inquisitors had incinerated so much paper before it had been able to corrupt. Piree's eyes held her there in the latent fire of their madness. She knew that he had always been suspicious of her.

Elena ignored Piree's suspicions. They had been waiting for Dolores, she said, because they needed her books. They had to substitute the book jackets so that no one would recognise Piree's material for what it was. Surely Dolores would understand?

Piree stood there with one of her books in his hand: "You have no choice but to submit," he said. "The jackets have already been switched by your flatmate Barajo and myself."

Dolores could not resist the same words her father had used. She sat on the settee where just those few long weeks before the intruder had lain. It was clean now, thank God. Of course she understood, disguise and subterfuge were innate to any project to protect people. Everything was permitted, even the destruction of the order of her books, of her dreams. So little was off limits in the search for a crime which had not yet been committed.

VI

Fear was something easy to settle with and much harder to dislodge. A few days after finding Piree in her bedroom, so unexpected and awesome, Dolores saw fire engines in action at Paddington Station as she waited for Gabriel to finish his shift. The uniformed firemen beat back an imagined enemy and then retreated in order. After the false alarm the gleaming red engines swung up from the concourse at Paddington. Gabriel emerged, laughing at the panic which the alarm had caused in the commuters. Dolores should have seen their faces, he said as he loomed above her as normal, in imputed authority: they could not deal with it and fled in scattered bursts.

It was not amusing, but Dolores had lost the courage to speak out. She had submitted to Piree. She had not had the courage to speak out, and she wondered if she would ever have the courage to confront him with the evidence. His criminality might well unmask her, and she knew that perhaps with this one release she might also consider contact with others, with Gabriel or Pepe. She might even enjoy being touched. She had resisted for so many years but the prospect of a new leader like Piree was a reminder of other authorities now dead and gone but still living on like broken worms in her soul.

At Pepe's she told Sebastiana about the fire engines at Paddington. Sebastiana put down her pen and took off the thick-rimmed glasses she wore. She asked, had Dolores seen the fear? Why was she so obsessed by it? She coughed a little and offered a lewd smile. Didn't her nights with that African make her forget those feelings a little, just for the time being? Where had she learnt about fear, anyway?

But Dolores could not answer that: still she could not say, *in my childhood*. Instead, and more than ever, it seemed to her that everyone was above her in the hierarchy. Perhaps it was what she had always longed for. What could be more holy than abasement? Piree had stolen the jackets of her books in pursuit of this terrible crime which he longed to commit as he pretended to revile it. Sebastiana mocked her fears so real that they ate her, even though whenever she left Pepe for a few days and went to Coruña she remembered all about fear and how it could separate and burn families with its emotional napalm. And Gabriel still commanded her with this idea of a trip to Paris.

He came to see her at Pepe's the night before they were supposed to go and reminded her that the Heathrow Express they needed to catch left very early the next morning from Paddington. They could meet in the concourse at six o'clock, when it was still dark, he would see her there. He patted her wrist as it lay poised on the bar and then left her. She retreated behind the defensive line that tightened her smile, executing the commands of her superiors, prising away the empty glasses and the plates soiled with residues. She could see that Pepe with his rum and his paper had his place in a world like this. He looked at her that night, after

Gabriel had gone: his thwarted desire for contact almost appealed: perhaps she could touch it, just once.

"You still want the day off tomorrow, bonita?"

"I never asked for the day," she said.

"You said you were going to Paris."

"For the day, patrón, just for the day."

"So you're not going to spend the night with him?"

"I have my obligations here, do I not? I promise to be here by nine o'clock."

"That's too late." Pepe slammed the palm of his left hand into the bar. "There is work for you to do here."

"But you just offered me the day."

"I offered nothing."

He reminded Dolores of those bulls she had known as a child, sated by the tedious familiarity of the flesh which yet always retained an ingrained attraction, seeing to their half-formed desires and yet baffled, enraged by trifles. Those bulls had been in the farms of the neighbours, and her father had relaxed when near to them, as always talking about something else and yet referring to himself. *Imagine the lives led by those beasts*, hija, *all gratification on demand, without guilt, without the need for pretence day and night*. And then she flinched beneath the spotlights of the ceiling as Pepe filled the space behind the bar. The most intense experiences were so awful that memory shredded or reconstituted them. She saw before her the patrón, *ay*, what was he doing here, in her space? She could not resist the force that was in them both, driving them to the inevitability of hatred because what they really longed for was the pleasure of entry into each other and so into the world which for a moment would allow them to forget. *You must be here as usual*, he said, with those hateful words commanding her silence.

Out in the warm evening her silence was devoured by others. A crowd of young men veered across the pavement as they sang some song. She gripped her bag and felt for her alarm. Then she sat on one of the hard seats at the bus stop, grinding without thinking of it a cigarette end into the pavement. When the bus came it was crowded. She stood with the lights brilliant and reflections of brilliance in the transparent windows onto the darkness. She felt surrounded by faces and evanescence, by the pretence of a world shorn of foundations which ripened minds for their destruction.

She could bear it no longer. Pushing her way to the exit door in the middle, she pressed the bell and alighted in Camberwell. She walked by the bilious lights of the takeaways and minicab offices where drivers sleepless sat blinking into the dark streets and awaiting a client with whom to share their anxiety. Then there came the softness of the residential areas, the absence of light. Her tower was not too far distant, and when she saw it she turned from the main road and walked along the avenue between the concrete. Here was always a moment of fear for her on her nightly return from Pepe's. Assaults were common. The place was inhabited by filth. And yet what could one do except walk on in silence, in constant escape from what might be following behind?

Rising in the lift, Dolores felt that she could almost touch her fear. If the Argentinian was there, she would scream. But when she opened the door there was no one. She entered the ordered emptiness of her sanctum. The mice were no longer there to console her. There was nothing. The walls of books rising in precipices of paper, each page an attempt at understanding. Yet even here the order was a fiction. The covers had been substituted by Elena and Piree and she was still agitated by what they had done to her books, even though she had had to go along with it. That awful man and his book talk! Piree was a real madman. She knew she had to denounce him to the authorities but yet there was something about his madness that was attractive. She turned suddenly, but there was nothing behind. She lay on the bed. She could not sleep. She waited out the night, waited for morning.

She had decided to go to Paris. She would turn Gabriel's invitation into a refusal. She'd ignore him for the whole trip and thus reset the hierarchy onto its allotted path. And with her eyes sore she rose and reversed the journey of the night before, and continued on from Waterloo to Paddington. When she arrived, she crossed the concourse. She felt like she had the night before, that she was being followed. Dolores turned but saw no one familiar. It was so early that few people were about. She was her own pursuer. She continued and then turned again. There was Piree, directly behind her.

"Has she got the books?"

"The books?"

"You have come to oversee their export." It was a statement, and there was no answer. "There is no time to lose. The transaction is ready."

"I have had no part in this," she said.

Piree grabbed her wrist with unexpected force. "Oh you are implicated," he said. "Of course you are implicated."

"Implicated in what?"

"The jackets of the books." He had begun to drag Dolores along the concourse. "Of course it could be traced to you. We discussed it with you. You did not refuse us."

"I had no choice."

"My contact would know, in Buenos Aires, even if the customs' operatives did not pick up on it at the freight collection point. He sees through everything. He would help with the detection operation."

They walked along the concourse. He seemed always to be talking about this contact in Buenos Aires. It went with his obsession with that story, *The Garden of Forking Paths*. It made her think of the dead writer and librarian, the Argentinian Borges, always a hero in her household through his support for the military governments of Pinochet and Videla. Her father often told her how relinquishing his studies of this melding of literature and history was one of the things he had most regretted when leaving the Complutense. The homosexual elite refused to see it, but Borges's fascination for political order had simply mirrored his exalted literary interests.

"Your friend in Buenos Aires, your contact – did he know Borges?"

Piree ducked the question. His friend was an expert, that was what counted: "We want him to decipher one of Borges's stories," he said, "*The Garden of Forking Paths*. The location of the crime will emerge there, in the product we've prepared for export."

Dolores tried to pull her wrist free but the American's grip tightened. She didn't want to make a fuss in public. She remained, in submission. "This crime," she tried again, "can't you tell me what it is?"

"I don't know myself," Piree answered.

"Why are you so obsessed by it?"

"My whole life, I've been pursuing it. Since my retirement, I've been able to dedicate myself to it."

"But how do you know that the clue is in that story at all?"

"Because it's obvious!" Piree snapped, tightening his grip on her wrist. "Because the worst atrocities only exist when they've already been imagined. If we could just undo the imagination, or at least decode it, we might be able to prevent the fires of the future." He paused for a moment, loosening his hold. He sighed. "Sometimes," he told her, "I wonder if I'm not somehow creating that future atrocity through my fascination with it, by trying to stop it from happening. But I can't stop myself. I'm addicted."

"What's Borges got to do with it, though?"

"Ever since I read this story, *The Garden of Forking Paths*, I've felt that it has a ring of prophecy. I can't explain it and I don't feel I have to."

Dolores felt a sense of stubborn familiarity. Her father had so often spoken of Borges, of his intuition that it was the rigidity of literary order itself which could keep the fragile paperweight of the world from shattering; and here was Piree, telling her of his compulsion to decode the imagined order of the past in order to forestall the future. Yet beyond the familiarity there was something dangerous, a sense of the subversion of everything which Borges and her father had stood for. By changing some small details of a world, its moral content could be transformed forever.

"*The Garden of Forking Paths*," she said in the end, "that's a story about a sinologist, isn't it?"

"Someone like me. Stephen Albert."

"Perhaps that's why you're so fascinated by it."

"Perhaps it is." Piree stopped and looked at her, in revelation.

"In Borges's story," she continued slowly, "Albert reveals the secret of the Chinese novel he is studying to his nemesis, who has been pursuing him for years. The Chinese book contains two meanings in one text, and is both a labyrinth and a book about time. But his revelation is his undoing. Albert shares the same name as a city which has been targeted in an appalling crime. By killing him, his nemesis reveals the city's name to the Axis forces."

"You see," said Piree, "the sinologist is the hero, and his pursuer uses him as an excuse for an appalling crime."

She stood with Piree near the departure lounge for the Heathrow Express. Beyond them ebbed the release of departure. Still there was the constant pressure of Piree the sinologist in her flesh. She was almost used to it beyond noticing. The pain relaxed, and his hand left her. He had seen the books packed for export, he told Dolores, down there on the concourse, which was all that he needed. He seemed to want to pretend that their whole exchange there in Paddington had not taken place. He was confident that everything had been prepared as it should have been.

She went on without him, still not seeing Gabriel, far less Piree's boxes. She stepped off into the press of anxieties. Attention was directed at the ticket barriers, distant in their automated openings and closings, offering and withholding flight. She did not want to go to Paris. She wanted to escape herself and yet she could not. In a corner of the foyer was a coffee bar and she walked there to order an espresso, for once to be served. Standing by the bar she broke the sachet of sugar and dropped the granules into her drink. She stirred it with a white plastic spatula, and drank: bittersweet: London, before her, where she subsisted.

Many people were at the espresso bar fighting the early start. For a moment she forgot Gabriel and Piree. Sometimes such was her alienation from her environment that it felt as if her life was being experienced by someone else. And when one's own life had become a virtual reality, how could one care for others, or about the future of a world in which one was always a stranger?

Those books will fall! She heard the barman exclaim rapidly. A suitcase had spilled half a dozen books over the concourse near the advance check-in desks that the airlines kept at the station. There were shouts of anger. People watched the minor drama. Dolores rose to see more closely, and saw Gabriel and Elena. They saw her, too. The books! Of course, Piree had mentioned them, yet she had not paused to consider that this rendered the Argentinian's presence inevitable. Piree had even said that he had seen the books on the concourse. Yet Elena had not been there, at first. Had Elena hidden and then reappeared, merely to provoke fear? There was no escape from the crime or the criminal.

Gabriel and Elena walked towards Dolores. He said that it was an opportunity for healing, for dialogue. The Argentinian smirked. Were those two really moving closer together, in spite of everything Dolores had done? She would have to stop it, take advantage of Gabriel's weakness. For his eyes were wide, fearful. He was defensive. A cowardly act, this, controlled by the Sudaca. It was all so filthy, so restless, and Gabriel imagined that she, Dolores, would spend a day in a foreign city with that witch who always sought control, whom he had started to touch again. And inside a welling of all these feelings endlessly deferred, the outrage of everything suffered and repressed. *You bitch! You thief! You fucking bitch!* Grappling with her enemy. At last the physical reckoning, luscious to scrape her fingers over skin which repulsed her, to grab hair which she despised. How wonderful it was to tear. What pain there was felt sublimated in the final requiting of desire. *You bitch, you've stolen him and he's mine!* Of course

213

Gabriel intervened, attempting their separation. She tore at him as well, swore: *Of course you take her side, you're her slave. You're her fucking slave! Devils, the both of you!*

The security forces grappled with Dolores. *Don't you see!* She screamed, *We've got to stop them!* They did not understand. They uttered words of apology to Gabriel and Elena, who moved over to the check-in desks and began to register some large boxes. *It's the books!* Dolores yelled, *the books!* She was screaming, writhing. There was a tremendous noise, but she could not tell if it was from her or from beyond, something even more fearful. What if that was what they had all been moving towards, something atrocious which they had all had a part in creating? A fire as an ending which might send them all back to a fire in the beginning? She screamed again, kicking out. The security men dragged her over the concourse. One of them yanked back her hair. She did not care. She could see them at the check-in desk, she could see them! Perhaps the whole Argentinian ploy had been a decoy. She felt as if she understood it all at last. When Gabriel had mentioned Paris he had given the game away. That was where they were really taking the books. She would have to act! This time, she would go to the authorities as she had promised herself for so long. She would go and unburden herself of what was happening before it was too late.

And outside, a blustery day early in March, the city cold and hard to the touch like moonlit stones. It was still early. Pepe's would be shut, but she had the key to Pepe's. Sebastiana might be there for her to confide in. Dolores could not return to Peckham to the flat she shared with the Argentinian. Everything had closed in. The sun shone but she did not see its light. Three years her father had been dead but she could see him, chiding her for having left the patria behind. *What were you running from, hija? From your past, what was wrong with your past? From your name? The Madrid family is one of the noblest of all.* So lonely there on the farm, just the two of them to fend off the world entire, the inevitability of passing. The memories returned, all the more intense. People tried to destroy the devil within them and the devil jeered in triumph.

Her feet led her towards Pepe's, the streets a grey mirror of the sky. In the farmhouse the mirror had been ancient, had even developed cracks. Her father, uglier and uglier, his girth unsustainable. But he had been an upstanding citizen and other upstanding citizens had treated him with civility. Weekly, Padre Ramón had been invited from Arévalo, and they had eaten Sopa Castellana among the fig trees. And always the priest and her father congratulating one another, agreeing with one another, laughing with one another. *We're remembering the good old days,* Ramón would tell her. And she, ever more diminutive beside him, the hijita, naturalistic in her silence, which her father's friends pretended to take for decorum. Not once did anyone question.

The shutters of Pepe's were down. Dolores unlocked them, opened the side door and entered. Inside there was no light. Sebastiana was not there. She hesitated before pressing the switch, left it for a moment and walked behind the bar where she leaned back against the bottles of spirits, empty, full, lined up. One could personify them. They could become individuals, against a wall, like schoolchildren waiting to be chosen for football teams. Like prisoners stood before the firing squad. The same instinct, diverted only by circumstance. Morality both a reason and a threat, and above all, an excuse.

Dolores felt weak. She sat on a chair in the restaurant and closed her eyes. She dreamt but could not remember her dreams and when she woke it was to see that Pepe was watching her.

"You have been waiting for me, bonita."

"No."

"Do not deny it."

"Where is Sebastiana?"

"She has gone to the wholesalers'. You knew it was her day for that today. You wanted to see me in private."

"I cannot offer you what you are looking for." Dolores stood up.

"But you are here to be of service."

"I am here to clean." She moved behind the bar, located her cloths and made to begin; Pepe laughed.

"That's good, you'll be here a while yet."

He moved towards her, so she turned and shoved his chest. "Leave me," she said, "it's not the moment."

Pepe laughed again. He was like every bully, afraid of resistance, but desiring more. "What do you think!" he shouted, "That I want to sleep with you. You've got an evil mind, bonita, depraved thoughts."

He left quickly to buy the paper. Dolores tried to return to working with her habitual thoroughness. It was remarkable how after just a few hours' absence the dirt would return, how impossible it was ever to liquidate it. The grease and layers of dust sprang up as if they had never been eradicated. After a time the first customers began to arrive. She felt calm as she took their orders, returned with their dishes. Some of the dirt had gone, and she was ready to work again. Work itself was an amnesiac. The aborted trip to Paris with Gabriel seemed like a fantasy. The fact that those books might already be winging their way to Paris or Buenos Aires did not seem to matter.

Some customers ordered six cubas libres and she went to prepare the drinks. Pepe was busy reading *ABC*. He was fat. He was smoking. Everything was as it should have been. He rose from his stool by the bar, carrying his newspaper past the customers. She returned with the cubas libres and saw her father standing by the window.

"Put those drinks down, hija."

"Don't come near me!"

"How disgusting, to work among drunkards."

"I'm sorry. I'm sorry." He moved towards her, but she could not be touched. "I'm so sorry." He reached out. "Don't touch me! I'll never do it again!"

People were slapping her, chasing. Piree was there, and seemed to have a gun. People were shouting. Was this at last the criminal? She had known it, of course she had known it! Gabriel came towards her. He feigned concern. He took her hand, but she shuddered. He withdrew. *Ay*, what was he doing so far from home, in constant motion? Was he too in escape from himself? He should not even have been here, but in Paris! What crime had he committed there that he should return so quickly and come by her and her shame? One could not explain the smallest mysteries of life. Perhaps she would only ever be able to understand them if she left all this behind her and imagined the journey that the books might have taken to Buenos Aires or Paris. There she might finally learn if all this talk of atrocity in the future was true or had just been a fantasy which they all of them were responsible for creating.

* * * * *

217

Buenos Aires
2004

I

Witness Statement of Ousmane Agbyeni, Ezeiza Airport

I divorced my country about a year after the Fenobi affair. She was a beautiful woman: her hair falling about her in thick tresses: angular, poised and quick-witted. She was one of the most successful traders at Jos market. Both the men and the women ran to her and she sold them rice, spices and tins of condensed milk, all at prices inflated by the value added from her salesmanship. She had developed no small fortune and bought up houses in the new neighbourhoods which were taking wing like vultures on the outskirts of Jos.

Fenobi was quite happy to publicise her wealth. She wore elaborate bracelets, necklaces and silver rings. But it was her misfortune to come from the Ron, a wretched group from Bokkos where the husband has the right to all his wife's property if he divorces her using his rights according to native law and custom. Naturally, the lazy wretches lie around until their wives are rich and then cut them off with nothing. I had met Fenobi's husband a few times before the case, the man was a wastrel who was always hanging around in bars spending his wife's money, someone with the air of a consummate scavenger, a beast who would have seen off the hyenas without any trouble. His plan was obvious and the whole of Bokkos and the Ron neighbourhoods of Jos knew of it, so when the divorce papers were filed it was for everyone almost a relief that the worst had at last been made public.

Fenobi came to petition the court as soon as the case began. I accompanied her to her village in the car which the federal authorities had given me, even though I knew that there was little that civil law could do for her. We were surrounded by Ron people as soon as we arrived. They shook the dust from their eyes and spat it out as the cloud we had brought with us subsided. Both women and men were angry. The women wanted to show me Fenobi's property, the houses she had built with zinc roofs, proof to the rainy season, the cattle which her husband had managed (badly) scratching their backs against the fenceposts of the animal pens in the village. They invited me to the community centre which a church had built there and plied me with chicken, hungry rice and cow's milk. It was bribery but not the sort of bribery that I was used to. The men were also angry, and when I emerged from the community centre I was surrounded. Who did I think I was, a Yoruba from Ibadan, to meddle in their affairs? To surround myself with their women? What, did I think they were all whores and whoretouts? I stood in judgement but what rights did I have? I was a Muslim, they could see, so what right did I have to interfere? Did I not know that this was their culture? Could I not see that already they were sick of people like me, of my faith, and our extreme demands?

And the law was on the side of men. In the court the ritual of humiliation was executed. Civil law provided little protection for women like Fenobi. The traditions of each people were seen as sacrosanct which was as it should have been. And yet no one stopped to ask where cultural traditions had come from in the first place, where if not from some great, uncorrected historical wrong could such a tradition have emerged from? How if not by understanding the violent emotions bequeathed by our history could we be at peace with each other? Neither the Federal Authorities nor Fenobi's people cared for such nuances. Actually, they were more trouble than they were worth. They required you to think. *Look*, Fenobi's husband screamed in the courtroom, *look at the extortion that her family have practised, the bride price was robbery, they are rich from me, eating my fat, I demand justice.*

I had to rule in his favour. Fenobi disrobed herself there in the court. She unwound her red-and-gold head covering, took off her green-and-yellow print dress and slipped her feet from her sandals. She stood there naked, reminding me of the pointlessness of my job. Her family had brought her some other clothes. Probably they had paid for them from her old bride price. Soon she was decent again. But I had already decided to leave. This was not the first case of its kind that I had come across.

As we say, if you go to any country in the world you will find there a Nigerian. It's true, there aren't many of us over here. And if you ask me why I chose Argentina, there is no easy answer. I had saved plenty of money from my job as a judge and could have bought residence anywhere. I could have gone back to Ibadan too, but I had acquired a taste for experience. I had already spent time in London but had seen that that was not a place where I could do well. Then two or three months after the Fenobi case had concluded I met another judge at a meeting of the judiciary in Abuja.

His son was in Argentina, he said, in Buenos Aires, doing good trade in African artefacts. This country was awash with money back then, before the crisis of 2001, when the bribes still trickled down. The children of the corrupt became hippies. Some of them liked our stuff and even wanted to sell it to each other. The judge at Abuja told me all about this place. The climate was much better than in northern Europe. There were few Moslems but I had never cared much for religion. Nor would I have to worry about the tensions between Christian and Moslem Yorubas in Ibadan and Jos.

So I decided that Argentina was the right country for me. I cashed in everything I had and transferred it via my contacts to my European bank account. I flew to London, spent some time with my cousins there, and then took a flight to Buenos Aires, to Ezeiza Airport. I rented a house in Palermo near the Plaza Cortázar and went out to eat in Italian restaurants. I even got drunk on some of the Argentine wines, shed the skin of my heritage just a little. I had enough money not to have to notice the poverty of the southern suburbs, which were brushed out of sight. I had a good time. But then I invested some money in a new bar run by a Spanish exile couple. The man was a crook and bled the place dry. His wife was always shrugging at me, pretending she didn't understand finance. They ripped me off and left me with nothing.

This is not a good country for someone as I was then: a penniless African. Where is? Those Spanish crooks cleaned me out so thoroughly that I kept on having to wire transfers over from my account in Europe. I had something put by, since over the years all those small considerations had accrued into really quite a large consideration. One of my nephews in London saw to wiring the money over to me, but I think that he was helping himself on the quiet to everything that I'd saved and wasting it all in the hotspots of London, in our old colony.

As it was, two years after I made it over to Ezeiza my nephew answered the phone one day and told me that there was no money left. I felt as if the ghost of Abacha or of one of his relatives had stuck his hands into the little I'd put by.

"What happened to it!" I screamed down the phone in the call centre on Corrientes. "Do you know what can happen to me here now? Don't you know, there is poverty here too?"

My destiny had swum before me then, a foul turd rising in a sewer. I knew without knowing what it was like to have no money here, as everywhere. I was not going to live off bread and sweet tea, or be forced to listen to my neighbours beating their children and each other. I shouted again to my wastrel nephew, "Where's the money?" But the coward had already put the phone down. I stumbled out of the cabin and looked at the girl who worked there. For perhaps ten seconds I said nothing as she waited with my bill.

"You owe fifteen pesos." She said this two, three times, until I registered her. "Don't even think of running out," she went on. "Last week we had an English guy, like you he called London. He was blonde, smart, a charmer, and he ran out without paying, back into the city."

After the life I've lived I have my own rituals of respect before the law. I paid the poor girl, even though by that time I was down to my last 200 pesos. I strolled down to the 9 de Julio and just stood there for twenty minutes, watching the grey rivers of cars clogging up. After a time I turned right and started walking south, away from the estuary. I passed under an elevated road bridge that had seen better days. I stood in a lay-by, hailed a taxi, and paid the guy fifty pesos to take me to the airport. I'm not quite sure why. I suppose I thought I might be able to beg my way onto an aeroplane or wing a courier flight. It was a reckless decision. But that was how I came to Ezeiza the second time, and really I've never left since.

So you can see that I've come across my fair share of criminal cases over the years. I've watched the innocent robbed blind by their own people. Others have taken advantage of me in the same way. I wouldn't want you to think that I'm a cynic, that I have nothing but contempt for human nature. I'll never forget how, after the Fenobi case, an old cripple who spent his days begging for alms in the transport park of Jos came over to Fenobi and gave her everything that he had. I've seen the power of sympathy, learnt how it's so often those with the least who give the most, that those who have nothing are blessed to live without the fear of losing it. But while I can respect human nature I've also seen enough that I can recognise where it deserves suspicion, where a man needs to tread lightly or even turn back if it feels as if the ground may soon give way, the cross-pole snap into the latrine, if you like. That's a roundabout way of beginning, or even of beginning an ending, but I was raised on stories, my grandmother fed them to me daily as a sort of surrogate milk, and I've never quite kicked the habit.

So that's why I was on the alert when the whole business started, just yesterday. I was over by the freight collection point where couriers arrive from all over the city to collect the parcels which have been sent from the other side of the ocean. It was a quiet time of day, just before lunch. All the trans-Atlantic flights had arrived by then and disgorged their passengers. I'd found by experience that the freight collection point was a good spot for me. It never got too busy. Both the motorcyclists and the hauliers were quite proud of their uniforms. They didn't like to create unnecessary dirt. It was quiet, yes, a good place for me. But yesterday it was all different. There were several people waiting there, the usual crowd. But there was also someone who stood out almost as much as I did. He was quite an old man, which was unusual in itself, and very well dressed. He had a smartly pressed suede waistcoat and polished black shoes. He carried a cane but he was not blind, this one, no. He seemed harmless and if he had not been so different to all those who were around him I might not have registered him. As it was, though, I got a good sense of the guy and I'd have no trouble in picking him out in an identity parade.

Anyhow, after a few minutes there was a rain of shrill whistles. The couriers were sticking their fingers into their mouths because an old man had gone past them all and was nosing around near the front of the queue. He was wearing a smart linen jacket and a red tie, bearing his age well, managing to seem dignified in spite of his stoop. He was almost a mirror image of the other old man in the queue.

"Turn round," a motorcyclist called, "wait at the back *viejo!*"

"Hey," a fat haulier joined in, "you may be only able to look down but you sure as hell know the way to the front of the queue!"

The man ignored them. He began to talk to some of those waiting at the front of the queue. "Excuse me," he was saying, "I'm looking for a man called Kent Piree. A North American."

And that was when the snake jumped into the smoke, when I really began to pay attention to what was happening in front of me. The other old man in the queue swung round from his spot a few paces ahead: "Cesar!" he exclaimed. "Is it really you?"

They embraced with genuine joy. I went over to work near them. It's not that I'm nosy or that all I care about is other people's business, cleaning up their shit. But humanity is a curious species, and one type of happiness at least can be found just by satisfying that curiosity. Why not admit it? I wanted to hear what those two had to say to each other.

"But Piree," the one called Cesar was saying, "you've only just arrived."

"Time, Cesar. The issue is time."

"Well of course it can be done," – Cesar's head was nodding in repetition, in disease of agreement – "it won't take us much more than an hour to arrange the transfer, and of course, if it's a matter of safety…"

"After you told me where he was based, there was no alternative. It's as it has to be, Cesar."

The two old friends fell into silence. They seemed pleased to have seen each other. Clearly it had all been arranged beforehand. And that was when I began to feel that something sinister might be at work. We had been trained in security at the airport and had been taught to report anything out of the ordinary. The fat men and their womenfolk disfigured by layers of make-up were the ones who passed through customs without impediment. But when you came across real anomalies, people like Cesar and this Kent Piree, waiting at the freight collection point, you learnt to watch out.

Perhaps I should explain that I'm by no means an ordinary paranoiac, the sort you probably come across lying like fat red mangoes in the fruiting season about the police station early each morning, waiting to denounce their neighbours. I know what I'm talking about. I was offered an excellent training in divining and dividing paranoia from what was really worthy of suspicion at Jos. I received there accusations about witchcraft almost daily. If ever someone became rich they were accused of having alliances with the fetish. This was the main reason offered by Fenobi's husband for her divorce. *I will not spend the rest of my life married to a witch*, he declared to me as he filed his divorce papers, *there is no law on the statute book which requires me to do that.* I knew from my imam in Ibadan that the Qur'an accepted the existence of sorcery but declared that djinns were always capable of outdoing the sorcerers. Knowing thus that good could always trump evil, I never believed that women like Fenobi who did well in business were witches or any such thing. I recognised these accusations as envious paranoia, the sort which allows wicked people to justify their will for domination.

So my feelings towards Cesar and Piree were grounded in genuine concern, not in the desire to spread malicious tittle-tattle. I worked particularly hard at a spot just near to them so I could hear how their conversation developed. Soon they were at the head of the queue. Piree's suave exterior was beginning to fracture. There was an impatience in him, which had built slowly and in the beginning had hardly been noticeable. I think that everyone was becoming aware of it.

"Are you sure he doesn't know we're coming to see him?" he asked Cesar as they waited their turn.

"He's no idea," Cesar said. "He is oblivious to it."

"That's vital. Secrecy has been the key, Cesar. Otherwise the whole crime could begin from nothing, from chance, from someone picking out the hidden meaning at the wrong time." They waited for a moment, watching the courier in front collect a package at the counter. "I'm really very grateful for your help," Piree went on.

"It's nothing between friends. Old friends."

"Of course."

"One has the feeling now that friendship isn't quite what it used to be," Cesar said, "that among new friends there's so often an edge of mutual ambition, or rivalry, the sort of thing which is really anathema to friendship in the first place. That's why old pals have become so important."

"Yes, yes."

"I published your stuff for years, Piree. I wouldn't forget you."

"I'm glad you could help, Cesar," Piree said, looking away.

That gesture of his made me especially wary. Cesar was so stooped, he could never have seen it. And why look away from someone who cannot raise their eyes to see you when the motion would not be noticed? It could only have been a token of bad faith, of scheming. That's the sort of thing you learn as a judge, those little moments which expose us all. I don't mind admitting that I had moved my things right to the front of the queue by now, that I was barely pretending to do anything. I knew that no good could come of this.

Their turn came. Piree passed over his receipt to Elena, the girl who was serving there. Their eyes met. Then she looked away from him.

"The goods have come from Europe?"

"Correct."

"Contents?"

"That's a stupid question, señorita, I have filled in a customs form as you can see."

"Contents?"

"Books."

"Are they for re-sale in Argentina?"

"No."

"Are they for use in business or for pleasure?"

"No, neither."

"Sir," – Elena looked at him with fatigue – "are they for use in business or for pleasure?"

"For business," Piree answered after a short pause. "As you know yourself, señorita." He tapped his finger there for a moment. Cesar had a soft smile. Perhaps he'd always found his friend's impatience endearing, a treasure rather than an irritation.

"You know, Kent," he said, "you've never been good at dealing with people, that's always been your problem."

Elena left for the back of the stock room. Evidently she had no desire to requite Piree's impatience. They could both see her lifting packages without hurry, moving as if to provoke them.

"Your signature please, sir." Elena proffered a pen; she had returned from the back of the stock room pushing a trolley piled high with boxes of books.

"Why do you need my signature?"

"It's the regulation."

"You are observing the regulation?"

"Correct."

Piree turned to his friend: "Cesar, why don't you sign for it?" He began to exert pressure on other's forearm, bringing him to the counter. "Look. Just here."

"Oh no, Kent. I'm sure you'll find that yours is the signature that is required."

Piree flushed: "But this is absurd," he shouted at the clerk. "Just give me the books!" The muscle below Piree's left eye twitched. He took the pen from Elena. "Bring the books round," he ordered Elena. "We'll find a signature in a moment."

While she was gone, and the two men had gone to meet her and collect their delivery, I moved quickly. It was clear that this was going to be a case requiring an expert witness. I've sat through enough court cases in my time that I can spot the moment when crimes become inevitable. This Kent Piree was beset by such anxiety, every gesture of his was a denial, an attack. Why should he have been so reluctant to sign for the books? Why had he brought them to Buenos Aires in the first place? It was a mystery, and I expect you'll find the nub of the case right here in these questions. He seemed criminal to me, and I've known plenty of them. His obsession with books made him at the very least a likely pyromaniac.

I'd heard Cesar mention executing the transfer at once. It was clear that they would make for the taxi rank with the trolley of books. I picked up my bucket in a hurry and moved towards the doors out to the drop-off point, pretending that suddenly I'd spotted a blemish on the airport concourse. I wanted to be sure of getting there first, but I moved so fast that I knocked into another member of the team, Gabriel. He stood there, soaring above my head as he always did and trying to derive authority from that advantage when always he was beneath me.

"Watch out Ousmane!" he shouted. "You will dirty everything!"

"Ah yes, Gabriel," I replied, "you are always working, always hard at work."

The man makes me laugh. He is always inventing schemes and flaunting them as if he is a politician, making ludicrous claims for himself, for his life, for the gold bracelet that he wears on his arm and which is doubtless a fake. I share a flat with him and with my nephew Ismail out in the badlands, the poor suburbs of the south where I can no longer ignore the ugliness and injustice that I've ignored all my life. But our surroundings mean nothing to Gabriel. He doesn't care about the hunger or the violence that go with them. Once he has finished with his fancy tales, he is always reading. He says he is a Christian but he never touches the Bible. He wants nothing to do with Ismail and me when we talk of our anger at our situation, of our anger with the past. He says we must move beyond anger and hold to what is true, and beautiful. Yes, the old lapdog certainly makes me laugh.

"We must begin our work again," he said to me, picking up his mop.

I chuckled. "Look out Gabriel," I told him, "here comes your friend."

The clerk from behind the freight collection point – Elena – was wheeling the trolley of books towards us across the concourse. She was followed by Piree. She moonlighted in the bookstore at Ezeiza in the evenings to earn a little extra cash. People say that she comes from a rich Porteño family but has argued with them and lives in a small rented flat in Belgrano. I don't know about that. But Gabriel has struck up a friendship with her recently. They met in the bookstore and he says that the basis of their friendship is in books. I laughed at him outright when he told me that and he didn't like it. But I've come across many prisoners like him in the courtroom, people whose balls were faster than their brains if you please.

As Elena and Piree came towards us we both pretended to work. I noticed that Cesar had vanished. I hadn't seen him go and this seemed troubling, dangerous even. It could be that the disappearances had already begun, then and there, without any of us taking note of it. It's not impossible in a country like this, in a world whose whole history could be characterised as one of disappearance.

As they neared us with the trolley of books, Piree was gesticulating. That was when he tripped over my colleague Gabriel's bucket, almost fell, and splashed soapy water all over the floor. Yet it was not the accident which disturbed, but rather his reaction which was the most alarming. He looked briefly at Gabriel, and then the shouting began:

"You are all the same, all the same!" he yelled. "You try to make our lives a misery, to dominate us." He paused, looking at the pallets of books to check that they had not been disturbed. "You hate us, because you will never be like us!" Then he stopped, and looked at a piece of paper he was carrying in his hand: "Here," he ordered, "you can sign this!" It was the receipt from the freight collection point. And Gabriel was so afraid that he picked up the pen and did as he had been told.

Piree continued to walk on towards the taxi rank. Elena pushed the trolley of books behind him. As she passed Gabriel she leant over and whispered something to him. Perhaps it was an expression of affection, or desire. One can never be sure when one thing will not lead to another. And there was something in that moment of affection, poised above the violence of hatred, that took me back to my life in Jos, to Fenobi unsheathing her body of the elaborate bracelets in the courtroom, even as I stood there on the airport concourse cleaning white people's shit.

I have not even said how the Fenobi affair ended. It was actually one of the last cases that I heard in Jos before I came to Buenos Aires. One could not keep such a woman from success. Soon after her divorce she had reconstructed her trading networks. Her business was building up and she had no shortage of suitors. This time she had decided to look beyond her own people from Bokkos. She was courted by Luke, a Christian Igbo who was a powerful trader in Jos. They excited gossip, as some of the Igbos in Jos said that Luke was an Osu. Luke and Fenobi did not try to hide their affair, and it was probably this openness which inflamed the tongues of the market. Naturally her ex-husband was angered by all the talk. He was seen one afternoon at the bush taxi stand, shouting at her, warning her. But she just laughed at him. Two weeks later she was killed with a knife one evening. Everyone knew who the guilty party was, and I tried him two months later in the courtroom in Jos.

That's how I've learnt to look at humanity with detachment. I've been confronted with enough tragedies that I'm wary of stepping in at all. I can't be sure of the emotions that run between Elena and my flatmate, Gabriel, but I know you need to examine this Kent Piree character thoroughly. His peculiar behaviour yesterday was there for all to see. Why all the subterfuge, the deceit? Why manipulate my flatmate into signing for his books? Was he trying to blame Gabriel for something, some appalling crime? You need to be like the dog in the rubbish bin. I can't help feeling that just digging hard enough will unearth all manner of disgusting stenches, and perhaps even the root cause of all those strange things I saw yesterday at Ezeiza.

If I were a policeman, in fact, I'd already be putting this report aside. I'd be patrolling the streets of the centre, around the Plaza de Mayo, the Boca, the football stadiums there and along at River. For Piree is out there in the city right now. I watched him help Elena and the taxi driver unload the boxes of books into the boot of the car. I watched him drive off. I can't help wondering where he went, or what happened to Cesar. Both those old men were talking about a crime and declared that the books had to be secured at once. There's something dangerous afoot, a firestorm about to ignite, and someone needs to step in and prevent it from starting.

II

Did I tell you that my husband's a murderer, gentlemen? It's not something that he brags about, mind you, I've never heard him talking to the clients about it, rolling up his sleeves to show them the blood on his hands. He's not talked much about it with me, either, if I'm honest. I haven't touched him for the details about the sound a bullet makes on flesh, twisting in the innards and shredding the brain. There's been no need.

There was once, I'll admit it, shortly after we arrived in the country forty years ago. We lived then in a room in a rented tenement in Boca. The landlady, Mrs Livecchi, was a Sicilian from Catania. She was a cat-lover and her stinking house crawled with them: ginger tabbies, black-and-white roans, tomcats and cowards, bitches on heat. They hunted mice and fought on the broken paving slabs of the street in the middle of the night. They must have driven the neighbours wild, all those immigrant families from Sicily and the Mezzogiorno living six to a room with

236

their washing draped over their balconies like the family crest.

I think there was something about those cats which touched us, too, as we lay there night after night. The scratches and the shrieks of the cats, the stench of their putrid shit, the disembodied ghoulishness of their noise, all of it seeped in through the thin blind onto the mattress where we lay, that lumpy, rotting mound that had probably been rescued from some bankrupt estancía during the great depression so that the landlady Mrs Livecchi could pick it up for next to nothing at a flea market and torture her tenants with it for years afterwards as they sank into it while they tried to make love.

Somehow all those thoughts, smells, and feelings, everything of which I was aware but couldn't articulate to myself just then, it all spilled over. One night I asked Pepe what it was like to kill.

"I know you had no choice," I told him when he did not answer straightaway, "but what was it like? Did you enjoy it? What did you do when you got back to the city? Tell me, amor."

"We took them out in the truck," he said in the end. "Ten of them, once. Just three or four usually. Soon they were thinking of nothing."

After that, he held me harder. And that was it, gentlemen, that was all he was able to say to me. We lived with Mrs Livecchi for two years until my husband got a good job as a foreman at the docks and started to save money. That was when we moved out of the tenement.

It's strange that I've told you all that. These weren't crimes that were ever tried and at the time they weren't crimes at all. That was just how things were in Spain in those days. My husband did his bit and it's not surprising that he's quiet about it now and doesn't discuss it with the clients. He's a man who is older than he looks, already he's turned seventy, and they wouldn't believe him. And there's no point in being judged by people who can't understand life, who think that peace is possible or even desirable. There's no point. Silence and forgetting are much the best way. What good comes of remembering the past anyway? It only brings back loss and anger.

That's my usual policy. But last night I had to alter it when the visitors turned up. There was something about them that brought the past back. I knew that we were in for trouble as soon as the taxi pulled up outside the bar. The guy sitting in the back wasn't the usual sort of customer we have in here, not at all. He was smartly dressed, I'll give him that, and his bearing was that of a gentleman. But I could tell otherwise. I could see that he was having a violent disagreement with the taxi driver. They argued for several minutes until he got out and came in to the bar. He sat down and Dolores, the Spanish waitress we've got over here from Madrid, went up and asked him what he'd like to drink. He ordered a good bottle of Mendoza, something strong, and sat there for five or ten minutes draining glass after glass until he'd drunk most of it up. He made no effort to look over at the taxi driver waiting outside, far less invite him in for a drink.

"Sir," I said to him in the end, "will you be dancing tonight?"

He looked up: "Tell me, doña, do you have storage facilities here?"

"Storage facilities?" I swallowed. We don't like madmen in the bar. It never does business any good. Pepe's tried his hand at quite a few ventures since we moved out of Mrs Livecchi's all those years ago, but all too often madmen have got in the way and we've been left with almost nothing. That's how we've learned that we've got to look after ourselves first. "Sir," I replied at length, "we run a restaurant and a tango club here, not a storage facility."

"Surely you have a store room in a building of this size?"

"Not for public use, sir."

"Not at any price?"

He wouldn't give up, I'll say that for him. "Not at any price," I replied. I left him sitting with his empty wine bottle and moved along the bar towards Dolores. "Go and give him the bill," I told her. "Make it clear that we don't want his type in here."

She did as I'd said and I was already trying to forget this strange interlude when the taxi driver came running in. "Well," he shouted, "are they going to let you in or not?" His customer made no answer. The car monkey came straight up to the bar and slammed fifty pesos on the counter. "The man wants to know if you've got storage facilities," he shouted.

"And I've already told him that we don't."

"Well you're not a woman to help someone in need are you, then, doña?" the little car monkey said. "You're not someone to rely on in a time of crisis."

He slammed another fifty-peso note on the counter and this time, I'll admit, my eyes grew a little wider. I don't mean to insinuate anything, gentlemen, but I'd be surprised if in the course of your duties you haven't come across similar situations yourselves. None of us wants to be prompted by greed and yet there it is, we're animals with bellies to fill and we're happiest when we can fill them without stress.

I still played tough, though: "This isn't a time of crisis," I told the car monkey, "and we don't need your money."

"Of course it's a time of crisis! Just as it was when your lot started arriving here. And what did we do then? We let you in! We stood by you. A fat lot of good it's done us! What have you done for Argentina? You sit there with your revolutionary rolls of fat." People are always assuming that we were revolutionaries. It works to our favour, and I've given up trying to put them right. As so often, with this man silence was the best policy. I was proved right when he put another fifty-peso note on the counter. "I don't want you to think that I'm trying to buy you, doña. But I need your help, and I demand satisfaction."

There was a lot of money waiting for me just there. The car monkey had insulted me, but he had called this a time of crisis. People are shits when the need arises. You only have to look at history to see the proof of that. I wasn't offended, not really. Perhaps I wanted to see just how far he'd go.

"Well then," I said in the end, "what do you want?"

"Our customer," he said, gesturing at the man beside the empty wine bottle, "has just arrived in the country. He has won as much money as he has lost grace. I want him off my hands. He's got all these crates in the boot of my taxi, crates of books so he says. He's been talking about them ever since we left Ezeiza. Just take the whole lot off my hands, him too, and let me go."

On an ordinary day I would have sent the pair of them packing. But books are on my mind at the moment. I've always been something of a reader. Words may be dry but they can bear an emotional, primal charge. They can be exciting. And now, for several days we've had this group of Mexican poets staying in the rooms we let out above the tango dance floor. They say they've come to Buenos Aires for a literary workshop, a *tertulía* if you will, but I don't believe a word of it. You may as well arrest them, gentlemen; you'll find an excuse to justify yourselves soon enough if you do.

These poets, as they call themselves, they've been on my mind, so grating, that when the taxi driver mentioned the books I softened. Perhaps I hoped that if another madman joined in with the Mexicans he might shatter their egos just a little. I didn't want them to stop drinking – I've never been much of an altruist – but I wanted them to realise that they weren't the only fools in the world who could go insane just at the thought of a line of poetry.

"Well then," I said to the taxi driver, "if your client really wants to store his books with us, he'll have to rent a room."

"Of course," he said. "Hey!" he whistled, "she's changed her mind. Come on!"

The elegant old bookman stood up and followed the taxi driver out into the street. Within ten minutes they'd carried the boxes of books up the rickety back staircase and I'd shown the guy his room.

"You'll need to sign in with us," I told him as we went back down the stairs.

"That's impossible, madam."

"We can't rent a room without seeing a form of identification. Those are the regulations."

Back at the bar, he rummaged in his money-belt and located his passport. The taxi driver was showing his impatience all the time.

"Come on, professor! Time's up! The meter's running!"

"Yes, yes."

"It's five hundred pesos, that's what you owe me."

The bookman opened his wallet and handed a clutch of notes to the man. I supposed that's when I realised that something criminal was in the air, because at that price the taxi driver was a burglar, as anyone would agree, just a lawyer by another name. Oh, I know that there's money enough around Palermo Viejo, even these days, after the devaluation. There are some who can go out to the pizzerías, take taxis, come here and knock back the wine even at the prices that we charge. And who knows, no doubt things will get better soon. But I could tell that the taxi driver was a crook all the same. I would have stopped him, but I needed to make sure that the new guest filled out all his particulars correctly. From his passport I knew he was called Kent Piree, but when I looked at the visitors' ledger I saw that he had used a false name, something which sounded even more foreign.

Years ago, as a child, I was fascinated by inspectors. The world seemed full of injustice. I'd read detective novels and secretly longed to happen upon a crime like I found inside them. And that was why I did not confront Piree at once. I could tell that I was on the threshold of some great mystery, as if I had chanced upon a mnemonic for life itself. The veneer of respectability beneath which lurked craven, violent criminality had to be exposed. I did not want to frighten Piree off. If I followed his trail hard enough, I might chance upon the deepest, ugliest crime of all.

After he paid the taxi driver and I checked the visitors' ledger I gave him the key to his room. Then he left. It was a quiet evening. For an hour after he had gone upstairs we only had a few customers at the bar. Dolores saw to the washing-up and took a message from me to Pepe, who was helping with the sound check in the dancing room. By and by the place became busier. The Mexican poets arrived and ordered a bottle of *cachaça*. They'd bought some limes at a *feria* and began to mix up the *caipirinhas* brazenly in the bar. I sent Dolores over to their ringleader, a fellow called

Bontera, who to make things worse claimed that he was actually a Chilean living in Mexico, though God alone knows what the truth really was.

"Hey," Dolores said to him, "you can only consume drinks which you have purchased on the premises."

"We have purchased the drink on the premises," Bontera said.

"What about the limes? And the sugar?"

"Sugar is a mineral and limes are a fruit. And the *cachaça* we bought here."

I was tired of these smartarses who called themselves revolutionaries from the safety of a drunken haze so thick that they would never actually do anything.

"Hey, *boludos*," I yelled to them, "the army know how to deal with your lot."

But they just laughed at that and downed their *caipirinhas*. The worst of it all was that I could see Dolores smiling at that moment, thinking in spite of all the moral disapproval she imbibed as a child that Bontera was stylish, hell, that he was sexy. I could see that that was the moment she considered sleeping with the Chilean pimp. Probably it was the only time in her life that she'd had a thought like that, and she seemed to flush it out as quickly as it had appeared. But Bontera had sensed her feelings too. He was canny, the Chilean, I'll give him that. You know the saying, gentlemen – "He sleeps like a Chilean": I don't think anyone takes it as a compliment. Bontera put his arm around her and asked if she'd come to dance tango with them all when her shift had finished. *Her shift finishes when this place closes and you all go to bed*, I called over, and that put a stop to it.

I didn't think much about the fraudster Piree for quite some time after that. The slow roll of the evening's beginning quickly unravelled. People kept on pitching up at the bar, their stomachs filled with meat and alcohol. They walked down the steps into the *tanguería*. The dancing got going quickly and never let up for hours, except when the tango band paused to refresh themselves. The room was dark, which was how the dancers liked it, intimate, musky with cigar smoke and perfume, those concealers of more carnal scents. Most of the dancers were stylish, well-practised. They drank with moderation, with the exception of the Mexicans. Two of them – Bontera and one of his sidekicks – made fumbling attempts at taking part. But they were too drunk to be graceful and too proud to extend their failure. They ordered at least three more bottles of *cachaça* and Bontera flirted wildly with Dolores each time that she went over but she just stood there with a gentle smile on her face as if pleased or in some twisted way released. She is a curious girl, that one: she even keeps the books she has in her room in a strict alphabetical order.

"They are insulting you," I said to her when she came back with one of their empty bottles.

"No, it is nothing, doña Sebastiana."

"We will put a stop to this," I said. "We cannot have these Chileans and Mexicans insulting us here, in Buenos Aires."

I walked down to the dance floor and pushed my way through to Pepe. I explained the situation, and in some detail, because I was alarmed that it might deteriorate. Call me suggestible if you like, but there was something in the air just then that smelt of decay. I'd already been confronted by two crimes that evening – by the taxi driver and Piree – and these poets and their visceral drunkenness did not bode well. It felt as if we were on the precipice of some terrible change, something colourless and formless and perhaps not even tangible as yet but oppressing us in all its inchoate mystery. Perhaps, it may be true, I overstated the situation when I described it to Pepe. But that may have been as well. He went over to the poets and asked them to go back to the bar in the foyer. *You're not dancing*, I heard him shout above it all, *you're just getting in the way*. He got them to move in the end and we all went back to where Piree had arrived just a few hours before.

The professor was there when we all came through from the dance floor. He wanted to pay for his room, but I refused.

"Don't worry," I told him, "I'll just put it on the tab."

He was quite drunk from all the red wine. His eyes were wide and clouded. "It's dancing in there, is it?"

Bontera overheard and called over. "*Viejo*, I'll show you what's what if that's your desire."

"Who's that?" Piree asked me.

"A poet." I shrugged. "A Mexican-Chilean called Bontera."

"What's he doing?"

"There's a whole group of them over here for some literary workshop, a festival if you will."

Piree rose and went over to them. They began to engage in discussion. I couldn't hear what they were saying, but the conversation was animated. Arms flailed. Bontera ordered another bottle of *cachaça*, probably just so that he could leer at Dolores again. At one point I heard Piree shouting, "I insist upon it," over and again. But I couldn't spend my time watching them. Customers were flowing by like wind gusting in an open-topped car, a ceaseless flow of the breath of the world. They ordered pisco, whisky and gin. The dancing was winding down. People had split off into the couples in which they would disappear to bed to requite all that unspoken feeling, all those urges which had swilled in that room along with the scent of drink and smoke and the sheer animalism of being. The foyer was becoming crowded and I could hardly make out the poets any more.

That was when Pepe came and took my hand. He often does so late at night. We danced. He pressed into me with his humanity. Perhaps that's why I don't ask him much about killing, as there's only so much humanity that we can take or that's good for anyone. I knew he had been on the right side but that didn't really make him different to those who lost in the end. Violence has always been part of the territory. Let's not pretend that it's the province of Left or Right, Fascists or Communists, Peronists or Neo-Liberals. I don't have to explain myself. You understand, gentlemen. And doubtless you've seen how easy it is to submit to a gentle force, like that, like Pepe guiding me about a darkened, emptying room as "el mono" Javier plays the bandoneon. We're none of us saints, and a gentle sinner may be the best you can find in this world of ours.

Usually that dance is the end of the evening for Pepe and I. It's been like that ever since we were at Mrs. Livecchi's, even in the last place we ran, a restaurant just around the corner which we part-owned with an African crook who never told us where his money came from. But last night as we went through the foyer we were stopped by Bontera and Piree.

"Don Pepe!" the Chilean-Mexican kept shouting, until he had our attention. "This man wants to buy a book of mine and I want you to draw up the contract."

"It's no business of mine," Pepe said.

"What's the book anyway?" I asked.

"We can't tell you, madam," Piree answered.

"Why not?" my husband demanded. "And why do you need a contract anyway?"

"Because everything has to be done correctly, Doña Sebastiana," Bontera said. "I don't want to be accused by Professor Piree of robbery." He snapped his fingers and whistled to Dolores. "Hey, *bonita*. Go up to my room and fetch the book that is on the bed. Here's the key."

"What's the hurry, anyway?" I asked when the Madrileña had gone. "Why are you so desperate to have this book?"

"The book has to be protected," Piree said. "We all have to be protected."

"You're buying up books to protect people?"

"That's right."

"How much are you paying?"

"The book's worth a thousand pesos," Bontera told us. "I picked it up in a bookstore in Madrid a while back. I was planning to sell it anyway, to help cover the costs of our stay."

"I am really very lucky to have met this young man," Piree told us then, with gentle authority.

As I've already mentioned, gentlemen, we don't encourage madmen in our club. It does business no good. But we were putting up with Piree. He was smart and had plenty of money. He seemed to have a calm demeanour. He'd drunk several bottles of wine and Dolores had just told me that he was paying the tab for the Mexicans as well. He owed us at least 3000 pesos already. And there's nothing to be gained from treading on the toes of a madman who owes you 3000 pesos. So Pepe and I just smiled at the two criminal literati and waited for Dolores to return with the book. The men agreed on the exchange and Piree handed over his money. Then he bade us all good night and went up to his room with the book. Bontera was about to rejoin his circle when I touched his sleeve:

"I think you'd better pay the bill for your rooms," I told him.

"Ah, Doña Sebastiana," he lamented, "can we not enjoy ourselves just this night? You're supposed to be a socialist, aren't you?"

"Who told you that?"

"Everyone knows that that's why you and Pepe found your way to Argentina, to escape from Franco. You're idealists, like us!"

Pepe had been listening by the bar. He hated it when people made assumptions about why we had left Spain, about our hatred of fascism, for God's sake. He mocked Bontera: "Ah, you know all about us, don't you *boludo*! You know how wonderful we are, that we will give you free board so that you can write childish poems about the collective ownership of *our* business. That's your idea of socialism, a free ride!"

"What is it, Don Pepe?" Bontera asked him. "Have I offended you?"

Pepe laughed. "I try not to get too angry," he said, "not to lose my cool."

I felt for my husband then. He never wanted to leave, gentleman, not really, but once he had gone too far and the municipal officials from our godforsaken corner of Galicia had advised us that a quiet exit would be the best solution. He's always reading about Spain in *ABC*. I think it was the contrast between our forced exile and Bontera's wilful road-trips that enraged him then.

"It's a thousand pesos," I told Bontera, stepping into the awkward silence. "That's what you owe."

He handed over the money. "What happened to your idealism, *doña?*"

"I learnt that idealists are just like everyone else. They're just as crazy, paranoid, and in need of food in their bellies as the next man. That's when we started in the restaurant business."

"It's an education here, *doña,*" Bontera told me, "but it's not the sort of education that I wanted."

"What did you want to learn?"

"We came to Buenos Aires to learn about culture, but we've drawn a blank. All we've seen is that some of the rich Porteños can still afford to manicure their pets and hire dog-walkers, they can still go and watch polo at the Hurlingham Club when it suits them. But for everyone else, it's misery."

"That's true at the moment, but with the new President, things may get better. That's what they say."

"I don't believe it."

"You've learnt something then."

"I suppose so."

"Well I want you to help me in turn. Tell me what that Piree is up to."

Bontera threw back his head and laughed. "You'll have to give me a bottle of *cachaça* on the house," he said. I motioned to Dolores, and she did the necessary. "Piree." he smiled. "Who knows? He says he's imported a stash of dangerous books, that he's desperately looking for somewhere to examine them. He thinks that some terrible crime's in the offing, but he can't say where it's going to be committed. He's looking for a clue, anything at all that will help him to solve the mystery. He says he knows someone who will help him to decode them, someone who lives out in the Tigre delta. At least, that's what he's told me." Dolores

249

brought over the bottle of *cachaça* and handed it over to him. "So when he saw that I had a copy of the books that he was carrying with him, he told me that he had to have it at all costs."

"That book," I said to him: "you stole it, didn't you?" He just laughed at me then. "I knew you were a thief," I told him, "I always knew it."

"Anyway," he said then, "I'm going to forget about all this for the time being, *doña*. I'm much more interested in going to bed with your waitress."

"You can forget it," I told him.

But Bontera was excited by a challenge. He shrugged at me: "Life's a mystery, *doña*, and you can never tell when one extreme state of mind won't transform into another."

He wasn't put off in the slightest. He continued to play the gallant about Dolores, sharing his drinks with her now that it was so late that business had died for the night and even the other poets had gone to bed, sharing also that firelight in his eyes, shooting stars of lust oscillating there in the sombreness of an establishment like ours when all the clients have left, when there's only one light left. He didn't know, couldn't know, the level of repression he had to deal with, though. Dolores had first shown up in the bar as if she was being hunted. In fact, when she arrived she even told us that she was being pursued. There were some real crazies out there, she told us, people who wanted the world to burn in flames, and they had to be stopped. She reminded me of some of the people we'd sailed over to Argentina with when we'd arrived in the early 60s, people who'd been pursued for so long that they couldn't believe that this escape might be real and that they might at last be able to live in peace. If you brushed against her behind the bar you could feel her body shake. She was like a Chilean, always ready to shake at the thought of an earthquake.

It was late by then. It must have been five in the morning. Bontera and Dolores were the last people in the bar. Pepe sat and had a coffee. I was intrigued by Bontera's chances of success, I'll admit it, and I kept on sneaking a glance over my husband's shoulder. Pepe's passion had dissipated after his confrontation with Bontera and the urgency had gone out of our conversation. We were relaxed. Perhaps I'd even forgotten for a moment the crimes of earlier on, of Piree's forged identity and the taxi driver's robbery.

Bontera and Dolores rose and came towards us. "*Doña*," he addressed me, ignoring Pepe, "we must wake Piree at once." The mad bookman had slipped my mind. We both stared at him. "Those books are dangerous, as I've been explaining to Dolores."

"Dangerous?"

"You don't think it's just any book that's worth a thousand pesos do you, *doña*? Piree paid a premium because he knows something we don't. You shouldn't allow him to stay here a moment longer without coming clean."

"What's he going to do?" Pepe asked. "Burn the house down?"

"He might do just that. Perhaps he's the real criminal in all this. All his talk of detection is just a distraction, an alibi."

"Bontera, the *cachaça*'s talking," I said. "You're drunk. Go to bed."

"That's fine," he said. "It's your hotel, your business to lose. But I think you should call a taxi and send him somewhere safe. Out to Tigre, where he says he's going anyway. If the worst comes to the worst we can throw the books into the delta there and no one will ever find them.

Then it can be as if they've never existed, if we train our memories towards silence and all the records are lost. Perhaps if people just stop talking about this atrocity, stop fearing it, stop imagining it, it will never happen."

Dolores laughed then, bitter, but also triumphant: "Or perhaps it's already happened," she suggested. "There might already have been an explosion somewhere."

"Where?" Bontera demanded.

"Who knows?" she returned. "My home city. Or yours, wherever that might be. Or maybe the sun exploded eight minutes ago and we don't know."

I looked at her. I don't think I'd realised until then what she was really like. "I'm not paying for a taxi," I told Bontera in the end.

"Do what you like," he said. "I give up here. I'm off to bed."

He left us, but my husband became agitated at his last words. Perhaps it was the effect of the lateness of the hour.

"The poet's right," he told me. "We must get Piree's bill together." He got up and went behind the bar to do the sums. "He owes us six thousand pesos, plus five hundred for the taxi to Tigre. Dolores, go and wake him."

"I'll do that," she said, "by God, I'll do that at last."

The Madrileña went upstairs. There was a commotion, some shouting. We weren't worried about waking the poets. The way our charges are rising, gentlemen, they can't demand a good night's sleep into the bargain. Privileges are bought with money these days and they haven't got enough money to have the right to anything.

While Dolores was waking Piree, we rang Pedro Lascar's taxi service, a few blocks away. My husband asked for a 150-peso commission but told Lascar that he could keep the rest. Lascar arrived double-quick. His old Chevrolet was waiting out in the street when Piree came down with Dolores, and I could see him smoothing his moustache as he looked with tired eyes in from his decrepit car out in the street.

"What's this?" Piree demanded.

"The poet says you must go," Pepe shrugged. "We don't know what material you've brought with you. You must show it to us, or leave."

"I can't show it to you."

My husband handed him the bill. With a gesture of fury Piree took out his wallet and gave over everything he had.

"That's not enough," Pepe said. "You're almost a thousand pesos short."

"It's all I've got."

"Don't forget," my husband said, moving very close to him, "that if the police come to investigate, we'll be implicated."

Piree looked pale; I could not tell whether through fear or anger. "I am helping you, and you are robbing me blind."

"That's the price, sir, and if you won't pay I'll have to call the police."

I had begun to feel sorry for the book slave, gentlemen, perhaps I should admit it. I'm not quite sure when our prices started to rise like this. Piree seemed so rich when he arrived in the evening, but we'd cleaned him out. Of course we've all had to live with inflation since the devaluation. We're all subject to forces we don't understand, whether in our workplaces or in our beds. But the man was standing there as if a hologram of himself, so pitiable, struggling desperately to believe in what he still held dear.

"Come," I told my husband, "he's paid more than the Mexicans."

"He has not paid his bill."

Dolores intervened, pushing the trolley with the boxes of books out towards the street where Pedro Lascar's taxi was waiting.

"Anything else he owes can be taken from my wages," she told us.

Piree followed her. He did not even ask for the return of his passport. He staggered out into the darkness where only the rats and the drunks wove their paths by that time of night. He stared emptily at the shopfronts across the way, all of them sealed by their grey metal shutters. He moved out to the silent road and toyed with a crack in the tarmac with his shoe. Lascar and Dolores loaded up the books in their carefully labelled boxes. When they had finished Dolores took Piree's hand and squeezed it. It was almost as if she desired him, even though that was surely impossible. They climbed into the taxi and drove off towards Tigre. As they turned out of our street towards Libertador Pepe ran after them, whistling and shouting.

"Hey, Madrileña, Madrileña!" They'd gone though. He turned to me. "She's got no wages owing, she can't pay the rest of the bill. Thieves!"

He left me there in the furious silence. And that was when I determined that I'd have to come to discharge my conscience today. One can see that I was mistaken when I thought that Piree had been robbed on his way from Ezeiza. He's the real criminal, a man who uses a false identity – takes some African's name, just to pass the blame on to them - and leaves without paying his bill. But quite apart from that, it became obvious last night that he's at the heart of a far greater crime, a mystery without end and as yet perhaps even without criminal and victim. I couldn't help feeling that he was some kind of ghost stalking through our lives, a figment of our imaginations come to remind us of some appalling act of violence in the past and of another one, perhaps imminent. I'm hoping that you might be able to find some answers and put my anxiety to rest. At the moment I can't help worrying that something awful's going to happen, that everything Pepe and I have so carefully built up in the years since we arrived - our businesses, our new outlook on life – all of it, it's about to go up in smoke.

III

Witness Statement of Carlos Delgado, Tigre

My childhood was interred on an *estancia* twenty miles from Azul. There in the province the emptiness was suffocating. Our minds rose blue in endless sky into distance. There were still lots of kids on the farm in those days. We all played with each other. Sometimes the *estanciero*'s son would invite us to the big house. We'd go into his playroom. We'd take turns being his horse as he rode us round, whipping us past his toys.

I used to be called "dormilón" on the *estancia* – sleepalot. I'm like a dormouse, I think sometimes, always happiest if I can curl up in a warm corner. I've always felt that nothing bad is likely to happen to you in sleep. Even a murderer might be stilled by the sight of those closed eyes. When I read of victims, atrocities, I often catch myself thinking, "If only they'd been asleep, if only life really was sleep, a dream." Then we wouldn't be ashamed by our fragility.

Today I woke early from my camp-bed in the converted store and boiled water for maté on the stove. I prepared the bitter herb in its gourd, turned off the radio and went out into the forecourt. There were some cars there, parked by owners of villas in the delta who were staying out in the water for a few days. The night was greying, like death. Gulls skated around our small harbour crying in hunger. They reminded me of some of the voices I heard last night as I fell asleep listening to a debate on Radio Continental about the co-operatives in the *barrios*. Some people were complaining that they hadn't stopped the indigent sifting through the rubbish at night or assaulting their neighbours if they drew a blank. They complained, but they had no answers. There are no answers to this terrible poverty which has come down upon us like a shadow from the sky, since the devaluation.

In these circumstances it's inevitable that we're all scavengers at the moment. Few of us grow our own vegetables or hunt our own meat. We're like the gulls, dependent on the skills of others. As a child I always grew food on our plot of land, behind the windbreak of ombú trees that separated our family from the *estancía* house and my humiliations in the rich kid's nursery. But I can't grow anything now. I haven't got the time out in the delta and my son's too estranged from me to care to help with growing food. And then here among the motorboats the main forms of life appear to be weeds in the concrete and tarmac. The only time I'm ever brought to think of the grasslands is when the Pampero wind comes up from the south. It smells of all that hot emptiness and silence. Usually I turn my back on the wind when it comes. Probably, I'm afraid of the past. I burn easily.

I dwelt for a moment out on the forecourt this morning. Perhaps I was waiting to see if the Pampero might blow. More likely, I was still a little tired. I wasn't expecting any clients yet, since the sort of people who store boats here are still doing well, and will benefit when things get better, and they are not the sort of people to head out along the motorway from the city before ten. I began to make towards the warehouse, preparing to activate the switch which opens the shutters and then to go in to the little office where I marshal the administration of the motorboats. But I was disturbed when the car headlights swung in off the road and a taxi drew up.

Two people got out – a woman and a man. It was the woman who seemed to be in charge, although one couldn't tell at first what the nature of their relationship really was. She had dark skin and long black hair tied up below her neck at the back; a muscle twitched in her cheek below her eye. He had a similarly agitated presence, an air of incipient crisis, although he was well-dressed like most of the people I work with. They stood there alone in the near darkness of the last of night. The engine was still running on the taxi, the meter ticking.

I chuckled. I put the straw of my maté to my mouth, drained the gourd, and then refilled it from my thermos. "Señorita?" I offered the maté to the woman, but she made no gesture of acknowledgement.

"We need somewhere quiet to rest," she said, "we've had a nasty experience on the train."

"On the train?" I looked at them both. The train from Buenos Aires to Tigre is a harmless commuter affair and I was sure it did not run at this time in the morning.

""Is there a quiet room?" she repeated. "Somewhere to rest for a few hours."

"There's my place." I pointed towards the low store where I had just spent the night. I felt that there was something suggestive in the offer as I made it. I didn't regret it. Her Spanish accent, so harsh to our ears, sounded exotic. It accentuated the Moorish features of her face. It incorporated her whole being as a sort of offering of escape from this quiet and repetitive life that I live in Tigre, that I've always lived.

"We'll go there," she said. "He's offered us a place, professor," she told the man, "let's unpack."

They had a brief exchange with the taxi driver, who turned off the ignition and opened the boot. They had heavy boxes, so I went to get one of the trolleys which I use to carry the clients' suitcases over to their motorboats. We stacked the boxes on the trolley. They were all sealed with brown parcel tape and marked "DO NOT OPEN".

"You pay the taxi driver," I told them. "I'll meet you over there."

I wandered over, pushing the trolley. I hadn't recognised the couple, but this was nothing unusual. The type of people who own houses out in the delta often have friends coming to visit from overseas. These international businessmen are dropped off here at the motorboat depot. Usually their friends are waiting for them, or else they've tipped me a few pesos to take them out once I've locked up for the day. I'm so used to this way of doing things that I don't think twice about it.

When I reached the converted store I turned, expecting to see them just behind me. But they were still over by the taxi. There seemed to be some sort of argument. It didn't surprise me. This often happened when people arrived by taxi. Eventually the car sped off and they came over. The man's face was as pale as early morning, as cold, as clammy, as desperate for life.

"You can come in here," I said to him.

He rested his hand on the topmost box for a moment and then withdrew it quickly. "You did not misplace any of them?" he asked.

"Misplace them?" I was not sure I had heard him right. "Between the taxi and here?"

"You did not misplace them?"

"No."

"That's excellent." He rubbed his hands together. "Take them inside."

I opened the door to the store and wheeled in the trolley. I stacked the boxes on the floor, but there wasn't much room after that. The man sat in the hard-backed wooden chair which was pulled out a little way from the small, square table next to the stove. The woman sat on the mattress from which I had risen only half an hour before; there was, after all, nowhere else to sit.

"This is excellent," she said to him. "We can wait for my flatmate and then go out with her to the house in the delta."

From what the woman had said it was obvious that they knew someone out in the delta, that this was where they were going. It turned out that the woman – Dolores, her name was, Dolores de la Madrid – lived with Elena, the daughter of the Barajos. She was helping the man to take some books out to the delta.

"You're his assistant?"

She shook her head. "No, my flatmate Barajo is. They met at the airport. She's invited me along so that I can see the delta."

"And you came out here on the train?" It seemed very unlikely.

"We've been robbed, if you want to know. This man here, Kent Piree, is a North American, a renowned scholar of Chinese culture. He was staying in the bar/hotel where

I work in Palermo Viejo. But the owners scammed him, packed him off in some taxi which dumped us at the station instead of taking us all the way here to Tigre as we'd agreed."

"I'm sorry," I said.

"They're bastards," she said. "They even said they'd call the police. That we hadn't paid the full amount."

"I'm sorry," I repeated – it's a word I've learnt to say often. I refilled the maté and offered it to Piree.

"No thank you."

"People!" I shrugged.

"The most important thing is that we've safeguarded the books," the North American told me.

"Yes."

"That's the most important thing."

"Of course."

"My wife wanted them, you know. That scheming bitch wants everything. She even followed us onto the train. She must have been conniving with the hotel people, the taxi driver. The whole damn lot of them." His eyes narrowed. "I saw her on the train, you know. She was coming towards me, down the corridor. Straight for me. 'I'll have those books, Piree,' she told me. I screamed: 'Thérèse!' Then she vanished."

I looked at his friend.

"We just need somewhere to rest for a few hours," she said, as if in exculpation, "until Elena gets here."

"You're at home," I told her. "Make yourselves some tea, or catch up on your sleep if you like. You can't have had much."

"I'm tired," Madrid admitted. "Tonight, it's like I've suddenly aged."

I had some paperwork to get on with in the office, but I told them I'd call back in a couple of hours to check that everything was OK. I closed the door and walked across the forecourt to the motorboat store. By now it was fully day. From the isolated, staggered growls of engines echoing from the centre of Tigre, it was obvious that people had risen. Buenos Aires had begun to recover its life. The grumble grew slowly into the soundless sky. Sometimes, if I stand in the forecourt for long enough and listen carefully, I feel that I can distinguish one sound from another: the *pibes*' motorbikes from the monotonous roar of the cars on the motorway that links Tigre and the city centre. When I pick out those sounds I feel content. The noise announces that everything is normal. I can't imagine the horror I'd feel if I woke in this city to genuine silence.

At length I reached the warehouse and went into my office, past the boats which were stacked five-high up to the corrugated iron roof. I switched on the radio and turned to the paperwork. It was the usual round of letters chasing payments and supplies. Here in Tigre I work with the plutocrats of this country although you'd never know it. Half of them own their house in the delta, their flat in Buenos Aires, as well as a place in Punta del Este or an estancia somewhere in Buenos Aires Province or Santa Fé. Money is still as plentiful for them as air, and perhaps with the change of government they'll know how to reinvest it to make it grow even more. And yet usually it's these same people who are so reluctant to pay the bills which are inevitable to such a lifestyle. I've learnt not to be surprised, naturally. Surprise often seems to me to be simply the admitting of a lack of imagination. But I have noticed that this tendency of my clients has only increased with the years. Perhaps money can buy you out of those irksome moral strictures, buy you out of humanity altogether.

The paperwork is tedious but I'm used to it. This morning I sat quite happily, sucking on my maté straw, listening to the latest discussions on the radio, and composing letters and emails to debtors. It was a pleasant start to the day and by nine-thirty I'd done almost half a day's work. I switched the computer to standby, turned the radio off and sat back in my chair. I had a paperback on the go, so I picked it up for a moment and read about seven madmen torturing their enemies, planning a revolution in society which would restore decency. Of course I'd read the book before. It's a classic, a book which never loses its relevance, since madmen always seem to be on the verge of assuming the reins of political authority.

After ten minutes of reading, the phone rang. It was Elena Barajo.

"Carlos," she said, "some friends of mine might come by today. They're going out to the delta."

"They're here already, Elenita."

She sounded put out. "Do you mind looking after them for a little? I'll be by with Gabriel in a couple of hours and we'll go out to the house in the delta."

"Of course."

"Thanks Carlos." She paused, her voice switching register. "Be especially good to them, if you wouldn't mind, Carlos. He's an important scholar of Chinese culture. He used to be a professor in a big university, Chicago I think. We're going out to meet Peter Halbtsen, and I'm acting as his assistant in all this."

I had worked out the Halbtsen connection already. As soon as Barajo's friend Madrid had told me of Piree's profession it had been obvious that he was heading for a meeting with the eccentric Halbtsen, who lives in the most ramshackle house in the delta. Halbtsen is also, from what I've gathered, a renowned specialist in Chinese culture, or a sinologist as he tells me to call him. He lives not far from my own house in the delta and I know him quite well. He's spent years studying a work of philosophy and literature by an obscure Chinese writer.

I reassured Barajo that I'd treat her friends well. I'm a soft touch for the patróns, I suppose, and especially for their children. I never used to complain about the bullying of the *estanciero*'s son. Some things just have to be accepted if chaos is to be restrained. And it's not as if he didn't grow out of his youthful thrill at inherited wealth and power. Eventually he left his years of riding us bareback around his playroom behind him. He became something of a hippie, which can be the way for those who've got enough money to afford altruism. Last I heard he was living in Recoleta and teaching yoga.

I'd always felt that Elenita Barajo was of the same ilk. Her family has made a fortune in insurance. There's something nervy and aggressive about them. They're the sort of people who spend their whole lives in fear and reaction. Elenita has always been different, though. About a year ago, I gently chastised her for following the will of her parents too closely. She's changed a lot since, too. She's thrown in her studies and got a job at the airport, started dating some African who's ended up cleaning floors there. She's even writing a book, so she's told me.

I carried on reading my book about the seven madmen for a while. Then at ten-thirty I toasted some bread under the grill on the small stove I keep in the office. I spread a thin layer of *dulce de leche* on a couple of slices and put them on my tin tray, the one decorated with a kitsch drawing of a guanaco in the pampa. I prepared two mugs of milky coffee and then took the whole lot over to the converted store where I'd left Barajo's friends. I knocked, and opened. The Spanish girl, Madrid, had fallen asleep on the mattress. The sinologist, Piree, was sitting in my chair. He hadn't even bothered to cover her with a blanket, and she was moving restlessly as she lay there, trying unconsciously to fend off the cold. I couldn't imagine why she was with him. He seemed such an unsympathetic character, just then, a man obsessed. Instead of looking after her he'd opened one of the heavy boxes and was holding one of his books in front of him. He put it back when he saw me.

"I've brought you something to eat," I told him. But before he took it he shook his hands, violently. "What's the matter?"

"They're hot. Too hot." He looked at the book he'd just set down and I saw that it was the *Labyrinths* of the old master, Borges. "Perhaps the crime is more serious than I thought. A general burning. Yes, perhaps it's that."

I held the plate out. "You're going out to see Professor Halbtsen, then," I stated.

"That's right."

"He's one of my neighbours."

"You have a house in the delta?"

"It comes with the job."

"Do you know Halbtsen well?"

"As well as anyone, I should say. There aren't many people who live permanently out there like we both do. I admire his single-mindedness."

"He's been working for years, deciphering an esoteric work of literature and philosophy," Piree said.

"He's told me something about its mysteries."

"It's a genuine work of art, of that there's no doubt. A book about time that never mentions time. A metaphor for the unmentionable."

"Do you agree with Halbtsen about its importance?"

He scoffed at the question. Then he began to eat the snack I'd prepared. Working out here in the delta, I've met my fair share of scholars and writers. But I've never met anyone quite like him. Even the old master Borges didn't make a celebration of his obsessiveness. These professional repressives may not have much money themselves, but they often have friends who do. Usually, in fact, they're supported by them. Borges used to come out with his rich friends quite regularly when he was director of the National Library. But even though they'd talk about all kinds of abstruse things they would always treat me with courtesy. His friend Bioy Casares, who only died a few years ago, used to try and involve me in their discussions. They pointed out new things I could read, and I tried to keep up. They were odd, there's no denying it, but there was a reach of humanity that sought to extend itself beyond their genteel obscurantism.

There was none of this in Piree, however. I felt anxious as I watched him eating blindly without thought or care for his companion. He was utterly single-minded. If Elenita Barajo hadn't said otherwise, he would have seemed more like a fugitive than a scholar to me.

I stood by the door for a while as he ate. I passed him the milky coffee, serving. Still we were in that hiatus of silence. Madrid stirred from time to time on the mattress, murmured in her sleep. He did not look at her once.

"Are you two old friends?" I asked eventually.

He shook his head. "We met by chance."

"Why didn't Barajo come with you if she's your assistant?"

"She was working at freight collection when we met at the airport." He shrugged. "We had to pretend."

"Pretend?"

"Yes. Everything is a pretence, isn't it?" He was silent. "You must have met Borges, working out here."

"I met him many times. I even saw him a few times after he went blind. Once he showed me a medal he'd been awarded by the military government in Chile."

"These were all rumours we heard, among the fraternity of sinologists."

"Rumours?"

"The whole damn labyrinth! The whole show!" I couldn't comprehend him. I thought of Borges again, of all that obsession with form and order – the idea that if you could just clean up everything once…Piree snorted. He was angry, just then, very angry. You could see it in his flushed cheeks, in the frown line which had suddenly appeared between his eyebrows. "Doubtless that's the same idea that's kept Halbtsen all these years living in isolation out here."

"What idea?"

"That if you try hard enough you might be able to spend your whole life without having to confront reality, and the violence of its mysteries."

I said nothing. I made an excuse, soon. I had probed as far as I could. The engines of the clients' cars were beginning to hum into the forecourt. I was expected to fetch their boats for them and take them out to the harbour. Several of them were waiting when I emerged from the store. "I'm sorry," I called over to them, "there was a power cut." They muttered, impatient, but soon I was at work, and their anger evaporated. It was the morning rush and they had learnt to practise a little temperance, even though it was not their style. I had learnt for my part to lower my head and avert my eyes. I made it clear that I understood the hierarchy. That was all they cared about. I usually managed to coin a tip.

The morning rush always falls away by midday. Most of them want to allow enough time to prepare a good *asado* out at their villas. It was the same today. Elenita Barajo was the last to arrive, with her African boyfriend Gabriel Cissoko. They drew up in a taxi which had brought them over from the train station. She was all smiles. Her long brown hair fell in curls on either side of her fresh, freckled complexion and the mole on her right cheek.

"Carlos," she said, "we're here at last." We embraced and I shook hands with Cissoko.

"It's the first time we've met," I told him. "You're the judge."

"No, no," he laughed. "That is my colleague, Ousmane. The Nigerian."

"And you?"

"I am cleaning floors. And so is the judge."

"Elena's told me a lot about you. You are welcome." Cissoko thanked me.

"Where are Dolores and Professor Piree?" Barajo asked.

"Over in the store. I can lock up for lunch soon and take you out to Halbtsen's villa, if you like."

"That would be perfect."

"How's the airport?"

She shrugged. "It hasn't changed."

"What about the novel?"

"I've had problems, Carlos," she said. "I had this idea. A crazy idea! For a book which can be read as if like a palindrome. You could read it either in the order of the parts in the book, such as from one to four – or backwards, from four to one."

"And what would the point of that be, then?"

"The book would contain two meanings in one text. Depending on which way you read the book, you'd find a totally different meaning."

"So?"

"So…" She took a deep breath. "So it's like the universe itself. Something that Piree was telling me, what he called a cosmic crunch. After the universe stops expanding it may crunch in on itself. Time will reverse, go backwards. There will be a new meaning, new perspectives. The deepest meaning of all may be hidden in the forwards progress of the story, and our universe, but it may become apparent as it reverses towards the original fire."

"Fire?" I asked her. "Why are you all always talking about fire?"

"Because that's where life started out," she told me slowly, "and that's where it has to end."

"Wouldn't you do better to write about life in the *Ciudad*, about what it's really like to live in these urban sores of ours, whose foundations are beauty and sadness, rape and hope? Or look into the history of it all, of how we got into the damn mess we're all in now in the first place? Write about the ancestors of your friend Gabriel, of my Tehuelche great-grandparents, of the greed and desire and, why not, the romantic love which threw them all together, and then sunk them."

"I want to do all that," she told me, "Just as soon as I can finish this palindromic novel, if I ever do."

"What happened to the book? What was the problem?" I asked her.

"I'm still struggling for my voice. I've read so much that I'm not sure it's possible to be original. There are so many characters in literature that they've started to walk through my dreams now, characters from the books of Bolaño, Borges, Canetti and Joyce."

"And what do publishers make of that?"

"They don't seem to like it," she told me. "Or to put it more truthfully, they don't think the public will. Oh they're very polite, of course. They're publishers."

"So what about those characters, then? Why do they obsess you?"

"They seem to convey the world I can picture much better than I can."

"What sort of world is that?" I asked her.

"Our world, Carlos," she said. "A story always pointing towards fascism in one sense, and heroic love in the other."

I thought for a moment. "Maybe you should just steal the characters then," I said. "You could change their names a little, use anagrams. Just by making some small changes you could create a different moral universe which yet appears familiar."

"Become a criminal!" She laughed. "Perhaps I will."

We walked over to the converted store where I'd left her friends. One of them had switched the radio on, and we could hear its tinny hollowness resounding across the yard as we approached: "It's twelve o'clock on March 8th 2004. Good afternoon. The news from Radio Continental". I opened the door. Piree was sitting next to the scarred wooden table, hunched up next to the radio and listening to reports on the forthcoming Spanish presidential elections. He did not even look up or turn off the radio for our entrance. He looked as if he cared, violently, about the news just then. As if it really did matter. I walked up to the wall and pulled out the plug. Madrid stirred in the abrupt silence, and opened her eyes from her dream. Recognition slowly overcame her, and she sat up, resting against the headboard.

"Elenita," she said, "here we are."

Barajo stooped and kissed her flatmate on the cheeks. "This is Gabriel," she told her. "You know him of course."

Madrid made a curious gesture, acknowledging the remark and dismissing it at the same time. "We can't worry about that," she said. "There are more serious things."

"We met at the airport here," Elena told her.

"At the airport?" Madrid asked.

"That's right," Cissoko told her. "I am cleaning floors there, and Elena works in the bookstore."

"In the bookstore?" Piree interrupted. "That wasn't what we agreed."

"Yes," Barajo said, turning to him. But a shadow had come over her. She did not look self-assured; her face had become frozen by lies. "I also moonlight at the freight collection point, of course." Piree said nothing: his brow had furrowed, as if in recollection of that feeling he so often had, of living in flight. "Those are the books you collected yesterday." Barajo gestured at the boxes. "You saw them too, didn't you Gabriel?"

"Yes," Cissoko said. "I was also working at the airport yesterday."

"Ah yes." Piree looked at the African with disdain. "It was your fault that they arrived at all."

"My fault?"

"You signed for them. Don't you remember?" Piree rose from his chair next to the radio. "And we've already settled the account. How else can you afford to buy a bracelet like that?" he sniffed, dismissively, gesturing at Cissoko's arm.

The African opened his mouth to speak, but then held silent. "Come on," he said, without awaiting a reply. "We must get them out to the delta. We must decipher the clue at once."

"Carlos," Barajo turned to me, "do you still have time to take us out there?"

"We must be quick," I said. "I only have an hour left before we re-open after lunch."

I threw the keys to the converted store to Barajo and asked her to lock up. Then I went to locate the Barajos' motorboat and prepare it. Elenita followed after me and so I asked her, what was all this about a clue in Borges's *Labyrinths*? The old master had hardly been a murderer, much less a detective. I had known him well enough to see that. Barajo shrugged at me, tried to disown responsibility. It was all Piree, she said, the sinologist. She said something I didn't understand, about the name of a character which also revealed an atrocity. There was something that they all wanted to prevent from happening, she said, but she had this strange feeling that as they pursued it they were bringing it into being. It was something like an explosion, she said then suddenly, an explosion which might already have happened so that all of this was too late.

I said nothing to any of that. What did it all mean, anyway? Within five minutes I had towed the boat out to the harbour and manoeuvred it next to the jetty. They were all waiting there with Piree's boxes piled up beside them on the tarmac. It was a scene I had seen often enough before, of wealthy clients standing beside their luggage and waiting for me to ship them out into the delta. Yet once I had hopped into the boat and turned to them, preparing to help them all in beside me, I realised that this was not an ordinary scene, not at all.

I turned to Barajo and demurred. It was getting late. Perhaps I didn't have enough time to take them out after all. But she pulled out all her persuasiveness. Yes, it's true, I really have always been a soft touch for the children of *patróns*. It must go back to Azul. I don't remember much of my childhood, really. Just the playroom, that humiliation. The horses, of course. And the wind, which still touches me now. I felt myself weakening as Barajo looked at me with her soft, floaty eyes.

"Can't you see, man?" Piree said abruptly. "Something awful's afoot, an appalling crime. We've very little time left if we're to stop it."

"A crime?" I asked. "Have you told the police?"

"It's a crime in preparation," Piree snapped. "We don't know where it's going to be committed or who's planning it as yet."

"How can we do anything about it then?"

"Because every one of us standing here is living in the awareness that what I've just said is true, that we must act. There's very little time. So little time."

He jumped into the motorboat, forcing the issue. The two women, Barajo and Madrid, stepped in after him.

"Gabriel," Barajo told Cissoko, "pass the boxes down."

Soon everything was loaded. I started the engine and we left the harbour. The channels between the islands were quiet. Just those few minutes of silence allowed the boat to mirror the world beyond it. What are people, after all, if not talented mimics? We looked up at those graceful, solid trees, rising as high as the blocks of flats in the city. The wake from the boat washed out against the shores, breaking down the mud, fragmenting the creek's boundaries. There was a skein of mist sitting above the water, moistening us with its silken embrace, touching us as we penetrated it.

273

Even Piree seemed magnetized by the scene. His grip on the boxes of books loosened. For a moment, he looked almost relaxed.

I recalled the last time I'd taken Borges out to the villa of one of his friends. He'd seemed happy, freed, as if at last, from the burden of his life's work. For years he'd been trying to get me to read a difficult book, Joyce's *Ulysses*, and at last I'd begun it. That pleased him. He even shouted to me as we made our way out to the delta, "You see, Don Carlos, it's all about heroism, about how to be a hero in the modern world, about who the heroes are." I agreed with him, of course. How could one disagree with Borges? He was sightless but saw everything. Nothing could escape his awareness except his own propensity for fascism and the way this influenced everything he did. But yet, I recalled, as I turned the boat into a new creek, the story he'd recommended was now one hundred years old. Its prescription for heroism needed renewing.

I was lost for some time in these thoughts, observing Piree, recalling Borges. We took some turns through the channels and passed the restaurant where the plutocrats go to dine when they haven't got anyone to make an *asado* for them. Elenita Barajo took my arm affectionately.

"Thank you Carlos," she said. "We're nearly there," she called out then, to the others. Cissoko smiled at her. He came forward and they held each other as they looked out ahead of the boat. I could see that they really cared for each other, something that's rare enough these days. And that was enough to lighten my day, to make me pleased that I'd taken them out after all. Souls need a helping hand, it often seems to me, if they're not to slip away like so much froth in the wake of our moving boats.

"There it is!" Barajo called to Madrid. "There's Halbtsen's jetty." Madrid came to stand beside them and we saw the shabby house approach. But as she did so, Piree began to scowl. I watched him out of the corner of my eye as we rounded the bend and approached the jetty. He took a sharp paper knife from his pocket, cut the tape around the boxes, opened them one by one, and then began shoving the books over the side of the boat into the delta, flinching as each one hit the water. The sight was enough to worry me. I looked at his eyes, those mad and circling orbs, and thought I saw a growing luminosity there, yes, a spark, flickering, transformed by desire into flame.

IV

For years I've observed changes as I've changed myself. The things I look at most often, of course, are the books. My collections moulder. The paper yellows in the heavy summer. It's almost moist to touch, and that excites me. Perhaps that's what I've been waiting for in this vernal lassitude. I turn the pages. But nothing happens, much, except in my mind. I'm always hoping that at least I might find my way through the labyrinth. Time's evaporating. Even though it's eternal, there's not much of it left now. That's frightening. I live in the realisation that I've almost grasped all the mysteries I've charged myself with and that I'm none the better for it.

It's obvious that I can't fight my way alone. I've known it for years. That book about time is too stylish. It's like a house of cards built by an angel and a demon. They're always bringing it to collapse and rebuild itself, always fighting, never resolved. I've read and annotated it once weekly for eleven years. I should know it. But it's like anything in life. The smaller the subject, the more mysterious it is. I could have been like my colleagues and written great comparative histories of the dynasties. But this way, I've learnt more.

Still, I've been hoping for help for years. Until today, Piree was the colleague I had most faith in. I met him once at a congress in Vienna, the city where my father grew up. It was also the city where Piree had been born, although his family took him away to America as an infant, for political reasons. In some ways, then, it was a home city for both of us, although we never said as much. Both of us understood and applauded the reticence we found in each other. We were children of the war and of the universal sense of exile which followed it. Our whole beings were bound up with it. He seemed at home in the city but I never once asked him about it. The fear of the past is too terrible to confront. The past itself is too terrible. And so we've been rootless. We've pretended the world's soil is too poor to thrown down roots anywhere. That it's getting worse. It's so easy to embrace pessimism when what you really desire is flight.

Surely that's why Piree never mentioned his Viennese roots when we met there. We went to a beer hall one evening. There was a group of us from the congress. Piree spoke impeccable German and conducted us with authority. We drank freely. He conversed in several languages. I could see in his diction the precision and rigour which adorns his scholarship. We spoke a little about our interests. But he was not at ease. At one point a filthy, ugly dwarf started loitering near our table, pestering us with requests and bits of advice. Piree screamed at him: "You're like a ghost!" he shouted, "hanging over us. We can't ever be free of you. Do you want us to be afraid?" He stood up, moved towards the dwarf with his glass of beer. "We despise you," he said, throwing the beer in the dwarf's face, "go! We'll forget all about you." But I looked in Piree's eyes and saw that we'd none of us ever forget.

At the time Piree's outburst was an irrelevance. And later, when we sat in a square near the concert hall and Piree began to mock a group of gypsy fortune-tellers, I still thought nothing of it. One notes these little details, indicators of underlying inclinations, or morality, and then tries to forget them. One hopes that one will never be found in the sort of instant of mortal stress in which they are acted upon.

There must have been something of worth in Piree. I did not forget him. Years after the Vienna Congress of Sinologists I moved to Argentina. For a long time I'd been working as a specialist librarian. My eyesight was not improving. I had been working on *The Garden of Forking Paths* for several years already. I needed somewhere quiet for sustained work. Through my tobacconist's aunt I heard of this house in Tigre. I moved with all my books. The ship called at Dakar, Conakry and Abidjan before crossing the Atlantic. In the humidity, the books suffered, slowly being affected by the salty air and a kind of mould I could not identify. But I was still able to work with them out here in the delta. I started submitting papers to scholarly journals and developed quite a reputation. Other scholars wrote to me, including Piree. The letters came via the journals. I always kept my location a secret, though it was known that I lived somewhere in South America.

Naturally, rumours circulated. The world of sinologists is small. It was said that I'd stolen books from the research library where I'd been working and had fled with them. Some suggested that I had a Nazi past. Why else flee to South America? There was even a whisper that I'd been murdered, the victim of some political crime related to a hidden meaning in a book that I'd been studying. It was all sordid. It was pointless to object. I just kept quiet, and submitted my research papers. I never thought anyone would find me. I don't know why I was so naïve. Most illusions, even our own, exist only to be destroyed.

Someone arrived at last, today. There was something familiar, as with a book you start reading and then feel that you've read before. Something eerie and disconcerting, as with anything that has the ring of truth. And with that thought I looked again, and that was when I saw that it was Piree. Probably relief was my dominant emotion.

He just turned up in Carlos Delgado's boat. I watched Delgado tie up the boat at the jetty. His passengers climbed out. Piree came first. As well as Piree and Delgado there were three others, Elena Barajo and two friends of hers, an African boyfriend and her flatmate. I knew Piree and Barajo, but not the others. Barajo was someone I'd only met in passing before. I'd never taken much notice of her, but she looked much more impressive this time. No one was going to push her around.

"You've come for lunch?" I asked Piree.

"Correct."

"What about the others?"

"They've come too. They'll arrange the food."

"Yes, but who are they?"

"It's all under control, Halbtsen. They're all people who've been carefully chosen. Barajo is my assistant. This is Elena's partner, Gabriel Cissoko, and her flatmate, Dolores de la Madrid."

"Don't worry, Professor Halbtsen," Barajo said. "I can vouch for both of them. And Gabriel is a good cook, he'll prepare something for us."

She touched him on the sleeve. "You're a cook?" I asked Cissoko.

"I can cook."

"But who are you?" We were interrupted by the engine of the motorboat as Delgado pulled clear of the jetty. "What are you doing here?" Cissoko's eyes fell downwards; he did not look at me or answer my question. "I just don't understand why you are all here," I said again.

"It's my day off," Barajo answered, speaking for him. "Gabriel and I are dating and Dolores lives with me. She'd never been to Tigre before."

"Have you brought any food with you? I'm not sure I've got enough to feed you all."

"We'll manage, Professor Halbtsen," Madrid interrupted. "But right now you must go and talk with Professor Piree."

While Madrid and Cissoko dealt with the food, I led Piree and his assistant Barajo to my study. They sat in two armchairs, beside the window looking out to the creek. I stood by my desk. There was nothing I wanted to say to Piree.

"We must talk, Halbtsen."

I walked over to the window and looked out at the creek. Over on the far side, Delgado's teenage boy was throwing stones at a tree. Some birds flew off. Their cries echoed sadly in their flight. I turned to Piree. "What do you want?"

"You have a secret."

"How did you find me?"

"Stop it, Halbtsen." Piree walked towards me. "You've always asked irrelevant questions."

"So why do you need to see me, then? Why couldn't you have left me here in peace?" I sighed loudly and turned away from him. The truth was, I hadn't thought of Piree for years except as a literary construct. He was a figure in journals, reviews, books. He existed *in print*. And this literary existence went hand in hand with his eradication *in reality*. One could just cross him out of existence. Destroy him. It was easy. "Why couldn't you just have left me in peace?" I asked again.

He saw me looking at my collection of off-prints, and laughed. "Well, you have been in peace, haven't you? That's how you've been so prolific." He looked at me carefully. "You have a secret, Halbtsen."

"What secret does he have?" Barajo interrupted.

"I told you about my contact who would help us to decipher the code, didn't I?" Piree said, turning to her. "Well, here he is. He's been working for years on deciphering the hidden meaning of an esoteric book written by Ts'ui Pen, *The Garden of Forking Paths*."

"What's that got to do with us?" she asked Piree.

"That book has a clue to the location of the crime. That's why we've brought the books out here, to be decoded."

This was typical. There had always been something of the paranoiac there. He had often voiced fears of crime. That evening at the congress in Vienna, after insulting the dwarf, he'd told me: "You can't be sure of people like that. They have small hands." I'd never thought about it before, but the sight of him discussing the crime in my study with Barajo made me see that, all his life, he had been overshadowed by a sense of his own betrayal.

"You know," I said to Barajo, "you'll have to ignore him. He's always talked like this. He's always announced his fear of a crime, that we'll have to act urgently. And when one crime doesn't happen, he fastens on another one."

"He's told me that we have little time."

"What have you told her, Piree?"

"The truth!" He began pacing up and down on the rotting wooden boards of my study. His face was pale. "That book which you are studying has a vital clue, I'm sure of it."

"Well, what is it?"

"That's what I came here to ask you."

"What's the book about?" Barajo asked.

I sighed. I had never before been asked to summarise my ideas in this way. That was one of the reasons I lived in solitude, out here in Tigre where such things do not happen. "*The Garden of Forking Paths* is a labyrinth *and* a book about time," I said. "The author left papers which suggested that he had written two books, one on time and also a labyrinth. But I've studied them for years, and I'm convinced that in fact they are the same book, that the same literary text in fact contains two books."

"He's written about it in journals," Piree said.

"And do you agree with him?"

"That's why I'm here."

I walked round behind my desk and sat down. There were piles of A4 paper there, filled with my scrawls. I could only just see them clearly above the paper. "The book is a labyrinth because it has been constructed without mentioning the word "time" once. And it is about time because time is never mentioned."

"That's absurd," Barajo said.

"Not at all," I said. "That was my breakthrough. I realised that if you really want to analyse a subject in any depth you must not refer to it in a work, or perhaps, these days, mention it once, twice at the most. If you want to know the character of a quality or object, even of a state of mind, it is in its absence that it comes through."

"His theory has caused controversy," Piree admitted.

"But what's it got to do with the crime?" Barajo wanted to know.

"Look," I told her, "I've already said, ignore him when he talks about crime."

"But Halbtsen," Piree said, "you'll admit that people have written stories about *The Garden of Forking Paths*."

"Of course."

"And in the most famous, by Borges, the scene of the crime was indicated by killing someone who shared the same name as the place where the crime was to be committed."

I rose. I was angry. You can't make a labyrinth out of sheer coincidences. "Yes," I said to Barajo, "that might sound meaningful if, like Piree, you've spent your whole life believing that someone is about to commit a terrible crime, and yet never quite locating them."

"It is interesting," she said.

I laughed. "Your boss – you know what he did? He burnt his whole library down. Now there's a crime." Piree said nothing. I snapped my fingers: "Like that," I told her. "Now you ask yourself, why does a man do that? What is it they can't bear any more about the world they've created, that they must destroy it?"

She looked at us both. A trickle of sweat was sliding down her forehead. It was a hot day. But it was not that hot. "I'll go and ask Gabriel and Elena how they're getting on with the food," she said.

"Why did you burn the library?" I asked him, when she'd gone. Still he wouldn't say. Probably he didn't know the answer to that question himself. When he talked of the great crime, the crime to come, I felt that he was always talking about the past, about the moral weakness and corruption that had stopped him from restraining his own crime. He knew, after all, how easily circumstances could come together for vileness to occur, to be spurted out into the world, to envelop it, invisible, never entirely to be forgotten. Perhaps he could see when these circumstances were coalescing again. "Why?" I asked him.

He sat down abruptly in one of the armchairs and looked at me in great sadness. "This is all a great joke for you, isn't it Halbtsen?"

"A joke?"

"You like nothing better than to mock my fears."

"I don't want to mock you, Piree. I didn't ask you to come out here to the delta. I didn't ask for this."

"No, you didn't." He rose and opened the door out to the veranda. He stood there for a moment, watching the creek. I joined him. "Do you like it out here?" he asked me.

"It's a good place to work. And there aren't many of those left any more."

"That boy's still there." He pointed across the creek, to where Delgado's son had not stopped throwing stones at the birds in the tree.

"Poor kid. He's never got over what happened to his mother at the hospital." I was quiet, thinking about Adriana. "There aren't many teenagers living out here on the delta. And there aren't any like him," I said to Piree.

"Like him?"

"The rest all have money. He doesn't have much. The other kids patronise and humiliate him. It's a pattern he can't get rid of. Who can blame him? It's their second nature."

"Why?"

I turned to him in disgust. "Because that's all they've learnt to do in life."

We were interrupted by footsteps on the veranda. Barajo had come to tell us that there was some food ready. We followed her into the house. She led us along the bare corridor to the dining room, where I have a simple pine table and some chairs. They'd prepared some sandwiches with the sliced bread that Delgado brings out to me every week from one of the supermarkets in the city. Cissoko had also made some rice, and served this along with some lettuce. When we all had enough food on our plates he went back into the kitchen and prepared his own food.

"Gabriel," Barajo called out, "you should have sat down with us. I'll do that."

He didn't answer and she didn't rise from her seat. She was too busy eating.

"You've used up all my food," I told Barajo.

"I'm sorry, Professor Halbtsen. But after lunch we'll go down to the store in the motorboat and get you some more."

"You know how expensive that place is," I said. "Look at the people who shop there."

"We'll cover it," she said.

Soon Cissoko came back in with his food. Madrid moved her chair up along the table so that there was space for him to sit. She slipped her hand through his and rested it on the bracelet he was wearing, as if about to try to remove it, and she had some claim on him that was greater than Barajo's. She'd almost finished eating. Soon she got up, excusing herself, and took her plate back into the kitchen. Everyone else was silent as they ate.

"Have you got the clue you were looking for?" Barajo asked Piree when she'd finished.

"Not yet," he said. "But I am still hopeful."

I didn't say anything to that. There was no point. Piree had never been hopeful about much in his life. He was obviously lying. Yet still his assistant Barajo listened respectfully to his response. She didn't understand him at all. When Cissoko had finished and the food had gone I realised that I needed to be rid of them as quickly as possible. I didn't want Piree hanging around. It would drive me mad. But I did want Barajo to buy some food for me, so I went to the shed, picked up the jerrycan of petrol and carried it over to the motorboat. I put some fuel in and whistled up to the others to hurry up.

They walked from the villa out to the jetty and climbed into the boat. Cissoko was last. I pulled the cord and started the engine. We circled away from the jetty, out past the overhanging branches of the willows and jacarandas and into the creek. It only takes a few minutes to go down to the store. It's attached to the restaurant. We passed one or two boats going in the contrary direction. They were steering unsteadily. Probably they'd come from the restaurant. They were the sort of people who had money. Piree was like them, or he had been. He said that he'd lost everything in the fire which had consumed his library. But there were others who said that the whole thing had been a conspiracy, a giant fraud of a solid insurance company. These people still thought him fabulously wealthy. He was still well-dressed, I noticed. He obviously had enough money still to indulge his imagination.

At the restaurant, we piled out of the boat. Señora Martín was in the shop, her fleshy arms crossed on the counter. She was smoking a Lucky Strike which she stubbed out in a decorative ashtray that was shaped like a horseshoe. "Señora Martín," I said, "have you any bread?" She laughed. Her cackle turned into a cough. She bent down below the counter and located a loaf of sliced bread. "Cheese?" She never spoke much. For a few minutes I enunciated my requests. She sliced the ham, fetched down the *dulce de leche* and the coffee, stood silent when she could not help and, at last, when I had done, stood there with her hand trembling slightly above the pad of paper where she annotated the cost of my purchases.

"Who's paying?"

"It's for me, Señora Martín," Barajo said.

"For you, señorita?" She looked at me. "You'd let a girl who could be your daughter pay for you?" She looked at Piree, then Cissoko. "It's too bad. What's happening to this country? It's full of *negros* and intellectuals. Shameless."

"Barajo offered, Señora Martín," said Piree.

"Of course she did. Her family has money. But don't any of you feel any shame?"

"What's the matter, Señora? Don't you like intellectuals?"

She looked hatefully at Piree. "We never asked for them in this country. The military government tried to clean them out but even they couldn't manage it. Mark my words, all these newcomers will bring us danger." I suggested to Madrid that she go over to the bar with Cissoko. "And who's going to pay for that?" Martín wanted to know. "Barajo again. You're like leeches in a swamp."

Once Elena Barajo had paid for the food, on account, Piree and I went over with her and sat by the window, looking down towards the creek. There were still quite a few groups finishing their meals. Some of them were eating desserts, a flan or a Martín Fierro. The room twisted through cigarette smoke. Children were outside, playing on the lawn. Their shouts drifted over to us, above the noise of the bar, of the motorboats, of the birdcalls from the trees. We looked out at them for a minute. Then Barajo rose: "You two talk," she said. "I'll be back in a minute."

I felt like getting up and joining her. Piree's presence was unnerving. At first it had all seemed normal. It gives fear when you realise just how soon the twisted and the strange can seem normal. My life in the delta seems normal to me, though of course I know it is not. And Piree's sudden arrival, our discussion, our stilted repressed silence at lunch – all of that had seemed normal. But suddenly it had become obvious that it was not. I knew nothing about Piree, not really. Mostly, I still thought of him as a printed cipher. I did not know what he was capable of, except that it was clear that he could pursue me, even to the ends of the earth.

"What are your plans?" I asked him.

"My plans?"

"Where will you go now?"

"I don't know."

"But you've got money?" I asked, voicing the feeling of the conspiracists.

He laughed. "No, I've lost everything."

"How did you do that?"

"You know, Halbtsen." He looked at me: his eyes were shining, wilful: dominated and violent. "I've spent it all in search of this crime."

"Oh, the crime." I watched him carefully. I could not expect him to leave of his own accord. I would have to enlist the help of Barajo. "And do you know what shape the crime will take?"

"Sometimes I have a dream," he said. "It's of a time in the future, always in the future. People are in their houses. There are groups of men, outside, well-dressed, smart uniforms. In order. They have lists. They knock on doors."

"Is that what you're afraid of?"

"I don't know. I don't know if I'm afraid of it, or of in some way it could be a release."

"That's why I live out here," I told him. "That sort of thing could never happen here."

"So you agree," he said, "you agree that it's possible. That I might be right about this crime."

"It's possible."

"You must help me, Halbtsen." He was whispering. Our heads were so close together, we were almost touching. For an instant I felt a stab of desire, of pain. "Before it's too late. You have the clue, I know it," he urged.

"You have it too," I told him. "You just have to think."

We were interrupted by Barajo. She appeared carrying a tray of drinks, with Cissoko behind her. They both almost looked like they worked there. I rose to welcome them. "Thank you," I said. But Piree was silent. His eyes were utterly empty. There was not even a breath of recognition, of sanity. He did not seem to recognise Barajo, his assistant.

"Professor Piree," she said hesitantly. "You remember." He shook his head. "We met at the airport. You met Cissoko there, too."

"Ah yes," Piree said. He looked at Cissoko. "You are working there, in the bookstore?"

Cissoko shook his head. "No, I do not work in that shop. I am cleaning floors there in the airport."

"You met him with the books. Yesterday, when you arrived at Ezeiza. You got him to sign for them. You created the evidentiary trail."

Piree looked at Barajo, in loss. "I met you there," he said to her, "as we'd arranged."

"And then we met Gabriel. You knocked his mop on the way to the taxi stand."

"And are there many like you at the airport?" he asked Cissoko.

"Two other Africans," said Cissoko. "Both from Nigeria. One of them used to be a judge. He is like Solomon, weighing each day's addictions, each night's needs."

"And how did you get here?"

"I was given some false papers in Madrid."

Yet it was clear that Piree did not remember. Was it such a mystery, the access to memory? We all knew that as soon as you struck memory from the unconscious everything was permitted. That was what life and politics were: the battle for memory. Piree had become an amnesiac in search of a dislocated crime. He was dangerous.

"Fall out! Fall out!" Piree had risen. He snapped his fingers in Cissoko's face, as if to wake him from a dream. He pushed him. "You have failed the test. You are not fit for entry." There was confusion. Piree turned to me, grabbed my arm, pulled me towards him. "Where are they, Halbtsen?"

"What?"

"The books. The books. Where are they?"

"You threw them into the river," Barajo said to him.

He turned to her. "Of course I didn't."

"It wouldn't be a surprise, Piree," I said. "You've burnt them before."

"That's a lie," he said.

"What books are these, anyway?" I asked him.

"The ones we smuggled from Europe, Barajo and I. The ones you were to help decipher."

Barajo began to laugh. She turned to Cissoko: "We're losing him, Gabriel. Perhaps he'll never find the root of the crime. Yes, perhaps Dolores is right." She took his hand, gently, but in command.

"Perhaps she is," Cissoko said. "Perhaps she is the one who has really understood what is afoot."

I'd overheard Madrid in the kitchen of my villa talking to Barajo, telling her that Piree was a lunatic, that he was the biggest criminal of all, that she must not believe him. Now she was over by the bar. I remembered, now. She had said something about working as a barmaid. She was coming over with a tray of drinks. Surely, Señora Martín had not hired her so quickly. The different layers of my life were beginning to strangle me. As everything became clearer, it became more complicated. Piree looked at Madrid approaching. She was a stylish woman, tall, dark. She was not out of place as a worker there. She was the sort of person that the rich in Buenos Aires paid money to be served by.

"Come on," Piree said to me, "we must go." He began to pat his pocket. He pulled out a gun, and pulled me outside. As we left, I heard a crash of glasses and a scream. "Let's get to the boat," Piree said. "We must be quick."

I tried to shake myself free of him. "What have you done?"

"There's very little time."

"What have you done?" I repeated.

"The murder," he said. "The crime."

"What about it?"

"This is your doing, Halbtsen," he said. "You've brought me here with Madrid."

I climbed into the boat with him. Curiosity always defeats willpower in the end. He pulled the cord and began to steer the boat out of the little boat park next to the jetty. "Where are we going?" I asked Piree. He turned right, in the contrary sense from my villa. "Where are we going?"

"I've just realised," he shouted, "I've made an awful mistake." He passed the inlet which led towards the mainland, and Tigre. We were headed for the River Plate, the grey belly of the great river. "For months, years," he went on, "I've suspected as much. I planned everything meticulously. I chose it all so carefully."

He loosened the throttle so that we no longer had to shout. "What did you plan, Piree? What are you talking about?"

"The books, Halbtsen."

"The books?"

"For months, I wondered how to smuggle them, how to get them past security. They've made that quite difficult, you know. Especially for dangerous weapons."

"I haven't left Tigre for ten years. I've no idea."

"But I succeeded," he went on. "The plan worked perfectly. For years I'd known."

"Known what?"

He smiled at me. The creek was widening out now. The islands were tapering off, and through the thin line of trees the flat end of the world appeared, the silver river, the River Plate. "Known where you were. Out here, in Tigre." He cut the cord and we drifted down towards the empty water into which the military governments used to throw their victims. An aeroplane droned overhead, twisted eastwards, out into Atlantic space. "Oh come on, Halbtsen. There aren't any secrets or mysteries left. Everything has its price."

That's how I found out how easy it was to smash solitude, today. All the peace I had worked so hard for, every moment of my life here in Tigre was in that instant devalued. "How did you find out?"

"I bribed the Latin America editor of *Ming Cultural Review*, right here in Buenos Aires. It was easy. But don't be too angry. It's a compliment to you. I knew you'd understand when I arrived with the books."

"But where are the books, Piree?"

"Barajo was right. I threw them into the river." He sighed. "What a mistake!"

I turned from him and looked at the grey light on the huge river. It was a sullen afternoon with the hint of a storm. There were breaks in the clouds and the sunlight played tricks on the water, bouncing, refracting, never still. Knowing that I was drifting out to the river estuary in the company of a lunatic, with a storm brewing which could easily electrocute me, I felt as if this was the end. But lifting that despair was also a quiet and unexplained joy.

"You won't help me, will you?" he said at length. "You've never believed in this crime."

"I haven't."

"You just wanted to bury your head and pretend it would never happen. That everything would be all right."

"That's how you see it."

"You're just a fantasist," he sighed.

"What are you, then?"

"At least I want to save things," Piree said, "at least I know that's still possible."

"Is it?"

He laughed. "Now we know where the crime will be committed, it's possible."

"Where's that?"

"In Madrid, of course."

That was when the extent of his delusions became clear. He had reached his conclusion because of the name of the woman he had drawn into his world, only to destroy her.

He pulled the rip cord and started the engine. The motor puttered half-heartedly, but did not yet surge into life. Piree pulled something from his pocket, and there was a golden flash as he cast it into the brine. For a moment I thought it was Cissoko's bracelet, that somehow he'd stolen it from the African in the restaurant, or that Elena had filched it and conspired with him, stolen it just to send it into the sea to join his books, all those mementoes of the struggle to preserve memories which no one cared for any more, which even Piree no longer believed in.

"What's that?"

He ignored me, and spun the boat in the water. I told him that he was too late, that we'd never make it back against the current. But we did. We re-entered the channel and left the estuary behind. In some uncanny way it felt as if we'd begun to go backwards. The world returned slowly, the birds returning, the greenery, life returning. We saw some villas. There were some shouts. Perhaps the most dangerous species of all is humanity, but it is also a beautiful one. So beautiful. Outside the restaurant, we saw Barajo and Cissoko. They had their arms round each other, perhaps in contentment, perhaps in the desperate need for comfort that occurs when things fall apart. I tried to see if Cissoko still had his bracelet, but the boat was moving too fast and I wasn't sure if it was there or not, if he'd managed to keep hold of it in the end.

"Aren't you going to stop?"

"There isn't time," he said, ignoring them.

"They seemed worried. Something might have happened."

"Of course," he said, slowing the motor as we approached my villa. "Something must have happened to Madrid. A crime."

I laughed. "What, you think she's been killed! Just because of that book, because of The Garden of Forking

Paths, because as in Borges's story her name might indicate a crime scene?"

"Yes. And Cissoko has realised that the finger will be pointed at him."

"That's terrible."

His expression stilled me. "No, it's irrelevant. Once we have that, everything follows. There's still time to save us, to prevent the explosion."

Really, he scared me. He drew up next to my jetty but left the engine running. I climbed out. "You're not stopping?" I asked him.

"There isn't time now. I must get to Madrid before it's too late. I must try to find some more copies of those books again. Everything must reverse now if the real meaning of all this is to be unmasked."

"You can have my boat."

"I'll leave it at the warehouse," he said.

"That's fine, then."

"Goodbye, Halbtsen."

He turned the boat away. I walked back towards the house half fearing that he might kill me from out there on the water, shoot me dead in payment and eternal recurrence of all my crimes in this, my life, my story. But soon the engine noise disappeared. For a moment I imagined Piree stopping further down the creek and diving into the water to look for those precious books of his that he had discarded. I could easily imagine him doing that, thinking that somehow this was a saving for him, for all of us, when his ego-driven madness and compulsion were merely driving us further and further towards disaster. I retained that image of his watery grave as I climbed the steps up to the veranda, opened the door and walked along the passageway to my study. It was still with me as I sat down in my chair and looked up at my companions out here in the peace I have wrought, at my books. But then that dream faded slowly into the gloaming and I was enveloped again in the condition that punctures my heart daily as I struggle, the unending condition in which I live, in loneliness, in terror.

END